SANDSTONE

An Anthology to Support This House of Books,
The Billings Bookstore Cooperative

Precious McKenzie, editor

CONTENTS

CONTENTS

ACKNOWLEDGMENTS

A BIG, HEARTY MONTANA THANK YOU TO ALL OF THE WRITERS WHO donated their stories, essays, and poems to this project. Your support of the arts is uplifting and inspiring. Also, my deepest gratitude goes out to Connie Dillon for generously creating the cover art for this anthology and to Craig Lancaster for giving his time and talent to designing the book itself.

Several of the works in this anthology have been previously published. Our appreciation and acknowledgment extends to:

Pete Fromm's "Pilgrim Creek," which first appeared in his book *The Names of the Stars* (Thomas Dunne Books, 2016).

Tami Haaland's poem "Every Morning the Squirrel Comes" was first published in *Life and Legends*, an online magazine.

Russell Rowland's "A Pair of Loafers" is an excerpt from his forthcoming memoir *Be a Man*.

Dave Caserio's poems "A Terrible Music," "Dublin Station," and "It Was Always Errol Flynn" first appeared in *This Vanishing* (WordTech Communications LLC, Cincinnati, Ohio, 2014).

Shann Ray's story framed in five chapters, "City of Hunger and Light," originally appeared in the journal *Five Chapters*, edited by Dave Daley.

Allen M. Jones's "A Remembrance" is from his novel *A Bloom of Bones* (Ig Publishing, 2016).

Precious McKenzie's poems "Know This" and "Iridescent" originally appeared as part of Tupelo Press's 30/30 Project.

Bernard Quetchenbach's "Baboon Mountain" was supported by the Artist-in-Residence program of the Absaroka-Beartooth Wilderness Foundation.

Keith McCafferty's "Aphrodisiac Graveyard" is excerpted from his forthcoming novel *Cold Hearted River* (Penguin, 2017).

Craig Lancaster's story "Slumpbuster" originally appeared in *Montana Quarterly* and is included in his story collection, *The Art of Departure*.

INTRODUCTION

IN 2015, ATTORNEY AND NOVELIST CARRIE LA SEUR HATCHED THE plan to create a one-of-a-kind independent bookstore in Billings, Montana. Even though Billings is the business hub for the state of Montana and the tri-state area, Billings did not have an indie bookstore that specialized in new books.

Carrie sought out creative people with a passion for literature: Craig Lancaster, Emily Stark, Andy Wildenberg. Former Billings mayor Chuck Tooley pitched the idea of forming a bookstore cooperative. The cooperative model would help disperse some of the startup costs and risks associated with opening a small business. From there, Carrie found additional creative innovators to get the bookstore cooperative idea off the ground. Jan Brown, Ryan Duffy, Russell Rowland, Adrian Jawort, Connie Dillon, Mark Taylor, Nina Hernandez, Gary Robson, and myself, were all on board for making this bookstore pipe dream a reality for the city of Billings.

In April 2016, the Billings Bookstore Cooperative, doing

business as This House of Books, received its official go-ahead from the state of Montana. The board began to sell shares of stock in the cooperative, and raise the capital needed to open the store. Along the way, more people jumped in to help: George Warmer, Randy Hafer, Lisa Harmon, Greg Krueger, Bob Wilmouth, Norma and Gary Buchanan, John Felten, Barbara Bernheim, and Bill Stearns. Member-owners even hosted house parties to help sell shares and spread the word.

In October 2016, the bookstore opened its doors to customers. By April 2017, the cooperative had almost 300 member-owners and a core team of volunteers to handle everything from painting bookshelves to planning cultural events. (Did I mention that our five board members are also volunteers?) It has truly taken a village, a generous, passionate, creative village to make this bookstore happen.

This House of Books, located at 224 North Broadway in Billings, is a unique business model that, like all small businesses, faces many challenges. The book market is risky and has razor-thin margins. The profits from the sale of this anthology will go directly to the bookstore cooperative, to help the bookstore buy inventory, pay daily operating expenses, and pay down debt.

From its very inception, This House of Books has been nurtured and supported by hundreds of generous people, including the writers featured in this volume. I hope this volume of contemporary Western writers surprises and delights you. On behalf of the board of directors of the bookstore, we kindly thank them for their work and their generosity.

For those who have not yet become member-owners in the bookstore, visit http://www.thishouseofbooks.com/ to invest and become part of our family.

Most of all, thank you for your purchase of this book. Your support will keep the culture of the book alive in Billings, Montana.

Precious McKenzie
Editor & Vice President of the Board of Directors
August 2017

PETE FROMM
Pilgrim Creek

THE BORDER AT THE NORTHERN REACHES OF GRAND TETON National Park is rough, steep country, doghaired with lodgepole, mostly unmarked, and almost totally unvisited. The minds down at headquarters, though, began to worry about hunters infiltrating from nowhere and decided that I, having worked the river for six seasons, was the perfect choice to delineate the riverless, pathless line on a map and mark it so solidly no trespasser would ever dare to cross.

So I cannonballed the old Dodge up the Wilderness road, the cottonwoods flashing past, tinged yellow by frost, the aspen flaring gold in the sheltered pockets amid the dark greens and blues of the spruce and pine. At the end of the road, nothing but wilderness before me, and beyond that, Yellowstone, I folded out the free visitor map and studied the line of the boundary. North for a while, with one little jog, then straight west for a long, long way. An impossibly straight line through impossibly unstraight country.

I threw my pack over my shoulder, glancing up toward the

scruff of lodgepole hiding the pick-up-stick deadfall underneath. Besides the hundreds of foot long plastic signs, blazed green with the buffalo and arrowhead, the warning, NATIONAL PARK BOUNDARY, the pack held rolls of bailing wire, a fencing hammer, hatchet, water, service revolver. All the normal camping stuff.

I started up hill and sweated and cursed the rest of that day, trying to follow the ancient broken line of old boundary signs, wiring my plastic signs at least within sight of the last one, the bundles of them diminishing more quickly than the miles. Afternoon crawled toward evening, my water bottle long emptied, not a scrap of clear ground flat enough or long enough to stretch out in, and my nebulous plans to make it all the way through to the creek grew more solid. Water, a creekside camp spot, some fish, maybe, for dinner.

Dusk closed in, early with the building overcast, and I finally came to the cut of Pilgrim Creek. On my non-topo map, it was a simple straggling blue line, the same one I could see from the top of the cliff I stood on. I swung upstream, looking for a gap, then down, until I found a kind of break, a chute anyway, a gravel pitch steep enough I could keep one hand on the hill behind me as I snowplowed down hundreds of feet, ending up in a pile at the bottom. Across the creek, the canyon wall rose just as steeply, but by sheer luck I'd found the lone flat spot, a cobble beach scraggled over with willow and chokecherry, even a stand of lodgepole crowded between cliff and water, a few big, old, dark spruce, their lower branches sweeping the ground.

The slice of sky I could see lowered and darkened as I strung a line between a downed spruce snag and its broken stump, hung my poncho over it, tacked down the corner with sticks I whittled with my hatchet, drove in with the flat backside. I slipped my pad and old down bag underneath.

Living a decade on the wages of a seasonal ranger, my camp gear was more under-the-bridge than REI. No tent, no stove, no freeze-drieds. Not even a flashlight, let alone one of the bitching new headlamps. Just a heavy, Vietnam era, rubberized poncho, a quarter inch thick foam pad, hardened and cracked with age. For cooking I had a charred black one pound coffee can with a loop of coat hanger as a handle. The menu? A bag of rice, dinner, bag of oatmeal, breakfast.

I set my pack against the spruce with the thickest, lowest

branches, the wind rustling down the creek tinged with the scent of rain. I broke off handfuls of the lodgepole's dead, dry lower twigs, scavenged for driftwood, fallen branches, building up a stock that would carry me through the night's cooking, an hour or so curled around the flames reading, enough for a small boil for the oatmeal in the morning.

Just before last light, I set up my fly rod. The creek was small, and low, but I cast to a hole the size of my backpack and brought up a brookie. Two more followed, just enough for dinner, just before dark. I squatted where I'd cast, slid in the blade of my Swiss Army knife, and tossed the guts into the fastest line of water downstream, a treat for the otters, or mink, or skunk, whatever was lucky enough to make the first stroll through here.

Building up a little fire, I grilled the fish, boiled my rice, and ate by the light of the flames. I pulled on first one wool shirt, then another, the cold coming up off the creek, breezing through the upstream pines, fanning the dying flames, rustling the needles and leaves against one another. Cracking my paperback, I read about Doc and the boys in Cannery Row, added more wood to the fire than I'd counted on, scooched a little closer to the flames. Gathering more in the morning would not be a problem.

Then, one rustle was different than all the others. I lifted my head, peered upstream, upwind, over the flames. Nothing beyond the touch of firelight on the first row of needles and branches but the dead black of a low night. I turned my head, straining to hear. Nothing but wind, trees, the creek.

I had spent more nights out like this than I could count. I knew a squirrel flitting across a camp could sound like a rhino. And a chuffing, stomping muley buck? Good god. T-rex.

I went back to my reading.

A crack of something, not just a twig snap, but something bigger, bent, then breaking. I forgot to close my thumb between the pages. I put Steinbeck down and rubbed at the back of my neck, the shiver there. I studied the few dimly lit branches, turned my head first one way, then the other, listening.

I put a few small branches on the fire, sticks that would flare up.

A twig cracked. Then another. Footsteps, nothing else. Something walking out there. Close.

I gathered my feet under me. Put a knee down, a hand. A runner in the blocks. A sprinter with no place to dash.

"Hello?" I said.

The steps stopped. Just the wind again, the creek. I listened for minutes. Eased back down a bit. I started to smile, shake my head. Spooked by nothing. I poked the fire up, put in another branch, just the end, in case I needed a torch, something I'd tried before, which never worked like in the movies. A few steps from the fire you stood holding nothing but a smoking stick, a few red coals glowing in the dark. But still.

Huffing then. Definite. Loud. Breaths taken in, snorted out.

I stood up.

Mule deer could sound something like that. An alarm. A timid challenge.

They didn't, really, sound anything like this.

I shouted, "Hello?"

A quick retreat. Not wind, not rushing water. A gallop. Something big. Branches knocked aside.

Maybe a bull elk?

Probably not.

But it had run away. There was that.

I looked around, sized things up. The fire threw out a wavery ring of light maybe fifteen feet in diameter, cut off upwind by the trees, downwind by my poncho's snag. Toward the river, the little band of willows, and away, the cliff, a few glimmers off bits of rock. Beyond that, in every direction, as dark as a pocket.

Rain began, ever so slightly, to patter down. "Fabulous," I said.

I went to my pack, the furthest reach of the firelight, towards whatever had been there, and pulled out my rain jacket, park service Gore-tex, green and whispery against itself. With the hood up, I'd be deaf as a stone.

I left the hood down.

I walked my perimeter of light, picking up what pieces of wood I could find, adding them to the fire. Whatever it had been, it was gone now. I sat back down, gave another look around, took a big, easing breath, let it out. I picked up my book, flipped through the pages till I found Doc and the boys. The bigger fire was great, easier to read by, though with the rain picking up, I had to hunch forward to keep the drops from pocking the pages.

Instead of huffing, what came next could only be described as a roar. A holy shit, straight to your feet, bowel clamping, MGM lion roar. Eyes wide, I stared into the wind, which kept anything out there from smelling how hugely dangerously human I was. I couldn't see an inch farther than I could with my tiny fire. The edges of the trees were only brighter, the darkness beyond them only blacker.

Another roar. Branches breaking. Something thrashing. Or being thrashed.

"Hey," I shouted. "I'm the top of the food chain!"

Silence. But no charging retreat.

"Goddamn it," I whispered.

And then a thought. Pancoast. If he'd managed to sneak up here during the day, camp out, wait for me... This was *exactly* the thing he'd do. Did bears really roar, anyway? Or was that cartoon stuff, Tarzan dramatics? He'd be standing just beyond the light, biting his fist, fighting not to pee himself.

"Pancoast?" I shouted. "I'm dying here. I mean, you got me. Hysterical."

Nothing.

I picked up my torch, held it up high and out front. I took a step toward my pack. Another.

The roar and the rattle of branches stopped me dead. I shouted, not quite quaver free, "The highest form of humor, Pancoast. I mean it."

One more step and I slipped my hand into the side pocket of my pack, pulled out my service revolver, a five shot .38, a gun the boss had chosen, insisting the river rangers carry guns, but wanting something that wouldn't get in our way, so going small, something that fit into the palm of a hand. We couldn't even shoot the same ammo the rest of the rangers used, for fear the gun would blow up. A cork on a string kind of gun, when what was called for here was a bazooka. An air strike.

I pointed it into the night. In my other hand, I held a smoking stick. A few embers glowing red. Was a flashlight really so expensive?

I tossed my stick back to the fire, and searched what I could see of the tree trunks, looking for one I might possibly climb. No real likely candidates. But, in a pinch? Grizzly canines clapping at my ass? Possible. Whatever was out there, though, would be on me before I lifted a foot off the ground.

I grabbed the lowest branch of the most realistic tree. Tugged. Just beyond the light there was a sudden tussle, a tearing sound. Something being pulled out of the ground, rending and gnashing. A chokecherry pulled up by the roots? An eighty foot spruce?

I lifted myself off the ground. But, if I could climb up, then what? When could I come down? Daylight? Spend the next ten, eleven hours perched on a branch I hoped could hold my weight? Ten hours in the dark, the rain, which was getting more serious about coming down.

I put my foot back on the ground. Pointed my little gun.

"All right, Pancoast," I shouted. "This is your best one ever. No lie. But, I'm kind of over it. One more roar, and I'll shoot your ass."

The roaring stopped. The rending and tearing and stomping.

What the hell was out there?

"Come out into the light now, bring your beer. I'll laugh myself sick."

Nothing but the breeze again. The creek. The rain.

I stepped backward to my fire, only glancing away from whatever might come out of those trees long enough to avoid stepping into the flames.

Footsteps, sounding closer. Huffing.

Not a roar, but I fired anyway. Up high, into the tree tops.

Small as it was, the clap of that gunshot closed in between the cliff walls and clouds, the rip of flame out the barrel end, startled me so much I nearly missed the freight train charge of full retreat through the trees. Not even Pancoast could make that one up. Nor an elk.

I pulled up my hood. The rain drummed down against it. I edged it back, tucked it behind my ears. But, there'd be nothing more to hear. Right? Thing was probably unconscious this very second, the spruce he'd crashed into cracked and listing.

How the hell do they get around in the black like this anyway?

I squatted by my fire. Threw in the last of my collected wood. Worked on getting my breathing right. Listened to my heart drum.

He'd been trying to get by me. On his way down the creek. The cliffs limited the options. He could splash down the creek, but that would only get him another twenty, twenty-five feet away from me. Or, he could just run right over me. How much did fire bug them anyway?

Or he could scare me senseless, make me run down the creek before him. Not a bad plan. If I had a headlamp, any kind of light,

I'd be doing that right now.

But without the light I'd end up in the same cartoon I'd imagined him in, conked out beside whichever tree I hit first.

We had no options. Either one of us.

Which is what I told him, when he came back.

He didn't roar this time. Just padded up close, knocked around a few branches. As if he'd been upstream doing some option exploring of his own, maybe hoping I'd gone away as much as I'd hoped he had. I thought maybe just once I caught a trace of movement at the very last reach of the fire's light, which was waning, closing in, the wood all gone.

I ran my finger along the tiny gun's trigger. It really was a ridiculous thing. I didn't want to shoot again, figuring it might take all of the last four shots to put myself out of my misery as the bear dined on my haunches.

But I stood again, not knowing if showing him my size was a good plan or bad. I retreated to the fallen snag of my poncho, and untied my boots. "I'm going to bed," I yelled. The poncho would be an even better hood, the rain against it deafening me to whatever might be taking place beyond it. I could not listen to this all night.

"You can take the creek, or just run past me here," I said.

"Or you can stay the fuck upstream and leave me the hell alone!" I shouted, firing once more into the treetops and ripping out of my rainjacket, dragging it under the poncho with me as I kicked into my sleeping bag, zipping it up tight, pushing my better right ear into the pillow of my wadded wool shirt, my not so hot left ear only inches from the steady thwapping of raindrops against the rubber sheet. The teddy bears could have their whole goddamn picnic right in my fire ring and I'd be none the wiser.

Trying hard not to imagine the crack my femur would make, the sucking tear of muscle torn from bone, I curled into a ball, back against the dead tree's trunk, and closed my eyes, only eight, nine hours till dawn.

STEPHEN GERMIC
Lichen

1.

A lichen is two things. I learned that today from a
Forest Service ranger with skin like fresh honey.

A lichen is a plant and a fungus. The plant does
what plants do: it converts sun and water into life.

I still don't understand what a fungus is, or does,
though I have the impression that, coming in the

form of a lichen, it is a thief of energy, eating what
the plant does. It would have been well to have

learned this very young, to know the drift of that
which takes from that which gives. The fungus

part, she explained, determines the form. Without

blushing she submitted that the fungus reproduces

sexually, the plant asexually. Forest Service rangers
now wear pants that fit maybe too snugly over their hips.

2.
In the morning she made a tea
from the leaves of a balsam fir.

She said there were some other things
I should know. *Mix in twigs and resin*
if you needed to cure a cough.
When they are green, eat cattails like

corn and when they turn yellow use
the pollen as flour. I wouldn't
have done it even without my
period. Be like other men.

Quit writing poetry and sleeping through
thunderstorms. Stop apologizing and
compare the movement of the clouds
to the wind you actually feel.

At the moment, I didn't feel any
wind, though waves were crashing
all along the broken shore.

3.
Lichens prefer sterility: alkaline soils or
the faces of bare rock. There are rare
species, or perhaps just individuals, that
thrive in moist heat. No one is sure.

Stephen Germic

And Then We Didn't Dream

There was nothing to hold
the ground to the ground.
We ate dirt, slept in dust, made
clouds by patting a haunch.

Clouds that did not rain. By
August even the rocks were
feral. They held our heads
in the night like witches,

bearded, howling something we
heard like final dreams. And
then we didn't dream. It was
the time of only actual things.

We ate the leaves of brittlebush,
which taste like nothing. After
a long discussion we concluded it
was the fifth of September

when we learned from a hermit

how to suck dew from the
desert marigold. The Earth
must have continued to tilt

on its axis. From where else could
winter have come? With its
burning snow, its indistinguishable
whiteness, its soft breath like love.

TAMI HAALAND
Every Morning
the Squirrel Comes

Along the ledge of the back fence,
around the corner, onto the small branches
of the sick elm, from the elm
to the poplar, across its scraggy bark,
it makes its daily heroic leap
into the fine stems of the maple
and there feasts on leftover
spinners from fall, each seed
curled with potential.

It's the wild leap I love, the branches
quaking like a bobble head,
snow or leaves flying in season,
and the happy squirrel bounding along
to solid trunk and then up

the next rung to light branches
nearer the sky, sometimes circling
or chasing in dappled sun.
In summer it splays along
the central trunk to cool, and then,
as if leaping tree to tree were
everything, it takes its flight.

Easy for a squirrel, no concern
for a slip that might send it
break-necking down or into the mouth
of the neighbor's cat who waits
in the shrubs twitching its full tale—
every day a leap and then another,
as if falling could not be
further from my mind.

RUSSELL ROWLAND
A Pair of Loafers

I'M TEN YEARS OLD, STANDING IN THE DOORWAY OF A SMALL trailer. Ten wooden desks are lined in two neat rows, facing a large teacher's desk and a chalkboard. Eight kids stand facing me, and I look at their shoes. All six of the boys are wearing boots.

I want to find a way to hide my own feet, and I wish I could go back to a couple of weeks before when I talked my mother into buying me a pair of black loafers. I had very narrow feet as a kid, and my mother was a stickler about buying shoes that came in narrow sizes. The only style available in narrow sizes at the shoe store where we shopped in Sheridan, Wyoming, was black oxfords. So for years, that's all I wore. When penny loafers became the big fad in third grade, I knew I didn't have a chance of ever getting a pair. But when we went to Gorem's Shoes just before fourth grade started, and learned that they had gotten a shipment of black loafers in narrow sizes, I begged my mother for a pair. I didn't mention that they slipped in the heel.

Now ... standing in that doorway, I wished I had waited. But we didn't know about this latest development then.

Just a couple of weeks earlier, my father had decided to take a job as a cowboy. Despite not having worked on a ranch since he was a teenager, he somehow landed a job managing an operation owned by construction magnate Peter Kiewitt, near the Montana/ Wyoming border. The ranch was right at the foot of the Big Horn Mountains, in one of the most glorious little valleys I've seen in my life. But there were some major problems with this plan.

First of all, soon after our arrival at the X Bar X Ranch, my father realized that Mr. Kiewitt had not informed the other ranch hands that Dad was going to be managing the place. Most of them had worked there for years, and one guy had been there for a very long time, and expected to take over as manager. So there were hard feelings, not to mention immediate conflicts. And because Mr. Kiewitt lived in Omaha, and came to the ranch only once every few weeks, Dad was left to deal with the tension on his own.

Second, the community along Pass Creek was very tight-knit. There were about a dozen ranches that lined the gravel road that turned off the main highway just north of Ranchester, Wyoming, and most of these ranches had been in the families for decades. They were not mean or horrible people, but every one of these families did have a certain standing in their community, and outsiders who came into that setting were subject to scrutiny. And of course, in a country where land is the most significant measure of a family's position, hired help did not exactly rank at the top of the food chain.

WHICH BRINGS ME TO THE MOST SIGNIFICANT FACTOR OF WHAT turned out to be the worst period of my parents' marriage. My mother grew up on a ranch, and she had no desire to ever live on a ranch again. When she married my father, she was thrilled with the prospect of getting away from life in the country. So she was not one bit happy about the move to Pass Creek, especially knowing that we would be considered 'help.' Whenever the opportunity arose, she made it a point to mention the fact that her parents' ranch was much bigger than any along Pass Creek, a nervous tic which I'm sure did little to endear my parents to the locals.

My sister Collette and I went to a one-room school during the two years we lived along that gravel road. And as is always the case, the dynamics among the children of that schoolhouse reflected those of the parents. It was a very confusing time, because it was clear, especially when we were alone with them, that the other children did not dislike us. But as a group, they made it clear that we were not one of them. We felt it from the first day we arrived, when I looked around the room and saw those boots.

The message was sometimes subtle, but always there. We were not invited to parties. We were ridiculed for petty things. Our second year there, I was one of two fifth graders, and there was nobody in sixth grade in our one-room school. The other fifth grader, Carl Caywood, gathered forces with the only fourth grade boy and two third grade boys, and they approached me with a proposal.

"Since you're so much better at soccer than anyone else in the school, we can't really split the teams up even, so it should be us four against you and all the little kids."

CARL DELIVERED THIS IDEA WITHOUT LOOKING ME IN THE EYE, and even then I knew that they were blowing smoke up my ass. I also knew that any argument would be overruled by this small but powerful majority. They had also appealed to a growing competitive nature in me. Part of me wanted to show them that they were making a big mistake, assuming that they could beat the pants off of us. I was going to prove that, by god, I really was the best player.

"Okay," I agreed.

Over the next several weeks, or perhaps it was even months, we played soccer every day at recess, and my little band of ragtag first and second graders and I lost every single game. There were many skirmishes, minor injuries, insults shouted, tears shed. I stubbornly refused to quit, and I think it ended up being a valuable lesson, and I'm not talking about futility. What I learned was perseverance, and about trying to become a graceful loser, which I often wasn't. But perhaps most importantly, I realized from this experience that, no matter how hard you try to be nice and get along, people are sometimes mean for no good reason. And that there are times when all you can do is keep trying anyway.

They beat us every single time, and after weeks of this, I started to show an explosive temper, sick of the constant humiliation as I fought to try and win just one goddam game.

This temper followed me for years afterward, although I don't think this was the only source. A lot of my anger bubbled up from some latent understanding of the unhappiness that was so heavy and omnipresent in our house.

SOMETIME DURING THAT SECOND YEAR OF OUR STAY AT PASS CREEK, my father drove to the Veteran's Hospital in Sheridan, and he went to the reception desk and told them that he needed to talk to someone. The nurse at that desk asked him what was wrong, and he told her that he didn't know, that he just needed to talk to someone. She told him that if he couldn't be more specific about what was wrong, she didn't know who to send him to, and that there was nothing they could do unless he told her what was wrong.

My father left that building, sat down on the steps and broke into tears.

WILBUR WOOD
Arriving

It is a young beach, perhaps twenty feet of sand between
high tide and the cliffs. At some points
high tide comes all the way to the cliffs,
which are constantly crumbling apart.

You stop. I stop.
We sit down on a cushion
of slick, rubbery lichens covering a large rock.
In a moment, farther down the beach, a chunk of cliff
breaks off and a landslide of rocks and dirt
showers over where we would have been
had we not stopped here
—as the dust and noise of the slide
settle, we hear our laughter
evaporating down the bright corridors of air.

At low tide vast rock and mud tidal flats

lie open to air

—walk lightly—
I reach to pick up a pearl-pink shell,
it comes away from the rock
with a soft, sucking pop!
and I am aware I hold something alive in my hand
and I turn the shell over and peer inside
and inside the shell a mouth is closing—

The whole beach is a mouth
opening and closing in rhythm with the tides
and the moon, the whole beach breathes,
and this whole long coast,
we pass through, inside the breathing—

Hawk

"God" I breathed
when I saw the hawk

now the word becomes not oath
but prayer

as the big bird wheeling
over the canyon

tilts his wing and
glides my way

closer, closer—
doesn't he see me?

am I the chosen one
or prey?

Kneeling on this ridgetop
I'm reeling him in

straight for my face
now he fills my sky!

I throw up my hands
I flinch away

deep in my fright
yet curious, staring

between my fingers
I glimpse the hawk's

quick casual shrug
of shoulder

lift him
over my cowering

stare—he
soars beyond my oath,

he vanishes
into my prayer.

Stumble

Listen. Listen.
We're all going to die.

Don't let the standing-up-too-fast
       Dizziness
       Deter you
From taking that next
       Step

Pause now.
Steady yourself.
      Breathe deeply
          In
          Out.

You know
How to do this.

Inhabit this body.
This gift

Haiku and Admonition

Warm winds melt the snow
into cold pools perched atop
icy roads and paths—

Walk like a penguin!

ELISA LORELLO
2.7 Miles

JUNE 20, 2015: I DESCENDED THE STAIRS OF BILLINGS LOGAN Airport to find Craig waiting for me. He sported the grin I hadn't seen in twenty-seven days. At least not in person. I'd been grinning since the plane landed, and not only because we were finally on the ground.

Twenty-seven days since he'd left Long Island following a week during which we had visited my old neighborhood, introduced him to several of my siblings and my mother, gazed at the Atlantic Ocean (it was too cold for toe-dipping), and ridden the Long Island Rail Road to Manhattan, where we had visited Prometheus at Rockefeller Plaza and the New York Public Library and FAO Schwartz and Eataly. We'd held hands the entire week. We'd fallen in love.

A four-year friendship had set the foundation for this moment, this arrival in Billings. Granted, that friendship had started in the most superficial of ways (Facebook), and at a distance, but it had grown gradually, innocently, quietly, so that when the time was right, physical distance wasn't as much an obstacle as it was a technicality.

Craig took me into his arms—he's got more than a foot on me, but I fold so snugly into him—and kissed me, brushing a strand of hair from my face. He could see the mental, physical, and emotional exhaustion not only from a day's worth of flying (I hadn't been on a plane in almost two years, and I'd rather poke myself with needles), but also the separation. I missed my lover, my best friend, this man who laughs at my jokes and reads my novels and loves my cooking.

"Welcome to Billings," he said, before adding: "You're in *Montana!*"

It was a bit of a head trip. Until June 20, I'd never been west of Chicago. In the months since, we've either visited or passed through fourteen western states together. And I've flown more times in the past year than I had in my entire life.

Craig retrieved my suitcases from the baggage carousel and walked me to his SUV. Seeing all the pickups in the parking lot, I knew I was far from home. Not that there aren't any pickup trucks on Long Island, but you were more likely to find a parking lot full of Priuses.

The airport is situated on top of the Rimrocks, he told me, so we'd be driving downhill into town. Before my visit, Billings had been a character in Craig's novels. It was the home of Edward Stanton and Jim Quillen and Hugo Hunter. And yet, the place had been anything but fictional because it was also Craig's home. He spoke and wrote about it not with worship, but with respect. Not without criticism, but with care. He loved Montana as much as I loved Long Island. His mountains were my beaches. His plains were my Hamptons. His open roads were my open waters.

We already knew that by the year's end, one of us was going to move across country. We didn't yet know which one.

Craig paid the parking fee, maneuvered around the roundabout, and began the drive down 27th Street. "We're about ten minutes from the condo," he said. *Ten minutes!* I hadn't enjoyed that luxury since I lived in Morrisville, North Carolina, a suburb of Raleigh and approximately 6.5 miles away from RDU. Also ten minutes. It had taken my twin brother well over an hour to drive me to LaGuardia that morning. It really is a long island.

I took in the sky. How could I not? Its vastness was unending, with powder puff clouds so perfectly placed I could have been looking at a mural, or those scenic backdrops used in old movies shot on Hollywood lots. I didn't care that I invoked the cliché: "Now I get why they call this Big Sky Country." It wasn't just the width of the panorama that captivated me, but the depth. Other than the ocean beaches on the East End, I'd never seen such distant horizons.

"So here's a better view of the Rims," said Craig, pointing to his left. He then pointed in the opposite direction. "Sacrifice Cliff is farther down." He pointed again. "The Beartooth Mountains are all the way over there—you can get a great view of them on a clear day."

Mountains. Many years ago, there was a point on the Northern State Parkway heading west where, if you were paying attention, you could see the tip-tops of the twin towers on a clear day. They'd been just as majestic to me.

I nodded, too preoccupied to speak. Too much surveying and studying to do. So far, 27th Street showcased a Billings that was not unlike Capital Boulevard in Raleigh, where I'd lived for six years. Or Route 6 in southeastern Massachusetts, where I had lived before and after North Carolina. Or Route 112 near Coram, New York, where I had been living for less than a year. I was renting a three-bedroom, two-bathroom "apartment," the upper half of a split-level house, the bottom half rented by my niece and her husband. Here on 27th Street I saw familiar places with unfamiliar names: a City Brew coffeeshop. A Cenex gas station. A grid of streets and avenues identified by numbers and letters and one-way signs. A smattering of casinos. *OK, so that's weird.* I didn't know gambling was legal in Montana; I've now come to accept these garish places as part of the experience. That day, I saw as many casinos on one street as there were delis or Chinese food takeouts or pizza places on mine. Grand Avenue was parallel to Central and Broadwater avenues, Craig explained. Like Northern and Southern State Parkway ran parallel to the Long Island Expressway, I mused. The interstate was at the other end of town.

Not a drop of open water as far as the eye could see.

I confess I was looking for familiarity, something that would better enable me to picture myself living there longer than the summer. Or, perhaps more specifically, something that would make me *want* to live there longer than the summer.

Montana has a population of approximately one million people. Suffolk County on Long Island has approximately 1.3 million. The entire island is 118 miles long. I'm still wrapping my brain around that. I'm still getting used to how much land separates towns in Montana, how far the interstate exits are from each other. I'm relearning the definition of a town, especially a small one.

Billings is the largest city in Montana, but it doesn't feel like a metropolis to me. Boston was Boston, Raleigh was Raleigh, but Manhattan was always "The City." No matter where I lived, one town never seemed separate from the other. I expressed no "Coram pride" or "South Huntington superiority." Ditto for Fairhaven, Massachusetts, and Morrisville, North Carolina. Would I feel differently about Billings? Would Billings seep into my skin?

Craig held my hand, caressing my thumb with his own. "We're entering the heart of downtown now."

Downtown is what I'd been most wary of. I wasn't the downtown type. No, I was a suburbanite through and through. Give me manicured lawns and wide driveways. Give me Target and Trader Joe's. Give me traffic jams and Honda Civics and PTA parents. I'd expected downtown Billings to consist of urban streets bustling with pedestrians, some shady and eccentric, others apathetic and focused only on where they were going or leaving. I'd expected lines of cars waiting at traffic lights, eager to get a jump on the green, edge out the pedestrian, beat the pack behind them. I'd expected activity. Instead, I saw empty streets and sidewalks. Cars parked rather than in motion.

"Where is everyone?" I asked. It was only Sunday afternoon. Was there some sort of curfew?

"They're around," said Craig. "We're almost home."

Home.

Not yet.

I was still overwhelmed by the big sky and Craig's FJ Cruiser and having just flown across the country to cultivate this glorious relationship. I was going to be living with a guy. And his two dachshunds. In a one-bedroom, one-bathroom condo. In a place where the bagels tasted like the Rimrocks. One of Craig's concessions, as he left Long Island nearly a month earlier, is that I'd ruined him for Montana bagels. "You're welcome," I'd said.

We crossed over the railroad tracks, turned onto a side street, and pulled up to two brightly sided box buildings with a gated entrance.

"Here we are," said Craig.

My heart pounded.

We unloaded the car and entered one of the boxes and Craig jingled his keys and opened the door. I stepped into the modern, studio-like dwelling with concrete floors and primary color accent walls and a kitchen that had half the space but twice the efficiency of mine.

This was where I'd be living for the next two months. 2.7 miles from the airport. Ten minutes, max, and usually closer to five. 2,100 miles from Coram, New York.

Within hours, I'd met Craig's dad. Within twenty-four hours, I'd met one of his closest friends. Within the week, I'd met more friends. Within the month, we were walking to the Big Dipper and the farmers' market and the Western Heritage Center. I was greeted with hugs and smiles and welcomes. Everywhere I went: "Welcome to Billings!" We took a road trip to Seattle, and I saw the Montana that Craig had fallen for long ago—the Crazy Mountains, Paradise Valley, Livingston, Bozeman, and Missoula. I developed tennis neck from the constant turning left and right to take in the scenery. I kept pointing, like a child, and exclaiming, "Look at that!" Craig sat and smiled, calm and close-lipped, yet content. "I know," was all he would say. And sky—so much sky! More sky and land than I'd ever seen. More cows, and fewer people.

I fell in love with Craig's friends. And his dogs. And huckleberry. I fell in love with all things huckleberry that summer.

And soon, my heart spoke what my head had yet to catch up to: *I'm going to live in Billings.* It was, indeed, seeping in.

On the other hand, it's really not about Billings at all, although that's now surely where I live.

"Home," though, is another thing. That summer, I learned that it was wherever Craig and I were together—a crappy motel room in Medora, North Dakota; a ferry ride to Bainbridge Island; It's A Grind coffeeshop in Cary, North Carolina; my former living room in Coram; and, yes, Billings, Montana.

Long Island will always be in my blood, my DNA. It's part of who I am. But it could no longer be home without Craig, and ultimately, life made the choice for me.

I flew back to New York in August, and packed up my belongings for the second time in one year. There were two more visits to Billings before Craig came to New York for Christmas and helped me finish packing the Coram house. Together, we drove across the country—ten states in all—back to that little condo. We lived there for three months and then bought a house in the Heights.

On a clear day, we have a great view of the Beartooth Mountains as we drive downtown. The airport is a little farther away now—five miles rather than 2.7—but it's still about a ten-minute drive.

I drive around town sometimes—I can get to most places without a GPS now—and still marvel at the fact that I live here. I admire the Rimrocks, and I like driving through downtown. I wrote part of a novel in the Billings Public Library. I meet my friends at City Brew. On a snowy day, rather than hole up inside as I used to do in the northeast, Craig says, "Let's go catch a movie," and next thing I know, we're in the FJ Cruiser, negotiating who's going to pay for the popcorn. We walk the dogs around our neighborhood on sunny days. And I always—always—take a moment to admire the sky.

I pull into the driveway of our house and into the garage and carry in groceries from Albertsons and I say, out loud, lovingly, "I live in Billings now." And Craig says once again, "Welcome home."

LORRAINE COLLINS
An Unusual Family Business

WHEN I WAS A CHILD, I SPENT FOUR YEARS IN A COUNTY JAIL.
So did my twin brother and older sister. Our father was the
sheriff, our mother was the jailer, and we lived in a building made
of thick sandstone blocks. It had been built in 1890. The front half
of the building had two stories and we lived in an apartment on
the second floor, though the kitchen and dining area and a small
office were downstairs. Mother could feed prisoners housed in the
one-story back part of the building by opening a small steel door
in the stone wall above the kitchen counter and pushing tin plates
of food through to the inmates on the other side. When we didn't
have any prisoners to look after, we three children were allowed
to play in that part of the jail.

There was a women's ward across the hall from the kitchen,
and this was also the laundry room. We didn't have a woman
prisoner very often, but when we did she had to sleep on a metal
bunk that was attached by chains to the wall in a cell in the room,
and could be folded down. The cell was never locked, so she could

use the toilet and sink and, presumably, the washing machine if she wanted to.

That's where we lived from January, 1941 to January, 1945 during the two two-year terms the law allowed my father to be sheriff of Butte County, on the western edge of South Dakota. Southeast Montana and northeast Wyoming were just a few miles away and our county had more cattle than people. Our town was a major cattle shipping point for this tri-state area but we also had a sugar beet factory and a brick factory. We were at the northern edge of the Black Hills with the famous town of Deadwood and the Homestake gold mine not far away. Our local bank had once been robbed by Butch Cassidy and the Sundance Kid. A street we all called Saloon Street provided a lot of activity for law enforcement.

When our father ran for sheriff in November, 1940, I'm sure he did so as a means of providing both a livelihood and a roof over our heads. Before the drought of the 1930s ended their intense efforts, our parents had tried to make a go of a Class A dairy, milking two dozen cows, pasteurizing the milk, separating and bottling it and selling half pints of milk to Civilian Conservation Corps camps and a cavalry unit stationed at Fort Meade. By the time she was ten years old, my older sister was helping our father deliver milk in town. It cost three cents a quart. My brother and I weren't much use on the dairy, but when we moved into the jail we were old enough to eventually be a little more help in what came to be our new family business.

We were nine years old and our big sister was twelve and a half when we moved in. I think these could be called formative years. At least, they were for us. It's hard to say which experience imprinted itself most on our tender psyches, but they were many and varied. Some involved blood and dead bodies. And one night there was an attempted jail break so our mother stood on the landing of the stairs leading to our apartment, armed with a .45 pistol, just in case any of the escapees wanted to come upstairs. It wouldn't have done them much good, since there were bars on our windows, too.

Our involvement as children in some of these experiences seems strange and exotic from the perspective of 21st Century America, but at the time it seemed much like any other family business, almost like a farm or a grocery store in which all members of the family do what they can to help out.

That's how it came about that one day a couple of years later we got involved in trying to clean up the bloody mess when a prisoner killed himself by slitting his wrists. That tragic event happened because a man had been taken to court where the judge had ruled that he was insane. The judge then sent him to the county jail to be housed until he could be transported to what we called the insane asylum in the eastern part of the state. All these decades later, the mentally ill are still housed in jails and prisons all over America, but things are little more civilized now.

It turned out that at some time somebody had smuggled a bottle of beer into the jail, no doubt through one of the holes cut into the steel mesh that covered the windows in the men's ward. The empty bottle was hidden and not discovered until that fellow found it and used it to kill himself. When he did not come to get his breakfast from the hole in the wall, Mom asked Dad to check on him. I don't think we had such a thing as an ambulance in those days. No such thing as a 911 number to call. Somehow, Dad got the man transported to the hospital. Mother went into the cell block where he had done the deed, and started to clean up the blood that was beginning to coagulate on the floor.

That's where my brother and I soon found her, clinging to the cell and holding a mop, sobbing. It was shocking to see our mother cry. I had seen that only once before, when I was about six years old. That time, I was alone with her in the house on the farm when she was washing dishes in a dish pan on the kitchen table. Something happened and the pan and all the dishes fell to the floor, breaking them all. I didn't know what to do then, so I just stayed in the living room until Dad came in.

This time, my brother and I pulled the mop away from our mother, held onto her arms and supported her, guiding her upstairs to her bedroom and then we went back downstairs and began to try to clean up the mess. I had a string mop. He had a shovel. We didn't know what we were doing, but I swished the mop around and he started shoveling. We were still doing that when our big sister and father arrived, and told us they would take over as soon as Dad went to check on Mom. The mattress was carried out to the burn barrel and somehow the mess was cleaned up and life went on.

I'm not sure what that episode taught us but it might have been compassion and endurance, though I hadn't heard those words yet. And I guess it helped us understand that fine British slogan I heard many years later: Keep calm and carry on.

The only other time any of us children had to deal with death was one year when my brother was helping our father look for a missing sheepherder out on the prairie. Dad asked him to go over to an old, abandoned well to see if there was any water in it. The Ford was overheating and they needed water for the radiator. When my brother pushed aside a board floating on the water, he looked in and there the fellow was, staring at him open eyed, though dead. While our father drove away to find a ranch home with a telephone, he asked his 12 year old son to sit by the well and wait. I guess that seemed the right thing to do, but it did feel like an awfully long time before he returned. Eventually, the poor fellow was pulled out of the well and wrapped in a blanket and put in the back seat of the Ford to take to the funeral home in town.

The night of the attempted jail break was exciting to us children mainly in retrospect because we were scarcely aware of it until it was over with. It did cause some personal embarrassment for me because I had inadvertently abetted it. We had a pretty full jail that night, including some with tough reputations. Two were in jail on charges of distributing marijuana and assaulting police officers, one had been arrested for murder in New Mexico but not tried, one had escaped from a Nebraska prison. There was also the 19-year-old who had escaped from a reformatory in Iowa and had slugged our father when he was apprehended. His sister occupied the women's ward after she was arrested for grand larceny and was discovered to also have escaped from a correctional facility in Iowa. At least two of the men prisoners had been known to carry guns.

Dad had installed in the jail a secret listening device called The Radio Nurse, manufactured by Zenith Radio after the Lindbergh baby kidnapping. When in the dark of night he heard activity and whispering in the jail that indicated the men were planning to break out, he called for reinforcements, got all of the men into the central cell block and locked them in overnight. In the morning a search revealed that the one Dad called "the escape artist" had fashioned a lock pick out of a bedspring, using a pair of pliers they also found there. Where had they come from? Well, the young woman in the women's ward had smiled sweetly at me one afternoon when no one else was around. She said that the sink had a leaky faucet and she wanted to fix it. I innocently gave her two pairs of pliers and one screw driver. Later she returned one pliers and the screw driver to our mother. She then slipped the other pliers to the men's ward through a hole in the thick stone wall near the ceiling that had a water pipe going through it.

It took quite a while for me to live that down, but at least I learned that sweet talking people sometimes might have bad motives, which is a useful thing for a young girl to know. The young woman who had willingly abetted the attempt to escape our jail, and her brother, who had slugged our father and tried to run away when arrested, somehow had to be returned to Iowa. Arrangements were made for them to be delivered to the South Dakota state prison on the southeastern edge of the state, about as far away as you could get and still be in South Dakota. This provided the last big adventure in our family business of running the county jail.

My 15-year-old sister was recruited to help deliver those young felons. Dad and Mother were in the front seat of the 1942 Ford and she sat in the middle of the back seat between the two handcuffed prisoners. They were not to touch her or each other and if they did, she was to tell Dad immediately. She was not to encourage them to talk to each other and was to report anything suspicious. It was a very long ride, travelling at wartime speed limits. Whenever they stopped at a gas station Dad would take the young man to the restroom, then Mother would take the young woman, then Mom and my sister could use the facilities, and finally Dad. Everyone was tense and nervous and it was a long ten hours before they finally arrived at the prison.

They all went into the prison, were met by Iowa authorities, went through two big steel doors that clanged shut behind them and then waited in a hall. Dad and some prison authorities took the young man away and then a woman came for his sister. Dad finally came back and it was with great relief that they all went to eat dinner and check into the best hotel my sister had ever seen. She was impressed that it had free stationery! They were all very quiet and exhausted, thinking of the young people they had just left in that grim prison. The next day, they had a good trip home. Yet the sound of those steel doors clanging shut echoed in my sister's head for days. That was not a typical teenage girl's experience and it's not the sort of thing you forget, no matter how long you live.

These memorable events were separated by weeks or months of more routine matters as men came into the jail and left again after a short stay, sometimes coming back again before long. Some became "trustys " and were let out of the jail to mow the lawn or hoe the garden. One man even built some lawn furniture for us. Now and then we would run errands for a prisoner, maybe going downtown to buy cigarettes for him, earning a tip of a couple of pennies or a nickel. In those innocent days, a child of ten or twelve could buy cigarettes with no questions asked.

Our friends often visited us in the jail and I remember one birthday party for my brother and me when we found a pair of handcuffs in the little office. We jokingly put them on one of our classmates and then couldn't find the key to release her. Mother didn't have a key, either, but she called Dad's secretary in the court house who did have one. We all ran out of the jail and across the alley to the court house, around to the front, up the marble steps outside, then the wide wooden steps inside, and into the sheriff's office. It was one of the few times we were ever there.

As Dad's second and last term as sheriff was ending, we had a sort of menage a trois in our jail for several months. In fact, two of the three were still there when we left, and living with them for so long provided a different sort of experience for us. The man and two women were from California and had been writing bad checks in several states before they arrived at our town, which was the first one they came to in South Dakota. They tried to cash a check at the local Gamble's Store. The owner became suspicious and called Dad.

I don't know how they tracked criminals in those days, but Dad soon found that the man was AWOL from the Navy and the three were wanted in half a dozen states. Their names were Bob, Justine, and Rusty. For some inexplicable reason, at first they claimed that Rusty was Bob's wife, but since Justine was quite pregnant, they soon all admitted it was actually she who enjoyed that status. Passing bad checks and crossing several state lines made theirs a federal crime and it took some time to get them before a federal judge in Deadwood.

Meanwhile, the two women were in the women's ward across the hall from our kitchen, a cot having been moved in to provide another bed. They could shut but not lock the wooden door on their side of the bars on the door, but they often left it open. Of course, Mom had to go in there to do laundry on a regular basis so the two women could come and sit in the kitchen or in the office. Justine got in touch with her parents in Iowa and they began writing to her regularly. Mom took her to a doctor for a pre-natal check up.

An appearance in federal court was scheduled and I think Dad was able to take all three there without any help. He did handcuff each of them. When Rusty said she was embarrassed by the handcuffs and asked if they were really necessary, Dad said yes they were. Bob wore a broad leather belt with an iron loop in it so his handcuffs could be secured to the belt and he couldn't raise his arms. When they returned from the courthouse they seemed a bit cheerful and relieved. Instead of prison time, they had been sentenced to six months in our jail, with credit for the month they had already spent there. They were with us for so long that they were almost like distant relatives down on their luck who had to be taken in for a while.

I remember our last Christmas in the jail because Justine's parents sent Christmas packages and they had to be opened in the presence of Mom and Dad to be sure there was no contraband. The three all came into the little office for the official present opening. Justine, feeling sorry that Rusty had no one sending her Christmas packages, had marked one for her. It turned out to be a dozen cookies.

Because Justine was due to deliver her baby soon, the court agreed that she could be released early, as long as she stayed in town. Mom and Dad set about finding a place for her to live as she awaited the release of her husband and the birth of her child. They found a small furnished apartment and began helping her find a few things she needed. They bought blankets and some things for the baby, a few pots and pans. After the little boy was born we all went to visit her and somebody took some snap shots of her and baby to send to her parents.

I've often wondered whatever became of Bob and Rusty. Justine and baby did get back to her parents in Iowa but I have no idea of the other two. We got Christmas cards from Justine for a year or two. Her son would be over seventy years old by now, wherever he is. It's strange that people we knew under such peculiar circumstances a very long time ago remain so firmly fixed in memory.

All these years later, I'm glad that we ended our unusual family business on a sort of high note, experiencing compassion and concern and trying to help someone that perhaps other people might think didn't deserve any help. Our parents showed us that not all people who do bad things are actually bad people. But of course, some are. It's good to keep both of those things in mind.

CRAIG LANCASTER
Slumpbuster

IT'S THE DAMNEDEST THING.

I'm crossing Montana Avenue, same as I do every other Tuesday for sure and a lot of the days in between. I've got my collar up against the cold because November's come on fierce, and I look back over my shoulder and see it. The Conoco refinery blazes up against the night sky, this blue-black color that I've never seen before, and I just stop. I stand there and look at it, and damned if it's not just about the most beautiful thing I've seen. I know that sounds stupid, a refinery belching who knows what into the sky, but that's what I see. True beauty, right there on the edge of the hardscrabble.

It startles me. All I want to do is stand there and take it in, think about it some, marvel at this perfect little moment I've been permitted to see, for whatever reason.

That's when the meathead in the Neon pulls up to me and leans on his horn. I jump back, staggering into a fighting stance, and he blows past me. "Get outta the road, dumbass." A middle finger presses against the frosted window. I scramble up the curb and give him the double six-shooter fingers, but he's out of there, and soon I'm looking across the street again. My perfect little moment, it's gone. It's all weeds in the sidewalk cracks and windblown newspapers and the bleary light that hangs over downtown, threatening, like an unpaid hospital bill.

I head for the front door at Feeney's and try to get my head back on my business.

"I TOLD YOU IF IT HAPPENED AGAIN, THAT'S IT," FRANK SAYS, POKING at me with a finger that looks like a chunk of polish sausage, and that reminds me that I'm about half starving, only I don't think about that too much because I don't know where Frank's finger has been.

"Yeah, but Frank—"

"But nothing, Hugo. That's it. I told you three years ago that you're too damn old for this, but you know, you did all right there for a while. But this—Hugo, this ain't all right. I'm telling you, for your health, you gotta stop."

He's looking at my right eye, which is no doubt mangled pretty good, but the eye isn't the half of it. I got laid out again, dropped by a left hook from a kid who, by rights, should have to ask permission to wash my jockstrap. Frank thinks I can't see the shots coming anymore, that the ones I used to duck or block are finding their way to my melon, and he seems to be right. Two fights in a row, I've been sent down. I don't think I lost consciousness this time; Trevor says I did, but that's the sort of thing Trevor would lie about. Whatever. I was down long enough that there wasn't any point in getting up. Frank's no dummy. He sees what's what.

"Frank, you don't know what you're talking about. A couple of bad rounds, man. It happens."

Frank's eyes narrow in on me, gaps in the slats. "Trevor says you was out."

"No, I wasn't."

"He says you was."

I have to be careful here. Trevor's a liar, a cheat. Trevor has a beef with me clear back to when we were kids, when we were both coming up, young, same age, same weight class, same path. It worked for me, and it didn't for him, and he's never forgotten or forgiven. Trevor's also the guy, now, who puts three hundred bucks in my hand every couple of weeks, fills the Babcock for his smokers on the basis of my name, and would never acknowledge the truth of the situation. Trevor's got a lot of reasons to see me done. Trevor is also Frank's only boy.

"Frank, I was there. I wasn't out. I didn't get up—no use in denying that. But my eyes, they were open."

Frank reaches across the bar with those sausage fingers and paws at the flesh around my eye, the one Trevor patched not thirty minutes ago, talking too much the way he always does. "Gettin' old, Hugo. How's that feel? That kid tonight, he's, what, nineteen, twenty? Shame to see you busted up that way. Real shame." I had to sit there and take it.

Soon after, apparently, Trevor called his old man, because Frank knew before I hit the door. "Stitchin' ain't that kid's strong suit," Frank now says. He brushes his thumb across the knitting, and I bite the inside of my lip. It may be days before I have the guts to look at Trevor's handiwork.

"Hugo, here's the deal: No more fights for you unless a doctor says it's OK—"

"Aw, Frank—"

Feeney brings his left hand down, a hammer on the bar. "Shut up. Just shut up. This is how it's going to be. You're gonna go down to the clinic, you're gonna see one of those nice doctors, and you're gonna ask for some of them head tests. I been reading about this. They do 'em for guys who play football, this whole round of tests where they ask you stuff like your name—"

"Hugo Hunter." I snap my heels together and salute.

"—and other stuff, too, smartass, and they brain-scan you or some crap. It's all scientific. Cutting-edge stuff. After the doctor does that and if he writes a note saying you can fight, you can fight."

I roll my shoulders inside my coat and look for some crack in Frank's delivery, some little opening I can move through and make him give up this idea of his, but Frank isn't showing any give here. I know this look. This is the deal.

"How am I gonna pay for that, Frank?"

I've seen this look, too. Disappointment. Annoyance. The look that tells me I have my hand out too much. I know this, and he knows it. The sigh leaves Frank like air squeezed from a tiny hole in a balloon. He sweeps the rag over the bar.

"Bring me the bill."

"Thanks. You'll see. It's nothing."

Frank runs the hose from the tap to the glass bottle without me having to ask. "You know, it wouldn't kill you to bring these back so I didn't have to give you a new one every time."

"I forget, Frank."

He sets the growler in front of me.

"Kitchen still open?" I ask. "Man, I'm hungry."

"I got some cold sandwiches. Turkey."

"Great."

He dips into the cooler and pulls up a cellophane-wrapped sammy. Wheat bread, moving hard from stale to ancient. I hate wheat bread.

"That'll do," I say.

"With the beer, seven-fifty," Frank says.

I look at him. No opening. It's Frank the Rock, a man with a face for poker but a leaning toward bloodsport. That face would drop in on me in the late rounds, there on the stool, when victory and defeat were an equal stretch. "Bear down now," he'd say. "It's yours for the taking."

"Put it on my tab?"

The face breaks. "Damn kids," he says, and he turns away from me. That's my signal to go.

I'm halfway through the door when the words hit the back of my head.

"You ever plan to pay this tab?"

I toss a backward wave. I want to come back with something quick, but nothing really occurs to me. My smart-assing has about kept pace with my fighting. I know what I want to do, but my body and my mouth don't seem to be cooperating anymore. Anyway, I'll be hard-pressed to pay for anything if I'm not getting in the ring, and even if I do, well, there isn't much to suggest that I'll be squaring that account any time soon.

I TAKE THE LONG WAY AROUND TO THE SOUTH SIDE, ALONG Montana Avenue parallel to the railroad tracks, to the underpass and on to the other side. It's a good half-mile out of my way, and I'm far past the turn-back point when the wind kicks up and the hooked glass handle of the growler starts grinding into my finger.

It's just as well. Cutting through downtown, even the little corner of it that stands between me and the house, means perhaps running into someone who just saw me get dumped on my ass, and I don't really want to face that. Or maybe it's just someone hanging outside the Rainbow or the Rex who wants to talk about the old days. I mean, don't get me wrong: It's nice to be remembered, especially after all these years, but some nights— and tonight is one of them—a guy just wants to take off his shoes, settle into the recliner and float away in a glass of beer.

The other benefit of going this way, and this one's a harder sell with the beer and the sandwich in my coat pocket, is that I'll get a little exercise in. When I retired, the running stopped cold. My knees couldn't take it anymore, and once you've reached the point where the good money's gone and never coming back, the motivation to get up and pound out the miles pretty much leaves, too. Life is no Rocky movie. I'll tell you that right now. Sure, I was like any other kid, screaming for ol' Rock to knock those bums out, but that scene where the kids run through the streets with him and up the steps? Straight-up lies. I know. There isn't an intersection here in Billings that I haven't crossed on the run, and not a single time did even one kid, let alone a whole neighborhood of them, fall in with me. I would've let them if they'd wanted to. Running is a damn lonely business.

GRAMMY'S HOUSE SITS DARK ON THE CORNER, A VIEW TO THE browned-over emptiness of South Park. It is, all at once, a welcome sight and a reminder of the things I haven't done. Time stands still around here. If I forget where I've been and what I'm carrying, forget about the piled-up years and the ache in my head, and if I pretend the porch light is on instead of busted out because I can't afford to replace it, then I can also pretend that I'm coming up on the house after an afternoon of chasing my friends around the park. I can pretend that Grammy waits on the other side of the door with a hot bowl of soup and a grilled cheese, that she'll make me bear down and do my homework, even the long division that's giving me fits. I can pretend that loneliness isn't welcome here.

But I draw closer and reality can't be dodged. The seasonals that used to bloom along the footpath are long gone, the dead husks of them whittled away by the four winters since Grammy last drew breath. Paint flecks away from the eaves, reminding me of the last promise to her that I didn't fulfill. I was laid up in the bedroom upstairs, blankets on the windows to keep out the sun. For three weeks solid I was in there after McGinley knocked me out—Jesus, McGinley. That lumbering ape. I could see everything coming, and it wasn't any use to me at all. He was so big, so much stronger than I was. I just couldn't keep him off. I'd hit him, move away, and he'd be on top of me again, crowding, leaning, that left hand crashing down on me, again and again.

Anyway, this isn't about that. I'm lying up there for three weeks, Grammy's bringing me my meals, because any kind of light hits my eyes and my head just feels like it's going to go off like a bomb. And she asks me, all gentle like, which was her way, if I'd mind painting the siding on the house. And I tell her, "Grammy, of course I will. As soon as this passes, I'll take care of it. I promise."

A week later, she's slumped over in the front yard, and a month after that I'm in Reno, fighting Olson just to pay off her funeral bill. And four years after that, I still haven't climbed up to those eaves with a bucket of paint.

I'll get to it one of these days. I told her I would. I will.

I SHOULDN'T HAVE DRANK THE WHOLE GROWLER.

Maybe it's the indigestion, or maybe it's the dream. Whatever it is, I'm standing at the toilet at 1:17 a.m. and I'm making a mess of it, aiming with one bleary eye under a single dusty light from the fixture overhead.

A lot of people might debate me on this, but I think there are four things in this world that deliver a cocaine high (four things besides cocaine itself, I mean): sex, sneezing, knocking a man out, and peeing. Still, I'm starting to think there could be too much of that fourth thing, as I stand here draining out what I put in just a few hours ago.

I give it a shake and head back into the pitch darkness of the attic bedroom. The blankets hung by Grammy over the windows remain in place, useful far beyond her intention. I can't take sunlight on its terms. The headaches come on too fast. Frank's been asking me about them for a while now, and it's been deny, deny, deny. I don't want to go to the clinic—a doctor's interests rarely match up with my own. But this is the path available to me, so I'll do what I have to do.

I fasten my hands together and reach for the ceiling beams. My shoulders groan happily in the tingle. I feel better. I consider a return to bed, but there's nothing there for me now. I head for the stairs.

EVERYTHING IN THIS HOUSE HAS A PLACE. MINE IS UPSTAIRS, OUT of the light of day. Grammy's is down here, in the bedroom she occupied from 1952, a bride who never saw her man come home from Korea, until she left us—left me—four years ago. I don't like to talk about her being dead. I mean, yeah, she is, but she lives here still. I can feel her moving through me in the silent moments, so much that I got rid of the TV so I'd never be distracted and never miss her. She finds me in my dreams sometimes, as she did tonight, and I'm frustrated that I lost her when I woke up. I can't bring her back. I can only wait until she returns.

I run my finger along the pictures and plaques on the west wall, her monument to me. It's a mashup of school portraits and boxing ribbons and stories from the Billings Herald-Gleaner clipped out and preserved in shadowboxes. And there, big as all life in the middle, is a picture of the two of us from March 13, 1997, when I rented out a ballroom for her seventieth birthday. She's silver-haired and beautiful, and she's kissing me on the cheek as I hold up a fist. Everything was looking up then. Everybody was happy.

I sit on the edge of her bed, and I breathe in deep through my nose, and she's there. She lingers still.

AN EARLY MORNING LIKE THIS, I MIGHT BE UP FOR A DRIVE TO THE West End and a corner booth at IHOP. But I sold the car, and I'm not sure where the next check is coming from, so I'd best hold tight to the money. I scrounge around in the kitchen and scare up some saltines and peanut butter, and I sit at the blue kitchen table and build me a few cracker sandwiches.

I eat them one at a time, peanut butter sticking to the roof of my mouth and ground-up crackers sinking into the fissures of my teeth. I sweep a finger through my mouth and loosen the residue. The back porch light casts a faint glow on the grown-over yard. Add that to my list.

I guess I'm going to have to start where I left off and talk it over with Frank. Yeah, he's done for me. But I've done for him, too, many times over. I need to remind him of what he owes. He won't open the place till the drink-at-lunch crowd starts milling around Montana Avenue, and that's a good number of hours away.

No matter. It's sit static in here or be moving out there. No choice at all.

I grab my sunglasses and charge the door. The light's coming up. The roasting of sugar beets, the smell of a sick child, fills my nose. The refinery belches into the morning sky.

Nothing changes on its own. You gotta change it, right?

VICKI TAPIA
Freedom

GRANDPA TAUGHT ME TO MILK A COW. HE MADE IT LOOK LIKE A breeze.

"Come-on, girl, it's time you sat yourself down on the milking stool." He pointed to the little wooden three-legged stool near the cow's udder. "Junie Lou won't bite!"

Junie Lou, a gentle brown cow, turned to stare at me, as Grandpa carefully looped her halter around the rail, tying it into a simple knot. Unconcerned, she began munching on the fresh hay Grandpa had forked into the front of the barn stall. I breathed in the sweet smell of that hay mixed with the scent of manure, and smiled, happy to be at Grandpa and Grandma's farm, the place I loved most in the world.

I plopped down and reached out for Junie Lou's teats, grabbing them and squeezing, waiting for the milk to begin squirting into the metal pail, the way I'd seen Grandpa do it a million times. He chuckled as I squeezed, watching as not one drop splattered into the can.

"Grandpa, this cow's dry!"

"Honey-pie, you move aside. I'll show you the secret." I slid off the stool and he squatted onto it. I watched as his thumb and first finger gently squeezed. He pressed down at the top of each teat to push out the milk, squeezing his fingers from the middle to his pinky. The milk magically spurted out in a steady stream, pinging onto the side of the pail. How did he do that? Grandpa grinned, turned and sprayed me in the face with the warm, sweet liquid.

"Ooh! Grandpa!" I laughed, as I wiped my wet cheek on a sleeve.

"Open your mouth next time, eh?"

"Okay, your turn!" Grandpa crouched behind me and held his old rough hands over mine, and helped me get the knack. After a while, he moved his hands away and I was proud to see the milk continue to stream into the bucket, all of my own doing. My hands grew tired before Junie Lou went dry, so lickety-split, Grandpa finished the job for me.

It was early April of 1961, the spring of my 9th year.

MAMA SAID LIVING IN MILES CITY, MONTANA, SHELTERED US from much of the world's turmoil. Still, whenever my 3rd grade class practiced the twice monthly bomb drills, it left me afraid inside. When the alarm blared, we had to crawl under our student desks and hide there until the siren quit. The thought of a bomb dropping out of the sky and landing on our town sometimes kept me awake at night, but I didn't tell anyone. Some might call me a sissy.

Miss Hicks told our class that we didn't know what the Soviets had in mind for us, but since we were in a Cold War, it was important for us to be prepared. As the crow flies, Miles City was smack dab in the middle between Malmstrom Air Force Base in Great Falls and Ellsworth in South Dakota, putting us in the path of any potential bombing raids. I didn't understand exactly how the United States had gotten in another war and why it was called "cold." Besides, hiding under a desk didn't seem like a smart way to avoid a bomb.

Our teacher taught us about the evils of communism. She told us some people in the United States had built bomb shelters in their basements.

If I had to live in one, I would worry about having enough food and where I might go to the bathroom, especially number two.

One day around the middle of April, after we had finished supper, Daddy read to Mama and me from the Miles City Star evening paper. Our country had wanted to help an island called Cuba resist the "scourge of communism." When I asked Daddy to explain a "scourge," he told me it meant the people under communist rule were often tormented and ill-treated.

I already knew from school that communism was a bad thing, so it came as no surprise that the newspaper reported the President had sent a bunch of rebel soldiers to Cuba to fight. They fought a battle in the Bay of Pigs and it had not turned out well. I felt sad when Daddy read that many of the men had died and secretly wondered what a bay of pigs might look like. I imagined the rebels swimming around a lot of dead pink pigs, floating belly-up in the blood-stained water.

I could forget about dead pigs, bombs and Soviets anytime we went to Grandpa's farm. For me, the farm was an enchanted land with interesting animals and endless countryside, where adventure always waited. On the farm, I could pretend to be anything and go anywhere. There was no other place in the world like the farm.

During good weather, Mama and I always spent Sundays at the farm, while Daddy went golfing. Sunday was his only day off from work and Mama said we couldn't hold it against him if he wanted to relax on the golf course. I would have liked him to come along, but I could see her point. Still, I knew I would never choose golfing over visiting the farm.

After early services at the First Methodist Church and a quick stop at home to change clothes, we drove south on the narrow winding road out of town, past the cemetery and down "lover's lane" to turn onto the highway. From there, we traveled another five miles south to the farm. My heart always skipped a beat when we came over the rise and there before me stood two houses and the old red barn.

Grandma and Grandpa lived in the tiny white house and my aunt, uncle and cousins, Bobby, Joey and Davey, lived in the bigger and newer white house.

One afternoon, my cousins and I tagged along with Grandpa as he walked up toward the highway. Grandpa needed to mend a short portion of the fence alongside the road.

After my cousins and I filled our jean pockets with interesting rocks, we wandered around looking for something else to do. I had an idea. "Let's go for a hike across the road," I suggested. "We can be pioneers. Is that all right, Grandpa?" I called over to him. I loved hiking up into the hills above the road.

"Yeah, but you kids stay in sight of the house, you hear?" Grandpa liked to keep an eye on us.

Standing on the edge of the road, we looked this way and that before trotting across the empty two-lane road. Few cars traveled this road between Miles City and Broadus.

On the other side, we skipped down a short stretch of dirt road and crossed the cattle guard between the barbed wire fence line. Once across, we officially became pioneers.

Along with our pocketful of rocks, Bobby and I both carried our pocket knives. Joey and Davey weren't old enough to have theirs yet. We all found walking sticks to use on our journey.

Appointing myself leader, I yelled, "Westward ho!" We set off down the dirt road, which went for miles up into the hills, where cattle grazed and windmills spun, drawing water up from wells to fill the water tanks where Grandpa and Uncle's thirsty Herefords could drink. Far off in the distance, I could see Signal Butte, with its tall radio signal towers and blinking lights. If I squinted, further away I could make out the tall, rounded peak with a mesa on either side that everyone called Angel Wings. Our wagon train wouldn't journey that far today.

Instead, my cousins and I headed toward the small bluff above the road, where wind and time had carved a forest of sandstone toadstools, taller than me, that stood side-by-side atop the hill. I knew exactly where Bobby and I had used our pocket knives to carve our initials into the sandstone last summer. That's when Grandpa had given me my treasured pocket knife, a three-blade one with a handle of pale-yellow bone. I hoped our initials hadn't disappeared over the winter.

All around me, spring showed her face. Baby green weeds and leaves sprung out of the cracks in the ground. Wildflowers couldn't be far behind. Silver sagebrush lined the pathway as we hiked up the rise.

"Rattle, clack. Rattle, clack. Rattle, clack." What was that? I looked down and to my horror, only inches to the left of my cowboy boot, I saw several tiny pinkish-grey snakes slithering unhurriedly toward me. I bellowed, "Rattlesnakes!"

Walking sticks flew in all directions and we hightailed it back to the dirt road, screaming bloody murder. Grandpa came running and met us at the cattle guard.

"What in tarnation? What are you kids hollering about?"

"Rattlesnakes, Grandpa! They were likely gonna strike!"

When we described how tiny and pink they were, he told us we'd done well to run fast, because snake venom from babies can be just as dangerous as from a full-grown rattler.

THAT SPRING THE NEWSPAPERS HAD BEEN FULL OF HEADLINES about space. "Yuri Gagaran, first man in space! Russia wins the race!" The US of A struck back a couple of weeks later when Alan Shepard blasted into space aboard Freedom 7. Glued to the black and white pictures on the television screen, everyone had watched as the gigantic rocket lifted off, soon becoming a speck in the sky. Fifteen minutes later, the space capsule had come back down and dropped into the ocean where it had bobbed up and down until a helicopter plucked Mr. Shepard out of his Mercury spacecraft. I found it hard to imagine being cooped up in that little capsule, shooting out into space like that toward the moon.

Our new president, Mr. John F. Kennedy, spoke to our nation on television about this very thing. He told us that next, we would send a man to the moon. After that announcement, lots of the boys in my class had decided they wanted to be astronauts. I didn't care about that. What I wanted was a horse of my own.

"Mama, I'll take good care of a horse. Please? We could keep him in the garage! Please?" My pleas continued to be ignored. We lived on the edge of town and didn't have a paddock or a barn. Several horses lived on Grandpa's farm, though, including a brown and white Shetland named Trixie. Everyone considered her the "kid's horse." Trixie's two main personality traits were a bad attitude and a stubbornness like nobody's business. Still, I'd rather ride a Shetland pony than not ride at all.

SCORCHING HOT, MAMA SAID IT WAS TOO EARLY IN JUNE TO BE this sweltering and that we could probably fry an egg on the sidewalk. After we parked Mama's little mint green Ford Falcon, she went on into the house to find Grandma while I hightailed it to the barn, looking for Grandpa. I figured that was a sure-fire way to get first dibs on riding Trixie, before my cousins even thought of it.

Stepping up and over the doorway ledge into the silent darkness of the barn, I shivered as the instant coolness tickled my skin. "Grandpa? Are you in here?" I heard noises coming from the tack room and went to find him.

I came around the corner and he jumped a little. Had I scared him? Knitting together his brows, he sized me up, "Betty? Is that you?"

My eyes widened and my head jerked back. I stuttered, "Uh, no, Grandpa, it's me! Betty is my mama!" Why would he ask me that?

It was as if his eyes suddenly cleared. "Oh, of course. I don't know what I was thinking," he laughed at his error. "How's my best girl today?" He could say things like that since I happened to be his only granddaughter.

"Well, Grandpa, I'm itchin' to ride today. Could we saddle up Trixie?"

"That old girl? Why, I suppose we could."

While I watched, Grandpa finished up his repair on a stirrup. He set it aside, grabbed the halter off the peg and scooped up a handful of oats, offering some to me. We walked out into the blinding sunlight and over to the corral. "Come' mere, girl..." We both held out some oats to encourage her.

She took her sweet time, but eventually the bribery worked and she wandered over to where we stood by the fence rail. Grandpa quickly slid the halter over her head. I thought she glared at him, but she also chowed down the oats we held in our hands. I liked the way her soft velvety lips felt as they brushed my palm.

By now my red and white checkered shirt had become damp with sweat, so I rolled my sleeves up. I was glad Mama had braided my long blonde hair into pigtails to keep it off my neck. I looked forward to being in the saddle and riding like the wind to cool off. Grandpa handed me the reins and together we led Trixie over to the barn. He ducked back inside to get the saddle and blanket.

I tied the reins up on the corral fence before grabbing the green and red plaid horse blanket. Standing on the bottom fence rail, I threw the pad over Trixie's back. Next, Grandpa helped me heft the saddle onto her. We flipped the left stirrup up out of the way before tightening and buckling the cinch. She immediately puffed up her stomach, one of her nasty tricks, causing the saddle to come loose and slip sideways when she exhaled. Grandpa chuckled, and muttered, "you crafty nag," as he expertly re-tightened the cinch, firmly situating the saddle in place.

Grandpa then gave me the okay and I led her out of the corral and into the shade in front of the barn. Carefully, I put my left boot in the stirrup and swung my right over the saddle and into the other stirrup. Trixie whinnied and shuddered a little. Grandpa stood back to watch me. At that moment, I had an idea. If I joined the rodeo circuit and became a barrel racer, Mama would have to let me get a horse. I planned to bring this up with her later.

"Come on, you big bag of wind! Giddy-up!" I kicked her in the flanks with confidence. She held her ground. I kicked her again. She didn't budge.

"Grandpa! She won't go!" I'd never met a more stubborn being. He walked over and gave her a little slap on her rear and she moved forward a few steps and turned to look at Grandpa, as if to say, "Excuse me?"

After a few more attempts to get her moving, I decided on a new plan. "Oh, all right, you ornery beast, have it your way!" I put my leg back over the saddle and slid off. Grandpa stayed behind, while Trixie and I walked to the neighbor's fence line, which put us as far away from the barn as possible. She moseyed along behind me, satisfied to move forward as long as I stayed off her back. I knew for a fact she'd not hesitate to gallop straight back to the barn.

I climbed back up onto the saddle and turned her toward the barn. I didn't even have to say "giddy-up." Just as I had expected, she took off at a furious gallop, and we rode like lightning, screeching to a halt in front of the barn door. She immediately started to buck. "Stop! Stop it! You bag of bones!" I yelled at the top of my lungs, pulling on the reins and holding on for dear life.

Grandpa laughed so hard, he could barely grab the reins and bring her under control.

"Good for you, girl! You stayed in the saddle. You didn't let her buck you off!"

I decided it was a good thing Mama and Grandma hadn't seen this happen because they would have scolded Grandpa for risking my life on that bullheaded pony.

Grandpa took the reins and led us around the barnyard for a

while. The heat started to get to all three of us, so we called it a day. I helped Grandpa put the saddle away and we turned Trixie loose in the corral. Grandpa went back into the barn and I wandered off in search of Mama and Grandma. I found them in the hen house collecting eggs. When I opened the door of that stale-smelling coop, the sunlight burst inside, revealing millions of dust specks spinning in the air. I sneezed three times.

I'd heard tales of chickens that liked to peck a person's hands if they even came close to their nest. Thankfully, Grandma had calm chickens that didn't mind when I slid my hand underneath to scoop out an egg or two. I helped Mama and Grandma finish up, knowing Grandma would use some of these eggs to make her mouth-watering egg noodles for Sunday dinner today.

"DADDY, MAY WE PLEASE BUY LOTS OF HELICOPTER BUZZ BOMBS? Oh, and we can't forget the parachutes!" I gave Daddy advice as we waited in line at one of the many fireworks stands on the edge of town. To my delight, Independence Day came on a Tuesday this year, which meant an extra day to spend at the farm.

I looked forward to this holiday all year. We always celebrated the 4th with fireworks and oodles of food. We would eat fried chicken and potato salad, plus birthday cake, because it was also Bobby's birthday. After we were all stuffed, we would take turns playing croquet that Uncle would set up in the yard. The best part was being allowed to stay up late for the fireworks.

Bobby, a year older than me, had bright red hair that stuck up in places and lots of freckles. "You're a firecracker!" I teased him. "That's how you got your red hair!" That got his dander up and he growled, pretending to be mad, and chased me all over the yard. Luckily I ran fast, right into Grandpa's arms.

Bobby got back at me later in the day. He strung a whole slew of Black Cats together in a tin can and set it off. I jumped nearly 10 feet straight up into the air. I didn't much like the ear-splitting rat-a-tat-tat when those firecrackers all let loose, one after the other. It scared me, sending me into Grandpa's arms for a second time.

By late afternoon, we kids started to beg, "Please, can we set off the parachutes?" We needed daylight, so we could see where to chase the little paper chutes after the firecrackers exploded. Plus, we had Black Snakes to light! The ash spirals they made really did look like creepy black snakes.

As the afternoon wound down, everyone breathed a sigh of relief when the thunderheads that threatened on the horizon skedaddled on east towards Baker. As soon as dusk settled, out came the sparklers. Using punks, my cousins and I took turns lighting each other's dazzling sticks, and then ran around waving them, sparks flying as we wrote our names in the air, trailed by swirls of smoke.

It takes a long, long time for it to get dark on July 4. Dark in the country is different than dark in the town. Dark in the country is inky black, so the fireworks look amazing.

Uncle and Daddy took turns lighting the fuses, while the rest of us oohed and aahed. The buzz bombs spiraled and squealed into the sky and sometimes the duds buzzed sideways, sending us running every which way. The fountains burst with color, while the Roman candles whizzed and sprayed sparks high enough to cast a glow on all our eager faces.

"Grandma, where'd Grandpa go?" I noticed he had disappeared. He usually helped to light the fuses. Grandma told me the loud noises seemed to be upsetting him tonight, so he had gone inside the house.

I went to look for him. "Grandpa, are you in here?" He didn't answer. "Grandpa?" I wandered a little further into the dark kitchen toward the living room. The old house creaked and groaned, making eerie noises and sending chills up my spine. Frightened, I ran back outside, pretending to be fine, but feeling sorry that Grandpa was missing all the pretty fireworks.

AS THE SUMMER WORE ON, MAMA AND I BEGAN TO MAKE SOME mid-week trips to the farm. This suited me fine. I noticed Grandma and Mama began talking on the telephone a lot more, too. What had me worried was that they always talked about Grandpa and how he was "failing."

Oh dear, what could he be failing? It confused me, but I was too afraid to ask. I thought about failing on a school exam, and how scary that thought was. I overheard Grandma telling Mama that Grandpa took the tractor and drove it in circles around the barnyard until it ran out of gas. He wouldn't listen to everyone telling him to stop. Were they talking about him failing to stop?

MAMA AND I DROVE INTO THE BARNYARD AS UNCLE WAS SETTING up the irrigation pipes one Wednesday morning in early August. "Oh Mama, look! Uncle is going to irrigate!" I bounced up and down in my seat, hardly able to wait until Mama turned off the car engine. I watched as he laid out the 4-inch pipe to irrigate both the vegetable and flower gardens and all the grass. The biggest thrill happened after he turned the wheel, releasing the water to gush through the pipes and out the umpteen holes, spraying onto the lawn. We kids stripped down to our underpants and ran around in Uncle's rainstorm, the cool, wet droplets softly sprinkling our skin. Running free filled me with such joy. "Catch me if you can!" I yelled at my cousins. I leaped over pipes like an antelope, before falling onto the wet, squishy grass, dissolving into giggles.

Just before noon, Mama told me it was time to head home. I begged to stay longer. Auntie said she could bring me later, so Mama agreed that I could stay the afternoon, bringing a wide grin to my face.

After lunch, Bobby and I decided to walk down below the big ditch to climb the tall haystack and afterwards gather some alfalfa from the field for the farm's pet bunnies, Blackie and Thumper. We found Grandpa in the shop and Bobby asked him if it was okay to take the hedge clippers to cut the alfalfa and Grandpa said "uh huh" without really looking at us. Bobby stood on tiptoe to reach up and lift the clippers off the hook.

We crossed the bridge over to the lower field, set down the heavy clippers and climbed up the haystack. I made it to the top first. "I'm king of the stack!" I called down to my cousin as he hurried up to where I perched atop the bales. Before long, we both ended up covered in hay, as we scrambled up the stack before bouncing back down, squealing "Yippee ki yay" at the top of our lungs.

After, side by side in the alfalfa field, Bobby was snipping with the hedge clippers while I tore the green alfalfa stalks by hand. "Oh! Ouch! Oh, my! Oh! Oweee," Shocked, I howled in pain, hollering louder than I ever remember hollering before. Looking down, all I saw was blood. My blood. My left pointer finger dangled from my hand, bleeding like a stuck pig. My horrified cousin had clipped my finger instead of the alfalfa. We stared at each other.

"We need to get back right now!" I wailed all the way back to the house, positively terrified my finger might fall off completely.

Uncle and Auntie took one look at my finger and before you could say Jack Robinson, I sat in the backseat of their car speeding into town to the Holy Rosary Hospital, with my hand wrapped in a towel, my finger throbbing. I didn't even faint, handling my injury like a true pioneer. Even the doctor, who used seven stitches to reattach my finger, told me how bravely I'd behaved.

Mama told me Grandpa got into a whole bucket-full of trouble with Grandma, Uncle, Auntie and herself. They asked what he had been thinking, letting us take those hedge clippers into the field alone. She said he had hung his head and apologized over and over. I was sad that he had gotten into trouble on our account.

While I recuperated, I didn't have to help do dishes or anything else that might get my bandage wet. I even got to take sponge baths a couple of times. It also meant no swimming until the bandage came off, which made me sad.

I didn't have much time to feel sorry for myself, though, before I heard the news from over in Germany. It was far worse than getting seven stitches and no swimming.

Those evil commies had decided to put up a long, barbed wire fence, followed by a concrete wall, to split the capital city of Berlin in two. They called it dividing the city, but what they were really dividing was families caught on either side. No longer free, the people on the East side could no longer cross over to the West unless they wanted to risk getting shot by the communist "scourge." I couldn't even imagine how awful it would be to lose part of my family this way. What was the world coming to, anyway?

MY FINGER HEALED AS THE SUMMER SLIPPED AWAY. Labor Day weekend brought the end of summer vacation, along with a heatwave. It thrilled me that Mama and I were spending the entire weekend at the farm.

Our car pulled to a stop near the fence in front of Uncle's house on Friday afternoon. From the car window, I saw my cousins busy building roads. I loved playing with Tonka trucks and hopped out of the car to run join them.

The four of us scraped and moved dirt, dug holes, and built roads going all over the place in the long dirt roadway leading up to the house. After Auntie and Mama saw how hot and filthy we'd gotten playing in the dirt, they easily agreed to one last swim in the big ditch.

"Last one in is a rotten egg!" I tossed my big black inner tube into the brown, murky water and jumped off the wooden bridge after it. My cousins followed me with their inner tubes. Grandpa watched us from the bridge. The water temperature was at its warmest of the summer. We floated on inner tubes, splashing and kicking in the muddy water. Even though the ditch was close to eight-feet deep in places, I liked the shallow parts where I could touch bottom and feel the mud, all squishy and mushy, ooze up between my toes.

"Now that looks like fun!" Grandpa called to us. In a flash, he had jumped into the water, but he still had on all his clothes and cowboy boots. He became a leaky boat taking on water, on the verge of sinking.

"Grandpa, Grandpa, what are you doing?!" Scared he might drown, Bobby and I tried to grab his arms. Somehow he managed to latch on to Bobby's inner tube and we paddled safely over to the bank. Crawling out was another matter, with the ditch bank so steep and slippery.

"Help, help!" we all called. Luckily, Uncle heard our cries from the shop and came running to the rescue. He shook his head twice, or maybe three times. I felt relieved he didn't scold Grandpa.

Nothing feels as quiet as night time in the country. I heard the squeaking of the screen door as it shut and Auntie's soft voice reporting that the boys were finally asleep. Grandma told her that Grandpa and I were also asleep. Only, I wasn't.

Grandma, Uncle, Aunt, and Mama continued to speak in hushed tones out in the kitchen. I listened to their soft voices from my fold-out, rollaway bed in the parlor. I overheard enough to know they were talking about Grandpa and all the strange things he'd been doing lately.

I crawled out of bed, tiptoed across the cool linoleum, stood by the door and listened more closely. I was afraid. I heard Grandma's shaky voice describing how she found him in the barn crying last week. And how, a couple of nights ago, a neighbor up the road found him out on the highway in his pajamas. I guess that's why Mama and I had come to stay overnight a few nights. We could help Grandma keep track of him.

What could be wrong? Why would he do that? It wasn't hard for me to hear the worry in their voices.

I'M 11 NOW, BUT I REMEMBER THAT SPRING AND SUMMER OF 1961 like it was yesterday. One of the last things I remember was the afternoon Grandpa and I were alone in the front yard. Mama and Grandma worked in the kitchen packing up the Sunday dinner leftovers to send home with us. I wandered out of the kitchen and into the yard to wait. I looked up to find Grandpa staring silently at me from across the yard, a scowl on his face. He seemed so peculiar. I don't think he knew me anymore. I remember the last of the cicadas humming in the trees. I remember the weeping willow that he stood beneath, still full and green in the late September sunshine. I remember the heat of the day closing in on me as I cried for Grandpa, wondering what took him away from me.

THAT AUTUMN THE DOCTOR SENT GRANDPA AWAY TO A PLACE called Warm Springs. Grandma thought he might hurt her accidentally, and she was scared of him. Mama told me Grandpa had something called hard arteries, and we couldn't keep him at the farm any longer. The doctor told us it was for the best. He said that Warm Springs was where all people like Grandpa were sent. I hoped and prayed he would get better and come back home to all of us. I missed him so.

He had been sent to the East Berlin of Montana. I cried and cried, but he never came home. He died. I never got to see him again. There was nowhere else for him to go. He lived the last two years of his life alone without his family. I sometimes wonder if he died alone too.

I imagine him laughing when the horse bucked. I remember him teaching me how to milk a cow. I try not to remember him staring at me from across the yard, looking fierce. I loved my Grandpa.

I wrote this all down to remember, just in case my arteries get hard someday.

ELIZABETH HUGHES WOOD
Digging Carrots in Early Winter with Cats

Still air
in long sleeve shirt, thick vest
digging carrots, early winter.

The yard full of cats stretching in play.
Pounce on fluttering grass blades
chasing
in this unexpected mild pause
from the rigors of cold.

Sunlight abruptly shoots through the dark cloud cover
fills the garden with white light
true heat in that sun,
I unzip my vest. Stoop, shove the fork deep
expose another handful of carrots

clinging to earth and ice crystals.

Warmth on my shoulders
the great whiteness gilding the earth
suddenly swept away
by fierce clouds.

That startling heat.
That uncanny bright
this incandescence within.

Stretched out on pale grass
cat batting at my pencil
carrots a mere sweet bonus
inside this luminescence.

Morning Song

I come into your house
late
stumbling
drunk on life
forgetting I am a guest here.

Morning,
awash in sunlight,
forgiven by the night rain
I gather sage.

If I Don't Go Out Under the Night Sky

If I don't go out under the night sky
I forget to be human.
Moonless night, winter stars.

This pause between sky
and cold feet planted in frozen grass,
respite for a troubled soul.

Ensnared far from the center
breathe in the cold
hold still this small mortal frame
so near the infinite dark.

JAMIE FORD
Madame Blavatsky and the Three Ascended Masters

with Tefvik Metrovitch

AUTHOR'S NOTE: DUE TO MY ROBUST TRAVEL SCHEDULE I WAS unable to get around to my story for this anthology. Fortunately, I made the acquaintance of an intrepid young author named Tefvik while riding a train from Tbilisi, Georgia, to Istanbul. After a careful examination of his literary curriculum vitae, as well as engaging in a stirring conversation about whether Orhan Pamuk, a Nobel Prize winner, should deign to become something as gauche as a member of the Cannes Film Festival, this fine young man offered to ghostwrite my story for free—*gratis—escritura libre*. Naturally, I was hesitant. But he insisted, and not wanting to insult him or his culture, I graciously acquiesced.

Well, much to my delight, young Tefvik is as talented as he is persistent. So here's his story, wholly original in its conception, and timelessly presented. In fact, I can almost picture the themes within distilled as a fable that might one day grace the children's section of your local bookery—but with a silver-haired girl and a warren of rabbits in the roles of the three masters. Someday, perhaps.

Nevertheless, here's Tefvik's quaint little story, approved by yours truly.

I hope you enjoy it as much as I did.

Jamie Ford
May 18, 2017

GHOSTWRITER'S NOTE: UM, BY THE TIME MR. FORD GETS around to reading this in print I have no doubt that we will no longer be "friends." We only met because he drank too much lion's milk (we call it *Raki*) and mistakenly passed out in my sleeping car. When I woke him and he found out that I was a writer heading back for my final year of grad school at Boğaziçi University (where I'm studying English Literature) he offered to "make me famous." And when I politely declined his slurring overtures and sent him on his way he proceeded to harass me on Facebook for two months! After skimming his posts I realized that he was far past his deadline for edits of his new novel—hence the menacing desperation.

But, as my mother often says, "*aç ayı oynamaz.*" Which means: trees bend while young. So I bent. I finally agreed and opted to share this curious tale, which was passed down from my great-great-grandmother. I'm told that on her deathbed she claimed this was more memoir than fiction. But even as a child I recognized the story's framework.

Mr. Ford, however, was not as discerning. He snapped it up immediately, promising payment at a later date. And I let him have it. Partly out of pity and partly out of a desire to be free from his ranting. Seriously. He frightens me.

Though I have to admit, it's not every day that a student in grad school in Turkey gets to write for an American audience. Even if under duress.

Tefvik Metrovitch
May 19, 2017

April 1868, Tsang Province, Tibet.

YELENA BLAVATSKY PASSED BENEATH THE GATES OF SHIGATSE, limping, and leaning on a wooden crutch made of lacebark pine. She'd lived outside the walls of Tibet's forbidden city for two months, begging in the streets, selling mulberry branches to be burned at Buddhist temples, and even posing as a mixed-blood Mongolian alley whore. At night, she'd slept in an alcove at the village cemetery, subsisting on a hidden cache of marmalade and stale barley. And by day, she hid in plain sight, never washing her clothing, her matted hair, or her dirty, wind-burned skin—knowing that the last Europeans to visit this sacred realm had been expelled more than a century earlier. Since that time, foreigners had been banned and those caught on the wrong side of the border had been tried and executed, and any unfortunate locals caught helping them were mutilated and tortured. So when the monks in the fruit market finally began calling her Scrapefoot and giving her bowls of old tsampa and rancid tea every morning along with the other mendicants, she knew her affectations—her ruse, had worked.

You've done it, Yelena.

Yelena never knew if the thoughts entering her head were her own or those of Master Morya, the Indian mystic who first appeared to her in visions when she was a child. She'd thought of the man as an imaginary friend, until she saw him in London and later Ramsgate, where he was part of a delegation from Bombay. As a crowd of people passed by he smiled and seemed to be speaking to her without moving his lips.

Why do you still doubt me, woman? I'm the one who found you.

"I...I don't..." Yelena caught herself before she said another word, remembering that Scrapefoot was also a mute. She glanced about to see if anyone had heard her voice, but the parade of people passing into the heart of the city was an assortment of the lame, the blind, the toothless, the aged and infirm—carried on litters by their families, and those stricken dumb, or cursed with lunacy, babbling and swatting at imagined nuisances.

This is your mission, Yelena—the first of many. Someday the name Madam Blavatsky will be known in the four corners of the world as someone who has learned divine wisdom at the feet of the ancient mahatmas, but first you must find them.

Yelena nodded and inhaled, tasting the dry mountain air. Her nostrils were filled with the comforting aromas of earthy, spiced incense, and roasted yak meat. But she didn't smile. Instead she coughed and spat—almost retching, and the nearest guards stepped away, covering their noses with orange scarves as she passed.

Because of her feigned limp she fell behind a line of barefoot orphans, most were clothed in rags, while some, the smaller ones, were naked. She regarded a small boy, rail-thin, on dirty, cricket legs, his hair shorn to prevent lice. Yelena chewed her lip and sighed as she remembered the illegitimate son whom she gave up three years earlier.

Yelena had known love only once, in the arms of a man who was not her husband. The stranger was a Hungarian opera singer, briefly famous for his performance in *The Gypsy Baron*, and for the encore in her hotel suite. But, like a malarial child, swollen with madness, her fever for this man had broken and the symptoms faded, replaced by morning sickness, aching feet, and a growing belly. And of course, the empty spot in her bed where the opera singer had once been. She'd shown no emotion when she heard that nicotine poisoning and fainting spells had ruined his career. And according to Master Morya, the singer died shortly before she gave birth. But Yelena still thought of that handsome man often, especially after the midwife, blind in one eye, took her baby away on orders from Yelena's father. At nineteen, she had fled an arranged marriage and her father had determined that dereliction of familial duty was scandal enough.

You mustn't ruminate on the past, Yelena. You're a Theosophist now, not a sentimentalist. You must give up all things of the body—your vanity, your pride...

Yelena startled and blinked as she heard the thundering bellow of longhorns echoing in the distance. She watched as the procession migrated toward the Shigatse Dzong, once home to one of the great Khans, but now occupied by a territorial governor and a Chinese advisor. From there the pilgrims would wend their way around the inner city on the eve of the Saga Dawn celebration. Because this was the one evening of the year when the poor, the sick, and the dying could touch the temple walls, humbly bow before the multi-colored prayer pole, and bask in the glow of thousands of butter lamps stacked higher than the rooftops. The rest of the populace would be allowed inside tomorrow morning, when the real festivities would begin and last an entire lunar cycle. Yelena eyed a simple building.

There it is, The House of Memories Lost, *built long before the age of Buddhism. The locals have forgotten its significance amid the smokescreens of dogma, ritual, and idolatry. The younger priests are caretakers of its occupants now, though no one has seen the mahatmas for hundreds of years—because no one can see them anymore—only you, my young protégée, if you are willing to see yourself as well.*

Yelena remembered the stories of Shambhala, a hidden country whose origin had long faded from the pages of history. Though a handful of survivors were said to have come to Shigatse, ages ago. If this is where the old masters were, Yelena thought the house looked plain, unimpressive—a simple dwelling of crumbling mud bricks, trimmed with painted wood. It had none of the elaborate gold and red features that the larger temples had, or their batik banners waving in the mountain breeze.

As she lagged further behind, Yelena limped down an alley until the procession was out of sight. Then she crept back to the front entrance where she found the door surprisingly unguarded and a mouse eating from a wooden bowl on the doorstep.

The young monks feed the spirits hemp seeds, one seed per day. That's all a real ascended master needs. What are you waiting for, Yelena? Go inside.

She hesitated, feeling her heart race as she imagined the many ways she might be executed if discovered—burned, beheaded, or tethered to horses and torn to pieces—the Tibetans had learned much from the people of the Steppe, not all of it good. Yelena shuddered and then slipped inside, closing the creaking door behind her. She drew a deep breath and slowly exhaled as her eyes adjusted to the darkness. The room smelled of burned incense, sour yogurt and ancient wool, and the air felt unusually cold.

"I'm in," she whispered to Morya as she found a single lamp, burning low. From that meager flame she lit another and then another until she could make out the features of the windowless room. There were three well-worn prayer mats around a primitive altar. Old furs and threadbare tapestries adorned the walls. And on the stone floor in front of her there were three circular, flowering *mandalas.*

Yelena wondered why they were still here. She'd seen monks

in the village spend weeks—even months, creating similar sand paintings, but they always destroyed the intricate artwork in a Buddhist ritual, sweeping the bright colors away to echo the transitory state of material life. But these magnificent creations were old and had remained untouched beneath a thick layer of dust, soot, and cankers of mold.

As Yelena got down on her hands and knees to examine the circles, she could make out the dark features of the largest mandala. She recognized the Summerian gods: Ki, Uras, and Annunakai, as well as Tatenen and Chronus, patriarchal gods from Egypt and Greece. The old deities were bowing to a larger, more fearsome being with scaly eyes and a mouth of serpents, a tongue of flame, rendered in coarse charcoal, sandstone, rust, burnt sulfur, and finely crushed gypsum.

"Morya," She whispered, trying to suppress her panic. "Do you see this?"

She looked about the room but saw no one. She listened, but all she heard was her heart beating. The lamp flames did not flicker. Their shadows did not move.

"Morya," she called again, louder this time. She closed her eyes, searching her thoughts. He was nowhere to be found. He'd abandoned her. *Or was this a test?* She grit her teeth and imagined that if he could speak, he would warn her not to remove the grime from the dark god's face. Fingers trembling, she agreed.

Yelena nodded, bowed, and solemnly moved to the next mandala, which was smaller in diameter and featured a pantheon of gods who were more familiar: Isis, Venus, Tacitus, Danu, Chaxiraxi, and Cybele—mother gods, all worshipping the sun. The bright colors of the sand painting shone through the dust, instead of becoming one with the image. The figures had been rendered in powdered roots, ground bark, bee pollen, dried flowers, and crushed seashells with bits of pearl. The mandala radiated beguiling warmth that was comforting, the artwork more felt than understood. Yelena didn't want to move away, but the smallest mandala seemed to be calling her.

Yelena suspected that the last sand drawing would represent a child, so much so that she hesitated. She steeled her resolve and finally allowed herself to behold the tiny rendering of Saharan animals and birds worshipping an infant. She looked at the toddler and allowed her broken heart to imagine that this child was *her child*. In fact, the child was a boy, and he had her eyes, he reached out toward her, wanting, pleading, a figure of crushed bone, wispy hair, fingernails, and dried, powdered placenta.

Helplessly, she reached toward the tiny hand, but when their fingers touched, the dust and mold atop the artwork smeared the image, and the more she tried to hold onto the little boy the more her desperate pawing destroyed him completely. Dark spots appeared and she realized she was crying and those were her tears dappling the flesh-colored stain where a child had once been.

She stepped back, wiped her eyes on her ragged skirt and called out to Master Morya again, and again. Pleading. Begging in the lamplight.

No reply.

In the absence of her spirit guide, Yelena did her best to calm herself. She decided that she would wait for further instruction. But as she regained her composure she realized that first she would need to do something about the stench of burning yak butter that had filled the room. So she approached the altar where there were three incense burners made of glazed brass, inlayed with fine runes that she didn't recognize.

By their sizes, she understood that they must correlate to the mandalas of the father, mother, and child. She tried not to think about their presences. Without Master Morya to sort fact from fiction—without his encouragement, his direction, she felt meek and superstitious, unsure. Even so, she smelled the long-stemmed incense in the first burner, which gave off a pungent aroma of tobacco and sweat and sex, like the sheets she'd slept on the night her son was conceived.

Her mouth felt dry as she moved to the next, smaller incense burner, which contained a circlet of pressed incense that smelled of milk and honey, with a burning sting of lye, like freshly laundered lace.

Then she opened the lid on the smallest burner, like the cover on a bassinet, and found that the tiny cone of incense within was still burning. A single ember had not yet died, and when she blew on it a flame appeared. She felt lightheaded as the incense smelled like her child, his thin tuft of black hair, sticky and coppery, wet with her own blood. She'd only held him for a brief second but that had been long enough for her to feel his breath, the gust from a butterfly's wings. Long enough for him to haunt her for a lifetime.

She blew again and watched the incense burn pink and then blue as tendrils of smoke coiled about her, ashen fingers touching her face. She closed her eyes as the fragrance echoed the cologne of the man she once loved. Her heart raced and her skin flushed and parts of her, long dormant, ripened in ways she'd long forgotten.

Feeling faint, she dropped to her knees and felt the largest prayer mat next to her. The mat was stiff, jagged, as though the red fabric hid a bed of nails.

The smaller, mother's mat, looked too soft, too comforting, she wasn't a mother anymore, or was she? She gave her child up, but surely he was still out there, somewhere. *Is my son happy? Does he think of me and wonder? Master Morya must know. Why does he never speak of my baby boy?*

Yelena had followed the voices in her head all these years. She'd been humble and obedient to those inner murmurings, but she'd been weak too.

Passing the straw-filled mother's mat, she found the tiny prayer rug of a toddler. It was too small so as she lay upon it she curled her body into a ball as her dirty hair fell across her face, hiding her from all but her own thoughts. She rocked back and forth, ever so slightly, eyes closed, wondering what she might have called her son if she had been brave enough to keep him, strong-willed enough to find him. To not just go against her family's wishes, but those of Master Morya who said the boy would be a hindrance.

As she rocked herself to sleep she thought about the scores of cities she'd visited: Paris, New Orleans, Ceylon, Quebec, Leipzig, San Francisco, Tokyo, Cairo, she lost count as she weighed that freedom against the cost of the many internal paths she'd ignored, the doors she'd left unopened, the rooms in her life that she'd left unoccupied, the chambers of her heart that she'd left empty and haunted. As she drifted she felt the incense smoke surround her, lighten her, as she felt her heart slow, and if she died here in this room, in this moment, filled with regret, it would seem just. She dreamed of Istanbul and the opera, of silk sheets, of eating poached eggs in bed, and drinking leftover red wine straight from the bottle.

She felt her burdens release, her ears buzzing, and a small hand brushing her hair away from her face, gently touching her cheek.

Yelena opened her eyes. She wasn't sure how long she'd been asleep. It felt like a moment—a fraction of a minute, but her body ached as though she had bedsores and her head reeled. As she squinted up, she counted three figures looming over her. An aged man with dark skin, balding, hat in hand. On her other side was a pregnant woman in Persian silks, her blouse unbuttoned. And above her was a child—her child, but older. He was touching her face softly but he looked down with condemning eyes. Then he was pulling her hair, pinching her skin, and when he opened his mouth and spoke in an unknown language she saw that he was toothless, ancient, frozen in this state, cursed. They all reached for her, feeding on her presence as though they'd been starving for a thousand years. They fought over her, tore at her, marveled at her foul clothing, tore clumps of her hair out by the handful and tasted it.

Yelena screamed.

She crawled to her feet and they edged toward her, inching like leeches upon bare skin. She stepped back, tumbling over the altar and spilling the incense holders to the floor where they clattered and sprayed hot embers onto the straw mats, which caught fire and filled the room with thick black vapors.

"Morya!" Yelena called through the smoke. She stumbled to the nearest wall and circumnavigated the room, feeling her way through the void, avoiding the hands and faces that dashed through the flames, searching for her, until she found the door and heaved her shoulder against the heavy wooden sway until it flew open and she was standing in the rain which felt cold and cleansing. It was night in Shigatse and celebrants were inside the nearby buildings, standing beneath awnings, waiting for the storm to pass.

She looked down at her muddy clothing, which was half torn. She unclenched her fists and found handfuls of her own hair. And in front of her appeared a pair of monks who must have been no older than eight. They dropped their metal lamps and ran, shouting for the city guards—orange robes flapping as though waving goodbye.

Yelena heard an alarm bell begin to ring and voices in the streets and in her head.

Run Yelena! Run.

Master Morya called her back to reality and she ran as fast as she could, past drunken revelers and pious pilgrims. She flew beneath the inner gate and kept sprinting, splashing through puddles, ignoring the strands of wet hair that stuck to her face.

And the guards who had rushed to see what was amiss, the sight of the lame beggar took them aback as she had been made whole, running free. They lowered their weapons and smiled. Some of them cheered "Scrapefoot! Scrapefoot!" while others fell to the ground, bowing deeply as though some forgotten magic had been unearthed.

But Yelena just ran, fleeing the city. Crying. Reconciling her gift, her universal truth, knowing with supreme certainty, with ancient divinity, that she would achieve greatness if only she could forget her child.

AUTHOR'S NOTE: HELLO, TEFVIK AGAIN.

I'm not really into Western fairy tales, but that's what Mr. Ford said he needed. So this amalgam of *Goldilocks and the Three Bears* and my great-grandmother's apocryphal tale seemed to suit both of our needs. (He actually wanted me to address him as Jamie, but that's a level of intimacy bordering on friendship that I'd rather not claim).

And yes, in case you are wondering, my older relatives still swear that my great-great-grandmother's story is mostly true. But, we are Moslem, so they stop shy of claiming Madam Blavatsky and her religious beliefs as part of our genealogical tapestry.

Speaking of outlandish stories, if you want to explore a real, Turkish fairy tale, I'd highly suggest the *The Boy Who Found Fear At Last*.

This amazing folktale appears in *Türkische Volksmärchen*, and has an ogre, a shipwreck, a sea-maiden, a boy king, and hands reaching from the grave.

On that note, I'd better sign off. I have a restraining order to update.

Görüşmek üzere,
Tefvik Metrovitch

DAVE CASERIO
A Terrible Music

When men go to war they break a terrible music
From the air, release the earth her charge of fertility
And nurture into blood-sod and wreck-rhythm, into deep-
Bass pounding of Stuka shriek and screech of shell, of the
Horse-bitted scream and the gritted teeth of wheel-lock
And rail into some great force voiced of their own
They break a terrible music from the air when naming
The names of those pitched from the living, whether
Blameless, or god-favored, frail or wicked, O'Malley or
Juan, Chia or Sean, Gertrude, Helmut, Mohammed,
Louisa, Edgar, eager the blood into the river of dying,
Ever to dark sailing, when men go to war.

Dublin Station

There is a Hearn, an Ahern,
A Barret, a Brit, Burrough,
O'Casey, Connell and Cody,
Dunn and Dundon, Tweet and Twohiss,
O'Callahans, O'Sullivans, six Kellys,
O'Brien, O'Rourke, Smith and Scully,
Murphy and Maycock, perhaps each of the stock
Of the rude fraternity of this morning's
Drunken me'boyo faces on ferry
From Holyhead to Dun Laoghaire,
On bus, now, to Dublin Station.

All night they danced—R&B and Disco,
Soul to Rock 'n' Roll, Euro-Tech, Pop
And Reggae—as they jerked and tupped under laser
Glitter and hull shudder, to the boom-bass hurled
And turgid smash of bow and wave hissing past
Under the lurch and squeak of their crepe-smirched streaks
Across a floor sticky with Budweiser, whiskey and soda.
But there is no flowering wiser in this morning in this year
Of the war in the Gulf—for there is one who was collapsed
In vomit, in the toilet stall; upon whom,
Young girls burst, shrieking: "Where's the Cock?
Come on, don't be shy. Give us a peak a' the beastie thing."
But he heaves as the ship heaves—Whump, Whumph,
Wump, Whumpwhump, as if channel fire—
A thump of guts, splash of water,
"Hey now, stop that puking, and show us your..."

"Cock! Cock! Cock-a-roo! Cock." But the young men
Are chanting now, from the open deck of the
Double-decker bus, down to the young girls below:
"Give us a whiff a' that yeasty bait,"
As we wait in front of the terminal ticket office window:
"And we'll give ya a peek a' the Cock."

Is this how my grandfather went to Gallipoli?
In cock and valor, in lust and song,
By hornpipe bands and their bantering chant,
A bluster of kisses as promises waved at fair dames,
Singing, "Who'll Go a Waltzing Matilda With Me."
And the beribboned flutter of their flags tacked to
Picket boats in line—The Irresistible, The River Clyde,
The Argyle. Did he go to those fields of corn, those gullies
Of thyme and red poppies, to rivers of salt and the blood-
Frothed hail of the Turk Ezine, to leap at the Munster's
First charging, of shamrock sprig, of the green and the pale?
Then Dubliners, then Hampshires, crying: "Out Aussies
Of Anzac, Gurkhas and Sikhs. You Lancashires,
Zealanders, Maoris, never retreat!"

So they died on the lighters, over the bloated dead and
Submerged, through the gore of the rocks to the ground
Of the beach, crying "Mother of God" in mother tongue all
The shrieking day of Suvla Bay to Sedd el Bahr.
And even the night: Shouts of, "Allah!"
Screams of, "Christ!" Of, "Hatun, Ana." "Ayo Gorkhali!"
Of, "Ka mate, Ka mate—Ka ora, Ka ora!" You shall die.
You shall die. All of you shall die in the shallow-mouthed
Plains with silver tin plates, in the hills and the knolls
With the shit of the flies, till all death-split tongues
Fold into one. The morning, in the year, Lords Kitchener
And Churchill gave the Turks a peek a' the cock.

But they will not stop, "Cock! Cock! Cock-a-roo Cock!"
Singing: "Tie a yellow ribbon round the old oak tree, the
Old oak tree, the old oak tree. And don't sit under the apple
Tree with anyone else but me, anyone else but me, anyone
Else but me. No. No. No. Don't send me off to Gallipoli.
Take anyone else but me, anyone else but me, anyone else
But me. No. No. And keep me away from Mortar Ridge
Or Shrapnel Valley. And don't be off to Dead Man's Land
Or Bloody Angle, Bloody Angle, Bloody Angle. Unless,
Unless, of course you want to be a putrid slimy sea of
Pustulate flesh, of lice and fleas, of myrtle, mud and gore,
A baking in the sun. Clap. Clap. A baking in the sun.

Clap. Clap. We all go off to No Man's Land,
With whistle and tin we go, whistle and tin we go,
Whistle and tin we go. Clap. Clap. We all stood up and
Over the top, over the top again. Clap. Clap.
Over the top we wend. Clap. Clap.

Over the top again. Clap. Clap. Went the bristle and spin
Of machine gun lead 'til we all fell down dead, all
Fell down dead, all fell down dead. Oh why did I join
The Infantree and the bloody Ar-ar-mee, the bloody
Ar-ar-mee, bloody Ar-ar-mee. Because, Because,
BecauseBecause, Because I was Bloody well barmy,
Bloody well barmy, Bloody well..."

And they clap, and they clap, and they clap again.
"Cock! Cock! Cock-a-roo! Cock!" In the House of Lords,
On the Senate floor, at the Arc de Triomphe and the U.N.
Door. To the deserts of Araby, we shout and sing,
Let freedom ring in this Silver Jubilee of Super Bowl XXV,
As we tie a yellow ribbon round the old flaccid tree
In the year of the war Saddam caught a peek a' the "Cock!

Cock! Cock-a-roo! Cock!" And it's two steps up a time
The conductor comes running: "Who's makin' war-whoop
And racket? Ye ain't goin' to fight.
Ye ain't goin' nowhere—yet.
So have some respect for mother tongue
Or it's off the bus I'll throw ya."

And their eyes slap his back cocksure and grinning like
The eyes of my grandfather and the eyes of those upon
First pink meat of sky over Dardanelles' lavender sheath;
First hurrah and last, rising over the stunned, unearthly
Beauty of wild rose and sage, of olive and thyme, and the
Faint glistening light of cypress and oak, hyacinth and
Grass, winking with spider webs and dew at the bejeweled
Sparkle of the bay; when rose the enormous globe
Of blood-fire over the last faery trace of phosphorous
Green water smoothed into a glassy, oily sea—
Surface of black eyes: a thousand ruptured fish aglitter.

Then the tidbit flecks of rifle fire,
The scintillating wobble of bayonets,
And the empty gauntlet of eyes'
Horizon-ward stare through the nothing
Between them and the pouring dead
Oozed in runnels of cankerous tongues
And gangrenous arms; legs a bag of mush.
Rain soaked, frozen, then rained again
They shudder in their own fly-buzzed clouds of shade
At the loveliness of Troy and snowcapped Samothrace,
Before Imbros' jagged scrim, crown of Tenedos,
Upon the ships' transfigured faces,
The stink of burning dead:

Through the hills of Gallipoli, in my land and yours,
In the deserts of Kuwait, by the waters of Babylon, in
The first holy cities, upon the flesh of mother tongue,
Cry: "Mam", "Ma", "Mutter", "Modra", "Mater",
"Mere", as all matter cries when first torn asunder.

"Cock! Cock! Cock a..." But the conductor turns
As my grandfather turned, in silence, to pints and sausage,
And spits: "Don't ye dare.
Not another fokkin' word, ya fokkin' bloody bastards."

Dave Caserio

It Was Always Errol Flynn

And when he played General George Armstrong
Custer in, *They Died With Their Boots On*,
And when Crazy Horse thundered across
The sharp grass of Little Big Horn hill,
He held what earth was his.

And whooped and tangled on a prairie lot,
Wedged between Pulaski's shack and the alley,
With little Paulie scalped and Kenny filled with arrows,
Or Benteen miles away or trapped and gutted, I stood
Flushed in the spirit-filled air, my imagined hair
Fluttered and gold as the feathers of the coming lances.

BLYTHE WOOLSTON
The Bone Dowsers

ASIDE FROM NAME AND OCCUPATION, THE TWO BETTYS WERE VERY different.

Old Betty smoked whatever was cheapest at the Smoke Shoppe. Other Betty was brand loyal to Salem Menthol Lights. Old Betty washed her hair with liquid dish soap once a week. Other Betty wore makeup and had kept the habit of having her nails done right down to paying for one-inch extensions with custom paint jobs on the holidays, like on Easter she had H E I S R I S E N ! painted on there, one letter per finger. Old Betty thought that was a bunch of crap, and everybody knew those nail salons were crawling with all kinds of crap, and someday Other Betty was going to end up having her fingernails die and fall off. Other Betty thought Old Betty should look at her own goddamn feet, because she had spit-green toenails thick as a saltine cracker and just as crumbly.

Anyhow, they were good friends and business partners.

That happened because one day Old Betty stopped for a beer at The Roundup Bar while Other Betty was tending. The two of them got to talking about how they wished they could make the world a better place, because who *doesn't* want to make the world a better place?

Other Betty was getting sick of tending bar, especially in the afternoons when the only customers who came in were smelly geezers with almost no teeth and a firm conviction that she would be grateful for a boob-grab because she was a widow and lonely. So Other Betty was ready to quit that job, especially now the insurance had come through from when the self-loader went on the fritz and crushed her Bill. But so far she hadn't pulled the trigger on that, because the thought of doing nothing for that many more hours at home? That thought made her feel blank inside.

So when Old Betty got to talking about how there were all these graves, pioneer graves, lost over the years because the boards that marked them rotted away, it struck Other Betty as heart-wrenching sad. Like that wasn't bad enough, now coal and oil development was happening and those graves were getting disturbed. The bones were getting all mixed up and crunched up and scattered around. That was the moment when Other Betty knew she had to do something about it. She had to make the world a better place than that.

As it turned out, Old Betty knew how to rescue those bones.

Old Betty's father had been a water witch, and, when she was a little girl, she had watched him cut a forked willow from down by the creek and peel it, all flexible and fine. He'd use that willow to show him where the water was hiding. People paid cash money for a witched well, a good well. It wasn't steady work, but it was enough to make it worth the effort, enough to get good and drunk once in a while without feeling guilty about it.

Her dad showed her how to shuffle along, keeping both feet on the dirt. He taught her how to hold the willow, which was a little tricky, thumbs under and fingers loose, sort of like holding reins, but not exactly. He said everybody could be a dowser if they paid attention, but she seemed to have a god-given talent for it. Her dad told her something else: a person could witch for graves, too. It was the same principle, but there wasn't money in it.

Old Betty thought about that when she was a little girl waiting in the car for her dad while he got drunk without feeling guilty. She thought about all the bones in the ground, right under there like the water, invisible but there. One time she got real thirsty while she was waiting, thinking about water and bones, so she licked the frost off the inside of the car window. That was a terrible idea because the frost was all mixed with her dad's cigarette smoke and she wanted to pull her own tongue out it tasted so bad. Maybe she should try that again, now she was a smoker. That would be a pretty cheap smoke, just licking windows of the smokers' shack outside Trixie's Casino.

Other Betty thought that was disgusting, but she wanted to know more about how to find the pioneer graves and rescue them.

Of course, Old Betty hadn't witched for years.

People were hiring scientists or buying bottled water these days. It was sort of a lost art. But maybe they should give it a try. They could practice in the cemetery, because that would be like shooting ducks in a barrel, which was just how it turned out—except for this one grave. The willow stayed dead-level when they shuffled over that spot. It was a puzzle, but then they looked at the gravestone and saw it was a boy who got killed back in the first Iraq War. That good as explained it. Those soldier bones might be somewhere else, half around the world, and all that was buried in his grave was an empty uniform in a military casket. So the willow switch was telling the truth the whole time, even if the truth wasn't what the Bettys expected.

Next day, when they were talking over how it went at the cemetery, a regular named Joe overheard and said he could sure use some help. He and his wife were fixing to move, trailer and all, to a new place a whole lot closer to the highway, which would sure make things easier far as snow removal went. Problem was the wife's favorite cat died about eight years ago. Joe buried it in the yard like the wife wanted, but over the years—with stuff happening, and the grandkids fooling around—the marker stone his wife painted got moved to the flower garden for some damn reason. Now his wife wanted him to move the cat's grave to the new place. She really did love that cat. Never got over it. She had five live cats, but the dead one was the all-time favorite. Joe, though, he didn't want to dig up the whole damn back forty looking. Maybe the Bettys could come over and give the place a once-over? He could offer them beer and barbeque, no matter if they found the cat or not.

They found the cat.

After that, they were busy as they wanted to be with grave

location. Not that things always went off without a hitch.

Once Old Betty had taught Other Betty everything about witching, Other Betty looked into it and showed up one day with a couple of pieces of metal clothes hanger she said she was going to use instead of cutting willow forks all the time. Old Betty thought that was a load of crap. Other Betty thought it was easier and besides it was recycling instead of destroying the planet. That first day with the clothes hanger involved, they, neither of them, got so much as a twitch. Old Betty said it was because the clothes hanger was interfering with things. Other Betty called bullshit on that and got in her car and drove off, leaving Old Betty there on a hillside between two creeks where somebody thought somebody was buried sometime. Old Betty just got her wand held right and started shuffling through and around the sagebrush. The dust the car kicked up on the dirt road blew away to the east and disappeared, not that Old Betty was keeping an eye on the car or thinking about how many miles she was away from home or how she was never going to let Other Betty drive her anyplace ever again. When Other Betty showed up with a cold six pack in way of apology, Old Betty had come to the conclusion there wasn't any grave. She had worked the grid pretty hard one way and the other and never got sign. So either what somebody heard one time wasn't true ever or the bones had washed away some spring at high water. After that, Other Betty always used her clothes hanger, and Old Betty shut the fuck up about it.

Then the high school track star got murdered.

She went out for her morning run, didn't come back, and then somebody found one of her shoes near the grain elevator. It was all over the news. Then it was all over the news that they caught two dumb sons of bitches from Texas who took her and killed her and buried her somewhere south of Canada or maybe east of North Dakota. Being druggies, their geography-bee knowledge and memory were crap. There was a lot of talk about if justice could be served when there wasn't a body. People remembered that guy who killed that other guy and, even though there was trace blood evidence inside the camper, he got off.

Sitting on her living room couch watching *Jeopardy* after the news, Other Betty couldn't stop thinking about that girl. Justice getting served was only the half of it; somewhere out there, in the high, wide lonesome that girl was lost. Who could forget the little family that went missing on the way to a funeral? And sure they found the abandoned truck and some bones eventually, but not from the baby. All the police ever found from that baby was a blanket and some bits of polar fleece snow suit. The police might have done better if they had been bone dowsers. They might have given that family a little more closure, something to put in a little white casket, at least.

So maybe they should branch out a little more, give finding that girl a shot since those who choked her out and left her in a shallow grave were so damn clueless: that's what Other Betty threw out there while the two Bettys were having a weekly business meeting over pancakes at the Daily Grind.

Old Betty was trying to talk Other Betty into getting paid money to find a grave. They could get paid cash money for locating a little boy's bones up by Glendive. It was a homesteader child who had a name and some family scattered around who even remembered how he died of blood poisoning because a boot nail was poking him. Being a kid, he didn't tell anybody. He loved those boots. And then he died. The family was about to subdivide that old homestead, but before they did, they wanted to maybe fence off a little plot and put a marker down. It seemed like the right thing to do—and it might jack up the price a little. Somebody from out-of-state might consider a tragic homesteader story a feature. The family was willing to pay a finder's fee. Other Betty wasn't too sure how she felt about that.

So now both of the Bettys wanted to take the business in a new direction. They bargained on it for a little while and then decided to diversify both ways. They could go find that little boy in Glendive and then head on up and do some looking around for the murdered girl. They'd give the whole thing two-three days and see how it went.

As it turned out, they found the boy's grave in no time flat. There was a patch of iris half-way up the hill behind where the first house used to be. The mother could have seen the place when she stepped outside to throw out the dishwater or pin up laundry. It was pretty much the logical place for that little guy to be, but the two Bettys went ahead and witched the site. They both got strong hits: the clothes hanger and the willow wand for once in total agreement. They marked the place, pushing day-glo flags on wire stakes all around. They had a hundred of those flags. They cost next to nothing at the big-box hardware store and were weather-proof and fade resistant. Other Betty liked the professional touch. So anyhow, the finder's fee was in the bag and they headed north to look for the murdered girl.

They spent all of one day prowling the gravel roads, looking for stirred up ground that might mark a recent grave. They figured the murderers were too lazy to walk very far with the body. It was a fair bet. It was Other Betty who first thought maybe it would be worth taking a look at some of the cutbanks where the road clipped a hillside. The dirt was looser there, and lazy sons of bitches could just have tossed her out into the ditch and then got the loose dirt and rock above to slide down and cover up that poor girl's body. Made sense. Plus Old Betty's hips were hurting her something awful, and she was in favor of anything that involved less walking.

When Other Betty found the thing, that was a time Old Betty hadn't even bothered to get out of the car. The wind was kicking up, and Old Betty said the willow was sensitive to weather. Other Betty took a minute to mention the superiority of clothes hanger dowser wands before she stepped out onto the loose slope by the side of the road.

She was as surprised as anyone when her dowsing rods jumped out of her hand and flew right into the dirt like arrows.

She was pretty sure she'd found something. Old Betty thought that was a load of crap, but she helped Other Betty start digging away at the cutbank. They had never needed a shovel before. They were in the business of location, not relocation, and bringing a shovel was more for grave robbing, if you think about it. But there were a couple of windshield scrapers in the car, and those did okay for trowels, plus the snow-brush end could be kind of useful if it got down to an archeology sort of deal that required a delicate touch. Old Betty wondered how long it would be before Other Betty broke a nail and they could pack it in and call it quits. Other Betty had plenty of practice, though, doing shit with those long extensions. Between the two of them, they moved a lot of dirt.

It was just a hub cap, according to Old Betty, and it sort of did fit that description, bulging out of the dirt, round and shiny. But then Other Betty picked up one of her clothes hanger dowsing rods, stood about ten feet away and dropped it. It flew, just like a dart, until it plinked into the thing and just stood there, trembling and upright. She walked over by the car, hunkered down and held the other dowsing rod six inches away from the rear tire. That rod just fell into the dirt, completely uninterested in the hubcap. Old Betty thought maybe they just used to make things better back in the day, but now the hubcaps were all made in Japan out of recycled gum wrappers or something.

Even if it did turn out to be just a hubcap, Other Betty thought it was worth digging it out. It was some kind of antique, maybe. She could put it in her garden or on the porch as a conversation piece. Old Betty was about to say how it could be a companion for the plastic goose Other Betty dressed up in seasonal costumes—fuzzy bunny ears, a lei and sunglasses, a tiny hockey mask—but the two of them had already collided on that particular subject several times before. Hurtful things had been said. Old Betty had no desire to watch the car drive away without her in it, so she let that go and resumed helping scratch the dirt with the windshield scraper.

It wasn't a hubcap.

Other Betty went to the car and came back with a tire iron. Old Betty was a little pissed that tool hadn't come out of the trunk before now. Could have cut down on the piddly-ass scraping time, which would have been good. Other Betty picked up a rock and drove the flat end of the iron down at an angle and started prying on the thing. The dirt gave it up, and the thing tumbled down the bank.

The cavity behind was cluttered with bones, all nested up in the dark.

Now both Bettys had dismantled enough chickens and deer to have a pretty clear idea about bones and how they worked. These bones weren't right. Old Betty reached in and picked one out. It was thin and hollow, like the abandoned shells after crab leg night at Trixie's Casino, but the surface prickled with little thorns, sharp little sons of bitches with a bite like nettles. Other Betty was getting the thing, because that was what she was after the whole time. It had rolled to the edge of the road and was sitting there, round side down. Other Betty picked it up, made a terrible noise of mixed prayer and pissedoffedness, and dropped it again. She held her hand out so Old Betty could see, and right there, stuck in her hand was a sort of porcupine quill deal, but bigger. Old Betty reached to pull it out, but Other Betty wasn't having any of that and jerked her hand back. Old Betty had to practically put Other

Betty in a head lock before she could get a grasp on the damn thorn. Then it wouldn't come out. It wouldn't budge. Other Betty was coming into her right mind, finally, and said there was a Vice-Grip in the glove box. The pointy end must have been stuck right in the bone, because it broke off. Old Betty was inclined to poke around a little bit and see if she could grab onto it again. Other Betty said hell no to that, she wanted a doctor. Old Betty saw her point. By that time, Other Betty's hand had started to swell up until her palm was round and her fingers were jointless as cheap hotdogs.

They hadn't even made it to the black top when Other Betty held her swollen hand in front of her, reached over with her good hand, and started pulling off her fingernails. They came away easy because the meat under them had started going soft and yellow. Other Betty placed them carefully on the dashboard, in order. Yellow mucus held them in position like glue.

A few miles later, Other Betty wanted a cigarette. Old Betty dug the menthols out and lit one in her own mouth before she tucked it between Other Betty's lips. Other Betty smiled around it, breathing in and out like she'd forgot how to smoke. Next time Old Betty glanced Other Betty's direction, the cigarette was smoldering on the seat between her legs and her head was drooped to the side

Old Betty reached over and picked up the cigarette before it burned through the upholstery, put it in her mouth, and took a long, deep pull. She was grateful for the cold smoke on her throat and the way it wiped away the dead bird smell in the air. The stars were coming out, popping into view like little blisters on the sky. The bone-nettle stings on her fingers hurt like hell. *Fuck the pioneers.* That's what Old Betty thought. *Fuck them for coming here. Fuck them for dying. Fuck them for leaving their bones behind.* Old Betty let her foot get heavier on the gas pedal. She wanted to be a little closer to home before she ended up just like Other Betty in the only way that really mattered.

SID GUSTAFSON
smallpox

1914 Springtime—Blackfeet Indian Reservation, Browning, Montana

It was not unusual after that manifest turn of the century for a child to spend the entire wind-driven day alone in front of the mercantile. Odd thing was, the child was white as the vanishing snow, white and left to fend the spring wind alone with nothing but the clothes on his back and a dog at his feet. When evening stole away the day's breezy warmth, robed Indians drifted their various ways. The boy sat and waited, the dog warming his toes.

Tess Ground Owl took notice after a long day's work in the store. She stopped to look the little stranger over and help him find his way. He asked the boy his name. He stood up, as if to be inspected, but did not offer an answer. "Come child. Your name." Nothing. She tried coyote French, and then Blackfoot. No answer, as if he'd been told not to speak with strangers.

The reluctant boy struck a chord with Tess. He would not relinquish a word, nor accept her urge to follow along to her room in Sherburne's mansion, the nicest house in town. She lingered with him on the street half a twilight hour, hoping to wait out some information, any information. She squatted down to pet his dog, giving the boy's faithful companion a good rub. The dog wanted to play, but the boy remained dispassionate. A gray chill listed in, giving Tess cause to turn up her collar. The sun settled behind the mountains.

Wouldn't give her his name. Didn't seem from around these parts. No one around to claim him. Not a word. She'd had a child once, a child taken away, a boy that could be this age, a French father.

"Listen, dear child," she asked, "if nothing else, please tell me what direction in this world you came from so I know which folk to summon." Three languages again. She swept her arm to the east, to the south, to the west. Nothing. That left north. North. She eyed the boy, caught his attention and swept her arm up the Front, north. Her gesture touched the boy, his eyes following her hand. A smile, a nod, a subtle affirmation. He gave nod with each tongue; English, Blackfeet, French, as if even he might understand all three languages, like Tess herself. She spoke French after the birth of her son, before the smallpox hit her and her husband fled with their child, fearing for the boy's life more than hers, having seen the smallpox. Scars remain, the loss of her child the biggest scar of all.

"Ok'i," Tess said in her Blackfoot vernacular, as if somehow it was settled that the boy would now follow along having made the northerly connection. But no, the child, be he hers or the world's, held his ground. Tess's coyote French seemed to interest him the most, giving her hope. French could likely make him mine, she thought. Has someone heard my prayers and sent him home to me? Perhaps he is afraid of me because of my pocked face, my shriveled nose.

She started to say something—but his expression stopped her, as if to say no, I am not yours, I did not come for you, but for another. Tess folded her arms ... trying once again to understand why her husband never returned. Her husband loved her. She knew he did. He knew she loved the child more than anything.

She measured the boy's features, looking for something of her in him, something of her long-departed husband. She tried to think of something unique, some identifier that time could not transcend—a birthmark, a scar, a deformity. Nothing. This boy had been spared of smallpox, but his parents likely had not.

He was a plain child, a bit light to have an Indian mother, skin bearing only a shadow of blood. She regretted not having treasured some feature. She remembered her child as a perfect child, and perfect he was until the day she fell ill. Next thing she knew, her son was gone. The French husband and his Métis people stole her child away to save the child, to save him from her smallpox.

She plied the boy with stories. She chanted. She sang, she laughed. She walked the street. In time, a rhythm entered her steps. She danced. She implored the boy follow along. A headstrong boy. Or maybe obedient. Perhaps that was it: obedience. He'd been told to wait for someone, a man. However willful, the boy came to admire her dancing. He looked her in the eye as she danced, appreciative of her intent to cheer him. If nothing, the boy knew she would help him find his way, even though it wasn't her way. Someone had another home in mind for the boy. This had all happened before. He was not the first boy she tried to make her own. She'd taken in a nephew. Tess bit her lower lip, motioned the boy stay put, and took off to inform the taxidermist. The crescent moon began its twilight descent, a butterfly chasing the sunken sun.

She looked about the town to see who might have watched her ply the child... no one, it seemed. Another boy orphaned in their street, nothing happening, reservation life some patched together thing, ancient ways half remembered, half lost; children forgotten, children abandoned. She looked back to the boy and smiled. She signaled 'be patient and wait, everything will be all right,' her gesture language his by now, linguists they were. He answered by petting his dog. He wouldn't be going anywhere. Reassured by the communication, Tess flipped her braids over her shoulders and trotted into the lilac night.

She stopped at the glint railroad tracks, her breath quickened by the whir of elaborated emotion. She not so much looked for trains as listened, her eyes fixed on Stuf's quarters. Before crossing, she turned and looked behind her—the town quiet and shadowless. An oil lamp flickered inside the building, illuminating the animals that hung from his walls. Encouraged, she stepped over the rails, crossed the open ground to the building, trotted up the steps and rapped. A long moment passed before his boots began their broken cadence across the floor. His gait had deteriorated, asymmetric as ever. Suspicious of callers at dusk, he cracked the door and peered over the security chain. "Who comes at this hour?"

"Napikwan waits for you in front of the store," Tess said, her singular voice identifying who she was.

"Napikwan?" the taxidermist answered, singing out the word in a language he seldom spoke.

"Yes. A boy pale as you."

"And you say he waits for me?"

"He waits for someone, but not for me. I tried to coax him home. But no, he wouldn't come."

"Wouldn't come with you?"

"Not this one."

"Why not?"

"Wouldn't say. Wouldn't say a thing, as a matter of fact. Wish I knew what he was all about."

"And you don't?"

"No, I don't," she echoed. "Not sure where he came from."

"He must have hinted at something."

"North. He nodded upcountry."

"Nodded?"

"When I pointed north, he nodded."

"What did his clothes say?"

"North too, maybe."

"Maybe he's Belly-Fat," Stuf said, referring to the Blackfeet term for an abandoned child.

"He's not fat. Thin as a rail."

"*Belly-fat*," Stuf repeated. "Life sprung from an unwelcome belly."

Tess's poxed nostrils snorted.

"I'll be down to get him."

"He has a dog."

"A dog. Maybe we can locate his people with the dog."

"Looks like any boy's dog."

'Stuf,' as the Indians dubbed the taxidermist, thanked Tess Ground Owl. He closed the door without ever having removed the chain. He often helped the orphans in town, especially the light-

94

skinned ones, finding them shelter, and then a home. Tess stepped off toward town. Out the door behind her, Stuf followed the pad of her testy footsteps. Bundled in his Hudson Bay blanket, he hitched his bones across the rails to retrieve the child of his alleged ilk. He moved along brisker than usual, nearly as fast as the nimble Tess. She hurried ahead to make sure the boy had stayed put. He had, huddled with his dog in the last hold of twilight.

When Stuf approached, Tess motioned him toward the child and stepped down the alley to her house. Stuf announced his presence with an authoritarian cough, which was unnecessary. The boy had seen him coming all along. Stuf stepped a bit closer and stopped. He raised an arm and lifted his chin. The boy popped up and bounded Stuf's way.

Tess watched from the gable window atop the Sherburne mansion. The boy's antics confirmed her belief that the child was told to wait for a man. The taxidermist turned about and headed back to his shop. The dog pranced and barked, happy to be found. Stuf marched across town. The boy sprinted ahead to the next crossroad. He waited for Stuf to catch up and show the way. Cat and mouse they crossed Browning.

Stuf stopped at the Great Northern tracks bridging the world. He looked east. He looked west. He listened. Nothing. He scanned the heaven for the meteor shower, the vapor of his emphysema catching the last light of a fallen moon. The boy looked up and down the shiny ribbons of rail. He observed Stuf gazing starward. The old man moved his fingers along the constellations, as if to count them, making sure all were there. He looked down at the boy, smiling. The boy looked from Stuf to the stars. He had his ideas why men looked up to them, and what might fall out of the sky.

No trains and no meteors. Last moonlight, a warmth to the wind, Chinook wind, most welcome wind in the world. Taking the boy by the hand, Stuf stepped across the steel and moved through the night. He climbed the barren porch and stood at his door, taking one last long gaze at the Heavens. The boy sat, humming and waiting, closing his eyes... dozing against the doorjamb.

Stuf stared starward. Maybe it was too early in the night. The medicine man Many White Horses had told him to watch the sky; that a comet approached. There, a wisp off Cassiopeia's chair. He looked harder, wishing for new spectacles. The faraway galaxy Andromeda twinkled in the wetness of his eyes, Andromeda and not a comet. The worn man sighed. He pushed open the door. The boy tumbled inside to catlike catch his fall, Stuf's animals suddenly upon him. The boy crabbed across the floor, frantic to comprehend the dismembered beasts. The taxidermist lit a kerosene lamp. The wick light made the mounts jump, if ever so slightly, and all in unison. The boy crouched and watched all the unblinking eyes, quickly understanding their death.

The animals stilled when the oil-lamp's chimney heated up, stiffening the flame. Indeed, most of the critters stared from their heads alone, only a few whole, some of them halved. The boy came from a land of the living. He had not experienced this aspect of animal afterlife. He looked from one to the other: grizzly bear, elk, coyote, mountain lion, wolverine. All animals he knew in life, prairie rock chimney, eyes rimmed with fear, dead.

Yes, Stuf had the touch to imitate life. He hobbled under his animals as if they were nothing. The child caught his breath and stood. He inspected each beast, touching, smelling; learning firsthand his or her fixed predicament. The wall behind him sported deer, mountain goat, mountain sheep, fisher, badger, lynx, grouse. Wolf. Everything made sense but their death.

The old man busied himself in the kitchen at the opposite end of the long room. The kitchen window offered a faint panorama of the plains rolling east. He finished his fixings and set out a bowl of corned beef and frybread. The boy chinned himself up to the table, continuing to marvel at the animals surrounding him. He spooned delicately and chewed carefully, so as not to disturb the incomprehensible stillness hung upon the walls. Manners, the boy had manners.

The pine fire at the far end of the room popped. A fierce gust of wind arose, shaking the room, trembling the animals on the wall. The boy knew wind and dined on. He finished his plate and eyed Stuf for more. Stuf dished out another helping of corned beef and cabbage, beef and cabbage raised on the reservation, beef and cabbage replacing buffalo and berries. When the boy filled up, Stuf showed him outside, pointing him toward the crapper, a hand-motion where to find the paper. The boy nodded okay, their sign language fluent, the moon lost below the mountains, the plains dark, Milky Way bright.

Sitting on the wooden throne of the outdoor loo, the boy watched a falling star slice the deep curve of night. His dog wandered off into the blowing prairie. The wind clarified the sky. He spotted another falling star, and another, and felt the movement of the universe. A meteor shower ensued. Enchanted, the boy counted the fallen stars until he could count no more. When he finally returned, Stuf led him to the washbasin and coached his little hands into the water and scrubbed them good. He showed the boy how to wash his face and brush his teeth, something the boy was not wont to do. Gums tingling, face aglow, the child climbed atop a bed Stuf had arranged. He tucked the boy under his softest buffalo robe and rubbed the little man's back. Another orphan searching for a life. The youngster fell asleep. It had been a long day of which we know only the half.

With the boy sound asleep, the taxidermist slipped back across town with a satchel of chokecherry pemmican. He went to Tess's and awakened her nephew, Butterfly, a reliable message runner. He fixed the young man up with the ancient sustenance and a bottle of Cola. He gave Butterfly instructions to head to Summerhome and deliver a letter to Madge and Betsy Bird; orphaned sisters Stuf rescued some time back. The young man caught up two horses and rode off to the Milk River, bringing Stuf's message that a boy had arrived.

The sisters arrived two days hence, carted to town by their team of well-wintered mules. Tess had the Bird sisters' spring order of ranch goods waiting at the mercantile for them as Stuf had arranged. Butterfly loaded the supplies on their buckboard. The sisters settled their bill with Sweetgrass Hills' gold dust and liveried the hybrids at the stable down the street. The two walked across town invisible to one another, yet somehow irrecoverably intertwined. Having survived the Baker massacre together, they were never able to part. Betsy limped. Madge strode alongside, her head canted to accommodate her one-eye way of going. The ladies crossed the tracks and approached the taxidermist's shop, a stop they made every time they came to town to visit their benefactor.

They march in without knocking to size up the child-find. Clouded sunlight pitches the animated room like ship's stronghold. "Come in, ladies, come in," Stuf says. "Make yourself at home, as your home it once was."

"New blood, eh?" Betsy queries, levering past Stuf with a sharp elbow. She trips on a bear hide ball, catching her fall with her fake leg, pegging the ivory into the wooden floor.

"Returned blood, more than likely," Madge counters, loosening the string that holds the musselshell patch over her smallpoxed eye.

"The Catholic priest said a white savior might show up someday," Betsy put in.

"So did the medicine man."

"Which medicine man?" Stuf asks.

"Buffalo Heart," Betsy replies.

"Yes," Madge adds.

"The beaver bundle man. Tess's grandfather, you know," Betsy says.

"The red papa," Madge clarifies.

"The dead papa, you mean. Black maybe, but not red. I still have his beaver bundle," Stuf puts in.

"We know you do. You just don't know how to use it."

"No. No one does. Not anymore."

"He might," Betsy says, putting her hand on the boy's shoulder. "This boy just might. The boy could learn. He might bring the buffalo back."

"A white boy bringing the buffalo back?" Stuf asks.

"Whiteman took them away," Betsy reasons.

"Oh, Stuf," Madge sighs. "Buffalo Heart entrusted you with the bundle for safekeeping. He knew what he was doing. You yourself were supposed to work the bundle during the wind and bone winter when our people became too sick and dead to work it anymore. You were supposed to bring us food to eat with the bundle. Even without the bundle, you and your government were supposed to feed us. You were supposed to bring doctors and medicine and you brought nothing. You took our buffalo away and left us to starve. Some bundle-keeper you."

Stuf winces at his failures, a pity that such smallpox epidemics had to happen at all. The Heavy Runner clan sick and hungry and camped on the Marias. American Indians dead and dying and freezing from the ravages of the poxvirus. The healthier braves and horses were off to the Sweetgrass Hills hunting deer.

Stuf left the Heavy Runner camp the day before the massacre in a bitter snowfall, riding horseback to Fort Benton for medicine to minister the Whiteman's Plague that blinded Madge's eye and took Betsy's leg. The horses were sick as the people, glandered and dying and weak. The young Stuf was a practiced horsedoctor. He traveled for horse medicine and Indian medicine alike. Medicine, he'd left the camp to bring home the medicine, he, the minister of medicine. Open sores on man and beast, fever and delirium, scabs, emaciation and death. Smallpox in the people. Glanders in their horses.

Stuf was warm in a hotel bed in Fort Benton when the soldiers attacked, early morning sub-zero weather, Colonel Baker in a frenzy to extract revenge for a white rancher allegedly killed by a band of renegade Blackfeet, a rancher married to a Blackfoot woman, the mother of Betsy and Madge. White men bent on war, whitemen on the warpath. An Army of well armed and well fed men. The Indians sick and cold, their men off hunting, an already- surrendered, peaceful band of Indians. Sick and dying, massacred.

Next thing the US Army had the blood of some hundred and sixty dead Indians on their hands. The cavalry savaged the pitiful encampment, shooting Indians, women, children, the aged and afflicted. Then burning their tepees. Snuffing out the infants. Madge and Betsy's mother among the dead, their murdered father the cause of the attack, Indians orphaned, smallpoxed, too many dead. Innocent Indians, the survivors freezing and starving, sick and hungry. Bitter cold. Sweetgrass Hills wind. North wind. Massacred sickness, some killings nearly humane. The Baker Massacre, a permanent tragedy for two cultures expected to live together forevermore, two races forced upon one another by the scythe of time and squeeze of space, the last free-living natives in America—smallpox sick and massacred, free no more, identity vanquished.

Stuf arrived back from Fort Benton that evening to the slaughter's remains. A blue hue to the river valley, the acrid smoke of burning flesh heavy on the air, smells and sights of death. Too late for his whiteman medicine to do much good. Survivors wept and struggled to stay alive. He helped the children best he could. Then the women. By darkness he attended the gutshot Medicine Man sitting next to his burnt down lodge. The soldiers burnt down all the lodges. He doctored the mortal wounds with special oils, giving the injuries a final unction. Stuf began singing. He sang the bundle songs Buffalo Heart had taught him. They sang all the bundle songs, singing until Buffalo Heart could sing no more.

The wounded Medicine Man lay next to the lodge fire. His eyes held a twinkle that belied his impaled body. Stuf drained and dressed the gut wound and applied a compress. Within minutes, Buffalo Heart sat up, grabbed the bundle, and placed the sacred wrap on his lap. He opened the bundle, removed a pipe and tobacco, and sang a final song. Stuf joined him in the sacred song. Buffalo Heart loaded and lit the pipe. He puffed and passed the pipe to Stuf, who smoked. The old man keened lightly. He took the pipe and tobacco, replaced them in the pouch, and removed two iniskim from the leather pouch, fossilized mini-buffalo, a white and a black. He held them out, one on the palm of each hand. He then closed his hands, put them behind his back and brought his hands out knuckles up. He asked Stuf to choose. Stuf chose the right hand. Buffalo Heart rolled his wrist, opened his palm. It held the black and the white buffalo, together.

The Medicine Man nodded, sighed, and winced; transfer complete. He replaced the iniskim and rolled up the bundle. In a slight of hands, he handed the beaver bundle to Stuf. His spoke a last word 'Napikwan.' He died sitting up, knees locked, arms limp on his lap, the bundle in Stuf's hands, ceded.

Stuf looked down at the boy. He searched for a clue yet unseen; a dialect, an identifying mark or facial feature, a map to his past. There, a nick in the ear, tiniest little nick near the top of his left ear, the cartilage wedged and healed. Distinguished and distinguishing. All who loved him must remember the ear.

The sisters switched to their native tongue, words sharp and sure. The boy leaned into their conversation, lips sealed straight across, a squint to his left eye; a bright child possessing a knowing demeanor, however mute. Stuf looked up to his animals. The frantic inflection of the sisters' diction took him back to their childhood. Their dialogue provoked happy memories. He tried to forget their scabs and fever and the loss of their sister. He tried to disremember the ulcerated tongue of the medicine man, the ooze from his belly wound, his crossed legs and frozen toes—Medicine Man dead, straight-up- sitting, dead. His people decimated, children orphaned. Blackfeet culture vanquished. The bundle held everything that remained.

The mounted animals loomed over Stuf like the sick hungry horses that lingered in the stench of massacre. Cottonwood riverbottom, slate light trapped in the back of his eyes, the smell of burnt flesh imbedded in the tissue of his sinuses. The lodges ransacked and smoldering, death everywhere. Smoke and suffering. Horses, wounded and glandered, gaunt and bleeding, redness flaming the snow about them.

They wrapped Buffalo Heart in a scorched buffalo robe and buried him in a tree. The bundle and Stuf escorted Madge and Betsy to a new home, this home that now harbored a boy, a new and different life with Stuf, a different world forever.

After the massacre, less-fortunate Indians ran away to die, the smallpox and violence too much to bear. Some fled with the Métis into Canada, to foment rebellion. A few went to work for ranchers, taking up with immigrant ways, denouncing their former freedoms. Others swallowed the tragedy and escaped to wherever they'd be left alone—Canada, Mexico, other reservations, other worlds.

"What's his name?" Betsy asked, catching her breath.

Stuf felt faint, flushed by the hazards of memory—a penetration his soul hadn't experienced in some time, decades now since Buffalo Heart had passed him the sacred bundle, uttering 'Napikwan.'

Stuf moved to his chair and sat, wheezing. He leaned back in his rocker to ease the heave of his lungs. Outside, clouds slid under the sun, dimming the room.

"His name, Stuf," Betsy ordered, fidgeting her ivory leg, remembering the smallpox and starvation as well as anyone could remember. She lifted her peg leg to a footstool and tightened the laces that held the prosthesis in place.

Madge sat down and one-eyed the ceiling. "Oh my, my oh my," she said. "What have those lost souls sent us?"

The boy listened and watched. He understood something had once gone terribly wrong in their lives, something they all withstood together. As Betsy finished her lacing the room grew quiet. She rested her forearm across her knee. The boy's eyes held on the tusk. What animal shared such a shiny bone? No bone he'd ever known. Betsy took notice of the attention the boy paid her. "Yes," she said, "to know me you'll have to know the leg. Don't be afraid of it. Nothing to be afraid of, nothing at all." Their eyes met. She eased the column of ivory to the floor with a pleasing tunk and stepped to him, grasping him by the shoulder. The boy smiled, falling into her touch.

"Let's have it, Stuf," Madge requested, tracing the boy's collarbone from his neck to his shoulder with her thumb, relaxing the child. "His name and anything else you know about him." She fussed at his dark hair with her free hand, and then held his head in both hands, examining the shape.

Stuf sat forward. "He doesn't have any lice, didn't have any when he arrived." She looked his way, and shook her head. "No, he doesn't have lice, but he has a name I bet," she said, giving the boy his head.

Stuf tapped at his teeth with the fingernail of his index finger.

"Luke," he announced, sitting to the edge of his rocker.

She sniffed, sensing a lack of conviction. "Luke? Did he tell you so?"

"No," he said.

"No?"

"The only name he uttered was badger. A name he repeated each time I asked him his name."

"Badger, eh? So how do you Luke that? Badger is probably his dog's name," Madge asked. Sure enough, the dog wagged his tail.

"I didn't exactly get Luke out of him outright," he admitted, looking away, speaking to the kitchen.

"How then?"

"When he wouldn't tell me, I read from the Bible. He looked up when I announced the Gospel according to Luke. That's all."

"Preaching to him from that Bible, eh Stuf? You ought to know better," Madge scolded. "When the whiteman arrived we had all this land, and the whiteman had the Bible. Now the whiteman has all the land, and we have the Bible. Some trade. Forget that damn bible." She circled behind the child, her arm the radius of a doting orbit.

"No preaching, I'd not call it that. Reading, just reading to the boy. He's a good listener, I'll say that for him. A fine boy. A good listener. Luke."

Luke smiled and nodded to the sound of his name.

"Maybe he doesn't understand all that Bible talk, a forked sort of English."

"Yes, I thought of that. I read scripture to find out if he'd heard that forked sort of talk before. Once you hear it, it sticks with you, whether you like it or not, especially if read with a certain heat. Some folk have Bible teachings in them, others don't. If they know the Bible, it helps trace origins, you know."

"Pft. Don't you wish?" Betsy said. "So, in the biblical sense, then, what do you make of the color of his skin here?"

"Well, skin's become sort of unreliable anymore."

"Really?" Madge asked. "You've come to believe that Indians come in a white color now?"

"Well, some do, or have, or will."

"Oh come on. You must have decided something a little more concrete than he's a white Indian, Stuf," Betsy prodded.

"No, he just kept right on a readin' his Bible, alienating the poor lost child," Madge put in.

"Madge, please. Be civil with Father. Stuf, what about your anthropology learning, your Darwin? All that high-minded science?"

"Couldn't bring myself to think of him as science. Madge is right, I just kept on with the Bible. He liked it, liked my reading. And from the way he listened, I suspect he is part Indian."

"From the way he listened?"

"You know, skeptical."

"So let me get this right. Even though he didn't tell you a thing about his family or people or anything like that, and he appears white, you think he might be part Indian because he listened funny as you read him the Bible?"

"Yes. That is correct. I figured you can only ask an abandoned child so much without making him feel like you might be the next to abandon him. I tried asking him softly, but he played it safe, didn't talk. He sensed I was trying to find someone for him, though. Content with that, he acted like he didn't have anything to say, like I should know what to do with him, that I shouldn't have to ask. That's when I sent word for you. My sense is that he should live with you sisters, that's all. God knows you two need a child."

"You just want a grandchild."

"Maybe. He knew I'd keep good care of him. He wouldn't speak, so I read. He listened, and listened carefully."

"And not a word out of him?"

"Not a word, save Badger."

"Badger. The dog, no doubt."

"And so you still—what has it been, three days now—don't know who he is, or where he's from?"

"What does that matter? He's a boy in need of a home. He won't stay with Tess. When no one else showed up, I sent for you two. I tried to find out more. Each day, instead of getting closer to what might be his ancestry, I got further away. What do you think? You tell me whom he came from. Tell me where, please."

"It might not matter, but then again it could," Madge said. "He seems to be under some sort of spell to not say much. Badger and that's it?"

"That's right, excepting all that talk he does with his body," Stuf said.

"What do you make of his voice?" Madge asked.

"He's an English speaker, alright."

"Maybe he speaks more than one tongue."

"Maybe. The Métis were through a week back, their carts howling louder than the wind, Métis from the North, yes ma'am. They traded in several languages, yes indeed they did."

"Métis, eh? Through last week?"

"Yes. Tess knows."

"She got to know them pretty well, I bet."

"I don't know how you mean that, Madge. Tess fixed them up with provisions like she does everyone, did the talking and trading she had to. Butterfly helped."

"Did you hear her talk with them?"

"Well, I suppose I did. I was around. They talked a lot, it seems. They spent a few days here."

"What were they speaking about?"

"Trade. Dealing. Money, you know."

"In what language?"

"What language? Well, all languages, you know what I mean. English, French, Blackfoot, whatever was handy. I didn't really pay all that close attention to which language, too much like my trading days, everyone spoke all the languages they needed to carry out their commerce."

"And what commerce was it brought them through?"

"Nothing in particular. You know the Métis. They remain the great nomads the Blackfeet and Sioux once used to be. Leaving Canada these days, they are, oui. Tried to make a stand up there. When that didn't work they started sifting down to settle whatever homestead or reservation wouldn't run 'em off." Stuf smiled at the thought of wandering Métis, their determination to live free.

"How was their skin?"

"Some of them are pretty fair, alright, whitefolk by all appearances. Others are dark, but not that dark, everything between. I suppose the boy could be of their blue-eyed mix- blood stock, Louis Riel's offspring perhaps." Stuf admired the Métis, he liked their independence. "Freestanding folk, those Métis. The boy could be Métis, fluent in their coyote French. English nouns, French verbs, nothing so cumbersome as prepositions or articles, the language of trade when buffalo migrated about the plains, a language vanished with the buffalo."

"Buffalo," the boy said.

"See there," Stuf said.

"Blackfoot, maybe there's some Blackfoot on his tongue," Betsy said hopefully, rubbing the boy's arms now, one, then the other. "Maybe he's been raised by those Bloods up North, init?"

"A white boy with those Bloods? Ha. Their Kit Fox society would doubtful allow that."

"It's in their stories. A white boy sent from some far reach to release the buffalo back out onto the earth."

"That's right."

"In our stories Napi is white."

"Those Bloods might have spit the boy out of some ghost dance then, init?"

"If he knows Blackfoot, maybe he came down through Waterton with the Métis. The Métis traded with Bloods before moving on down here to ply the Pikunni. You wouldn't think they'd abandon one of their own."

"What about the Heart Butte Blackfeet? Could they be up to something?"

"They could be."

"What about kidnapping or something? Maybe he's kidnapped and abandoned."

"A white child left to the savages."

"The boy knows the stars in the North. Knows 'em well," Stuf said.

"Must have came from the North, then." Betsy concluded.

Madge nodded.

"Lot of people up North."

"Over time."

"Through time."

"The Métis through the other day, and a lightskin sprouts out of nowhere?" Madge eyed the child, and then Stuf. "Same story as you, Stuf. Same story fifty-some years ago. Buffalo Heart divined you out of nowhere, smoked you out of the sky. Out of nowhere you came riding that elegant white horse. If my memory still serves me, Métis had been through a few days before your arrival. Out of nowhere you spoke the Blackfoot dialect of our Pikunni tongue, Napi's messenger himself come to save us."

"A fable," Stuf proclaimed.

"Ha," Betsy exclaimed. "What else were we supposed to think?"

"I told you that I learned the language living with the Blackfeet one winter at Fort Benton. We sat around all winter telling stories. A man named Blood and his wife Red Elk taught me all the Blackfoot I needed to know to barter furs, which is quite a lot more than you'd think. I learned some of the language listening to their stories. Other traders and Indians told stories as well. All winter long; stories. Three or four different tongues. Stories we needed to hear to get through the winter. Jimmy Schultz told stories in Blackfoot. He was a whiteman who knew Pikunni like his born language. After I heard him storytell, I knew one day I could speak fluent Blackfoot as well, and did. Buffalo Heart thought I was sent by Old Man with your language on my tongue, Napi at work."

"You saved us, Stuf."

"You saved yourselves."

"We know what happened, what you did for us. We'd be dead without you, and you know it."

Stuf fell back into his chair, his mind enfolded.

"So how do you suppose this blue-eyed child ended up at our door?" Madge asked the animals. Luke looked to the caped animals. The cobwebbed glut of immortalized creatures remained suspended in muteness.

Stuf lifted his heels and resumed rocking. "Luke, how old are you?"

The boy flipped up two hands, five outstretched fingers, plus, one at a time, two more, first the thumb, then the index finger.

"Seven?"

The boy spoke. "Seven."

His manner of counting out his fingers intrigued Stuf. The thumb as one, North European.

"Maybe we should ask if they want to take him in at the Holy Family Mission," Madge suggested.

"Forget that," Betsy said. Her walrus drummed the floor. "What about Tess?"

"He didn't want Tess. You ladies take him on home with you, now. He is a fine boy. He is going to be just fine if you give him love and a home. That's all a child needs. That's all you needed."

"He might need a Dad."

"We'll find him a dad."

"I'm too old, my goodness, children."

"We'll see about that," Betsy said.

Abetted by the blur of her harlequin eye, Madge considered Luke. "Maybe someone will show up to claim him before long."

"If that time comes, fine."

"Who else knows?"

"Tess."

"Tess Ground Owl?"

"The merchant's clerk."

"She had nothing to do with his arrival?"

"No, other than welcoming him. She found him waiting in the wind after work, all alone, him and Badger. That's all I know," Stuf said, understanding there could be more. "He wouldn't go home with Tess. She tried hard, wanted him as hers."

Madge sighed. She replaced the shell over her wandering eye, took the boy's hands and squeezed them, her thumbs on the top of his wrists a certain Indian way. With a torn-pocket smile Stuf stopped rocking. He built himself out of his chair a joint at a time, pleased the situation was moving forward in the direction he'd divined.

Goes around, comes around, he thought. The children he had raised couldn't refuse the boy.

"I'll help with the fathering," Stuf declared. He stood from the rocker—a half step to catch his balance—and hung his thumbs into his vestpockets. He coughed to clear his throat, took a breath, waggled his fingers, and sang.

"What will become of a boy as light as he? As light as me,

A boy as white and alone as me,

Arrived here from the land of the Cree."

Madge looked to Betsy. "Let's be on, then."

The boy dropped off the stool to stand between the ladies. Forty glass eyes witnessed the delivery. The threesome shuffled across the gallery, Betsy's walrus rapping the floor with glee. The sisters sidled the boy out the door in a deft display of teamwork. Their elk- teeth bracelets clacked as they scooted him on his way—their way—elk teeth excited; a child sent to make the world new again, to make the world real.

The taxidermist followed them outside. Low-moving clouds garbled the sunlight. Verdant air, green hills, beckoning mountains yonder—a landscape of hope. "Speak only the Queen's English with the boy," Stuf joked. "For his good fortune, you know," he added, shooting a finger to the sky, chuckling. A wind gust took his hat, wheeling the straw past the threesome, spooking the mules.

The ladies held Luke in check until the animals relaxed. In unison, one at each arm, the sisters elevated Luke's ribby frame to the seat of the buckboard. His dog jumped aboard after him. The wood squeaked against the wind, wind cleansing the world. Unfamiliar with little-boy antics and wary of strange dogs, the span of mules pawed, Summerhome mules eager to get back to Summerhome grass.

Stuf lumbered by, chasing after his hat. The boy laughed. The sisters laughed, everyone laughing in the wind.

Madge wrapped the reins around her wrists and clucked the mules. The hybrids charged into their hames, glad to be on with it. They trotted their cargo out onto the green plains. White coulee snow melted into the grassy landscape. The boy sat and rode and watched—happily squished—stock-still except to point out an occasional bird the wind flew by.

Beyond the middle of everywhere, into the yawning shadow of the backbone of the world, the sisters began speaking Blackfeet. The mules racked, their attentive ears rolling back to detect any command that might be directed their way. The sisters weren't talking to the mules, and the mules soon knew it. A swift trip home, singsong excitement— words darting across the grassland like windswept larks. The mules trotted the trio down the long coulee to Summerhome on the South Fork of the Milk River.

By the time the women unloaded the supplies and unharnessed the mules, the boy had uttered wind and bird and grass in Blackfeet. It wasn't clear whether he had just learned the words, or knew them all along.

The sisters scurried about the twilight making everything right—a lyric dream of beautiful promise, lost identity eager to find a home.

Thus ended the brief orphanage of Luke Tailfeathers.

MARK TAYLOR
A Year in Baker, Montana

"HANNAH, LET'S LOOK AT THIS GRASSHOPPER WITH MY MICROSCOPE."

"Okay, Madison. Ooh. Look at that."

"Uh-oh. Hannah, we'd better leave. Here comes my grandpa, and it looks like he is starting to suck in his breath to tell us another story."

"Hi, girls. Studying grasshoppers? Hey, did I ever tell you about the time I visited the Athenaeum, in Boston, with Ralph Waldo Emerson?"

"Grandpa, you never met Emerson!"

"Well, yes, Madison. You and I both know that, but it makes a better story if I tell it that way, doesn't it?"

"Grandpa, that story stinks no matter how you tell it! Besides, we are only ten years old and we don't really care about what Emerson had to say about the "sublime" of Longinus. And the whole thing is pointless anyway: I don't think Emerson ever said anything—"

"It's not nice to say 'stink,' Madison. And you know I felt very close to both Emerson and Longinus for many years."

"I know Grandpa, but Hannah and I both have heard that story before. Do you have another story you could tell us?"

"Hmm. You know, Madison, that grasshopper you are looking at reminds me of the time we lived in Baker. Did your dad ever tell you about that?"

"He mentioned it but he was only, like, seven years old when it happened. He doesn't remember much."

"Let me tell you."

"Is it short?"

"Yes."

"Okay. You can tell us."

"Well, it starts many years ago, when I got a job in Baker."

"Where is Baker?"

"Well, Hannah, Baker is in Fallon County, right at the eastern edge of Montana. If you go east from Baker for about 15 miles, you will be in North Dakota. To the north is Wibaux County, and to the south is Carter County. I was hired to work in all three counties."

"What did you do there?"

"I worked in the schools, Hannah. It was a job in special education."

"Did you have to drive a lot?"

"Oh, yes. And they had a big oil field there...Anyway, it was hard for us to find places to live in Baker because there were oil field workers coming and going all the time and they rented just about everything that was available. But the big reason it was hard for us to find a place is that we had some livestock, so we needed a place to keep them. We rented a small farm."

"What did it look like?"

"We lived in a small white house that was at the end of a dirt road. In the front was a little garden area. In the back, there was a wooden barn that was as big as a—well, you know how big a barn is right? Big. It was just about falling down and it looked like it had not been painted for at least 20 years. The barn had lots of cats living in it. Also, the farm had a chicken coop, a couple of steel grain storage bins that were mainly full of mice, and a metal pole barn full of pigeons where we kept the tractor and farm equipment.

"There were some steers, a milk cow, a few horses, a couple of goats, a few geese, and some chickens. Most belonged to the people who owned the place, but we were able to bring our animals, too."

"My dad told me about the goats and the chickens. He said the goats were smelly."

"True. One goat was the size of a pony. Your dad tried to ride it. It had huge horns that he could hold onto and steer the goat.

"We let the chickens out to wander around wherever they wanted to go. They generally stuck around the house and buildings. When they were laying eggs, they liked to go into the barn and find some out-of-the-way place to hide their nests. We would go in and have to hunt around to find the eggs. It was fun, like an Easter Egg hunt every day."

"Dad told me that sometimes when he was looking for eggs, he would look into a hiding place, and a chicken suddenly would fly out into his face."

"Yes, that kind of thing startled all of us."

"But didn't you have foxes or skunks that would come and try to get the chickens?"

"That is a good question, Hannah, but no, we didn't. The geese kept every predator away. Everything was afraid of the geese. Even snakes stayed away."

"You had a dog, too, right?"

"Yes, but she was a gentle, old, black lab. Frankly, she got to be afraid to walk around the barnyard because the geese and the goats would attack her. In just about the first week we lived there, she approached one of the goats in a friendly way, but the goat butted her in the ribs so hard you could hear the air being knocked out of her lungs. She learned right then to avoid the goats, and after the geese pounded her a few times, she just learned to avoid the entire barnyard."

"Oh."

"We moved there in the late fall. We faced quite a few challenges over the next year. One of the first was that the well-water we had smelled like sulphur, it tasted a little bit salty, and when we took a bath in it, it left our skin feeling slippery. People who grew up in Baker liked that feeling, but for us, it made us feel like we still needed to rinse off the soap.

"We brought about 20 houseplants with us from Billings, but the Baker water killed every one of them. When we made rice with the water, the rice came out yellow.

"The next challenge was that the winter was the coldest ever.

The temperature on the thermometer went down to -50°F, and when the wind was blowing, which was just about all the time, the wind chill could reach -100°F."

"I heard that when it is that cold, if you spit, it freezes before it hits the ground."

"Yes, Hannah, I have heard that, too. I was afraid to try it, though. It was dangerous just to go outside in that weather, so when I had to go out I bundled-up carefully. Once I was outside I never wanted to uncover my face enough to try spitting. Besides, I was afraid that if my lips got even a little bit wet they would freeze."

"Dad said the house was drafty."

"Yes, that is right, Madison. The house was old and the doors and windows were not tight. Even the walls were not tight anymore. The front door, facing east, let people into a little entrance hall, where they could take off their coats and boots, and then there was another inside door that would let them into the house.

"That winter, when snow fell and wind blew, the entrance hall piled up with fine, gritty little snow crystals that blew through small cracks around the door. The snow in the hall got to be as much as two inches deep, and the hall never got warm enough for it to melt in there. We tried to stop up the cracks, but when you are renters, there is only so much you can do. There were too many places where the snow was blowing in and we finally gave up. We just closed off the front hall.

"Snow was also blowing right through the walls and into the living room. Again, it would pile up and would not melt. The only way we could cope and keep some of the house a little bit warm was to close off the living room and not go in there until spring."

"Were the animals okay?"

"The animals had a really tough time in that cold. Well, actually, the geese did not have any trouble. They just settled down outside in places that were more sheltered from the wind and they were fine.

"The horses had some shelter from the wind in their stalls in the barn. Once they went out, though, and the hard snow crystals and the sand picked up by the wind blasted the hair off of their rumps."

"That is terrible!"

"Mmm. It was worse than that, Hannah, but I am keeping the story short.

"When things finally warmed up a little in the spring, we were relieved. The snow melted and we tilled the garden to get it ready for planting. We planted several things and started tending the garden. We watered and weeded and watched. Gardening was the third challenge.

"Things started coming up. The water was a bit poisonous for the plants, though, so most of the things we planted did not survive. We had just a few hardy plants that seemed to be making a start of it.

"The insects emerged in the spring, too. The ones we noticed more than any others were mosquitoes and grasshoppers. As the summer went on, the mosquitoes started to go away but the grasshoppers just got bigger and hungrier.

"There were a lot of grasshoppers. If you are keeping track, they were the fourth big challenge. If you measured off a square with about three feet on a side and then counted the number of grasshoppers in the square, you would probably find at least 100.

"I had heard about grasshoppers in the Dust Bowl in the 1930s, and how they would eat everything in sight. That is exactly what happened to us. They ate every leaf of everything in the garden and then they started eating the root vegetables that were still in the ground. They ate the grass in the pastures, and they even nibbled on the wood of the barn.

"At the beginning of the summer, the chickens liked to eat the grasshoppers, but by the end of the summer they were sick of them. When a grasshopper would fly by a chicken you could almost see her shudder with disgust, they all were so sick of eating grasshoppers.

"And did I mention it was hot? The poor chickens would walk around in the heat, holding their wings away from their bodies, panting to try to stay cool. It would have been funny to watch except that we were so hot and so sick of grasshoppers, too.

"Finally, in the late summer it was time in Baker for the Fallon County Fair.

"Of the things featured at every county fair is the county's agricultural product. Farmers, ranchers, and 4-H'ers will bring in their best livestock to show, and the best examples of the crops they raised. Gardeners will bring in their best produce and the best examples of things made from their gardens. There might be displays that are just plates with raw vegetables on them, each one showing five perfect green beans, for example. Or there will be displays of perfectly pickled beets.

"We wanted to compete at the fair, but like I said, nothing grew in our garden except grasshoppers."

"Grandpa. You didn't...!"

"Oh, yes we did, Madison. We went out and caught a few pounds of grasshoppers. We cleaned them, boiled them up, and picked out the best ones. It is amazing the variety of colors and different shapes you will find among grasshoppers when you have that many of them. You might think they are all just grasshoppers, but we found out there are dozens of different kinds.

"Anyway, we prepared a jar of pickled grasshoppers. The grasshoppers were perfectly arranged in the jar with little sprigs of dill that we bought at the store, and the liquid was perfectly clear. Our grasshoppers were beautifully pickled."

"Gross! No!"

"Yes. Not wanting to stop there, we made up some grasshopper candies. We chose some nice medium-sized ones and dipped them in chocolate. As the chocolate hardened, we were careful to make the surface look smooth and not all gloppy. Also, we arranged one back leg so that it made a handle to hold onto while you lifted the little confection to your mouth.

"We entered the fair but we did not tell anyone what we were bringing. We just said, 'pickles' and 'candy.'"

"What did people say when they saw what you brought?"

"We soon found out that we had no reason to feel particularly clever, and we needn't have been so secretive. It turned out that no one was able to enter the County Fair competitions with anything else except grasshoppers. There was not a single display of vegetables because nobody had any."

"Did you win?"

"Well, let me say this, we had a great time. It was fun to find that everyone shared the same challenges that year, and to find that we could all laugh about it."

"Grandpa, is that story true?"

"Yes, Madison, it is mostly true."

"What part did you make up?"

Grandpa smiled slyly, a little twinkle in his eyes.

"Grandpa, you are impossible!"

DANELL JONES
Aviator

the sharp salute of the windsock to a strong west breeze
little-girl thighs sticky on the crew seat

dad in the cockpit peeling off his cowboy boots
you can't fly in these motherfuckers

the sunbaked runway
radiant sendoff for sky divers and fire fighters

he sticks his hand out the window
goddamn wind blowin' like hell

then guns the Cessna
ripping us through gravity

as naturally as his fist
splinters glass

Bronzes in the Drawing Room of Sir Henry Basingstoke

The busts of cantankerous elder statesmen
gaze downward
from the carved mantle
foreheads rippled with important grief.

How they miss their colonial hotels
—Bombay or Nairobi—
the panting of ceiling fans in the damp air
the rustle of women dressed for dinner.

How they used to love lingering in the drawing room
with their cheroots and brandy
watching the girls shimmer by.

Is it any surprise
they disapprove the ungodly canvas before them:
    archangel escorting naked waif across rocky peaks
        —her slim, besotted innocence
        —his manly wings sweeping girlish breasts?
Is it any surprise
it rises the urge for a Reform Bill?

The Morning the Pasque Flowers Bloomed

Waking with magical powers
Tim strolls with his dog across Mumbai, Aleppo, and Kabul
off-capping to busy neighbors and offering Bella's amiable head
to children's' curious hands

Later, he'll oversee
the transformation of moldy leftovers into penicillin

He will make sure cobalt blue teapots adorn all gardens across
all continents
reminding people that the sky has not always been blue
nor love so complete

After that, he will see to it
that Dr. Watson outwits Sherlock Holmes

Basking in his successes, he'll try out the curse of the Bambino,
comma splices, accidents, illness, and heartache

He plans to do something about laundry and housework, generally

Tomorrow, just for fun,
he will see to it that on every piece of paper on every desk on the
entire planet a cat stops

If only for one day, every man will lift its tender body in his hands
and feel the grumble of love against his fingertips

Engagement

Today, I saw two flickers

tumbling one over the other
sharp beaks striking like angry drummers
a dazzle of wing on wing

they fought or they fucked, I don't know which,
in the street, on the grass, up the side of the maple
their contest needing no spectators

and as I closed the garden gate
I noticed one thing more
where one flew, the other meant to follow

The Wedding Guests

Wind cuts hard across the lawn
upturning clean white umbrellas
tilting hats and flitting ruffles.

Someone thinks of kites—
how this wind would twitch their tails
like suspicious cats.

The long grasses on the hillside
bend and wave like a fresh tide
cresting across the mild slope.

Thunderheads gather to the west
drumming their warnings.

We hold hands.

Voices carry.

SCOTT MURRAY
The Short Man

MY MEMORY OF THE SHORT MAN HASN'T FADED, OR EVEN BLURRED, in spite of the passing decades since I last saw him.

We called them rat boats, but they were officially if not affectionately called PBR's, for Patrol Boat River. The U.S. Navy didn't like the fact that we referred to ourselves as the "River Rats" either, so we didn't say that very often if we weren't out catching rays and speeding up the Mekong Delta.

I had gotten my own boat after my promotion to Lieutenant (junior grade), a living example of the hard working sailor rising through the ranks to ultimately sit in officer's country. My command was a skating little hunk of metal designated PBR 750, but we called her "Honey." Her cockpit was the ultimate in beautiful simplicity, consisting of the wheel and about five dials that showed oil pressures, engine revs, and fuel. But Honey had jagged teeth, in the form of twin fifty caliber mounts fore and aft, and she could skip over the heavy Mekong muck effortlessly on her unmuffled twin diesels.

We were part of the Brown Water Navy, in that stinking little police action misnamed the Vietnam War in educated circles. Our part of that exercise in futility was to patrol the sewer, or so it seemed to me. What they called a river I wouldn't have let my old man's pigs swim in. The Mekong was an infinite stretch of brown sludge channels, cutting back and forth through a densely matted jungle of crawling vines and shrubs. When the monsoons came, the river looked like a torrent of blood, bursting at the banks with all of the fresh mud washed down by drenching leaden skies.

For the most part, the members of my crew were great guys that I would have gone to the mat for. In contrast to my months of training to pilot a PBR, I found out that when the entire crew consists of five sailors, you didn't hear much of that "Yes, sir, aye-aye, sir, let go the lines forward" shit. We became more than comrades in arms. We were friends. Well, most of us, anyway.

"Dutch" van Ornum had been with me from the start, and I wouldn't have traded him for twenty other Chief Petty Officers. His bulging chest and arms conveyed all the authority he would ever need to keep my crew in line, and I relied on him for that. Dutch was sinew and muscle as hard as stone. Wherever a fight broke out, you could count on finding Dutch. If he wasn't there, he was on his way. And Dutch loved to take the fight to the enemy, which to him meant anybody that wasn't white Anglo-Saxon or Germanic Protestant. When he wasn't on deck, you could locate Dutch in one of many Vinh Long riverfront bars, trolling for a confrontation. Dutch had been the first in the River Boat Navy to talk a machinist into welding a grenade launcher onto Honey's forward machine gun tub.

"Got to kill them in numbers," he would say, baring pearly white teeth beneath his rusty moustache. "Only thing they understand. Got to take them out in droves."

Russell Fines was our lanky Kentucky born and bred engineer, who spoke with a painful drawl, but he kept Honey's motors purring. Slow and deliberate at everything he did, Sir Russell seemed too genteel to be an engineer, but he could nurture those valves and hoses like a doting young mother putting a newborn to her breast.

I had Bradley Jackson on the forward mount, a tough black kid from Watts, who loved to kill. It didn't matter where we were, even if we were only a few miles upriver, you could find Brad in his forward turret, massaging his twin magazines and greasing all of the moving parts of his death-dealing instruments. I have retained images of Brad, especially of the times we stopped for chow, and I can still see him scraping his long, human bone-handled machete over his lips, listening for action, pondering his chances of finding a target behind the swaying curtains of flora. Brad also had an annoying habit of cleaning his M-16 every day, and taking random shots into the brush.

"Got to know the sum-bitch is workin', don't I?"

Last, and most people would say least, was my rear gunner, Tim Witherspoon. Tim was a skinny guy, who wore giant horn-rimmed glasses with really thick earpieces, which would have made him look at home in launch control at NASA. His sparse brown hair had been cut very short, leaving major white sidewalls shining over his ears. While the rest of us were on either our second or third hitch, Tim had been drafted as soon as he had finished college, and the education bit alone would have been three strikes against him. But Tim made things worse by talking about his plans for graduate school, and how the fucking war had screwed his chances. Even at his best moments, Tim was clearly reluctant, and in the middle of a firefight he would often sit, mouth agape in terror, unable or unwilling to pull the trigger.

Dutch hated him, from the moment the kid's boots slapped Honey's deck.

"You wanna get us all killed, you pussy? What the hell's the matter with you? Didn't they teach you how to fire that thing in Basic?"

Dutch and Bradley rode his ass about everything. I think Bradley joined in mostly to deflect Dutch's hatred of blacks. They thought they could beat the cowardice out of Tim.

"You gonna get us in some beaucoup deep shit, white boy."

I was often caught in the middle, and did my best to mollify Dutch, with a little detached help from Sir Russell. Russell wouldn't ever have said anything derogatory about the kid. It just wasn't in the gentleman's nature. He had that natural wet duck ability to let everything roll off his back, and he believed more fervently than anybody I ever knew that the golden rule was the way to live your life.

But the other two kicked Tim around, and heaved him into the

Mekong a few times when he wasn't looking, and then chewed his ass for not being more careful on deck.

When Tim got short, with only a couple of months left before he was scheduled to be shipped back to the world, things got worse. Dutch tortured him mercilessly, calling him a worthless bastard, without any sense of duty to country. But I could feel for the kid, because I had gotten to where I didn't really believe in the cause, either. And Russell rolled his eyes and shook his head in his quiet, Southern way.

We had just finished a monotonous patrol up near An Trong, and we were on our way back to the supply and refit ship YRBM 21, or the Delta Hilton, as we called it, when Brad saw the cotton wadding that Tim had stuffed into his ears to blunt the constant staccato blast of the diesels. Without a second thought, he immediately informed Dutch.

What followed was the rudest, most humiliating head slapping I had ever witnessed.

"Fucking stupid college twit. Get that shit out of your ears, and keep it out! How the fuck you gonna hear when things get hot? Do you not give a rat's ass about any of us?" Frothing anger collected on Dutch's moustache, but he stopped his tirade for a few seconds, as if he really expected an answer. "You'd better start worrying about yourself. Anything goes wrong on this boat, and I'm gonna frag your skinny little ass."

I never jumped in, when Dutch was on the fever like this, mostly because I was really afraid he would kick my butt, too. Dutch wasn't the kind of guy you wanted on the other side of you. Looking back on it, I probably should have tried to cool him down, and I think Russell was always a little disappointed in me for not exerting my rank. He would look down that long, aristocratic nose at me, and scrunch his eyebrows up and down like he had developed a nervous tic.

In a lot of ways, Honey was really Dutch's boat, and I was her glorified pilot. I had reached the point where I had trouble interacting with Dutch on patrols, and I felt like I was always seeking his permission and approval.

But they all still called me "Loot", in deference to my rank, and at least pretended to respect me. Toward the end, though, all of us knew who was really calling the shots.

When Witherspoon was really short, down to four days, we

drew what should have been a candy patrol up to Chou Doc. Dutch was going on about having kicked some ass up there, in a floating pontoon bar at the harbor. Tim, on the other hand, was fidgety, and he got strung out on keeping his twin fifties spotless, greased, and ready for action.

"It's a cakewalk, man," I kept telling him. "No Charlie in this part of the Delta for next to a year now."

"Can't be that easy, Loot. I'm real short, you know."

"Yeah, I know, Tim. Four days and I gotta start working some greenhorn into your position."

"Damn pussy," Brad groused.

As I had predicted, we saw nothing all day, except lazy brown water bordered by sinister green vegetation.

When it got late, and the orange sun was kissing the tops of the jungle canopy, we pulled into a patch of grass and set Honey's engines back to idle. With Chou Doc only five miles upriver, Dutch had decided that we needed to get lit before we tied up and hit the bars.

In our ritual fashion, we gathered in a knot and torched some righteous weed, in the form of dripping Thai sticks Dutch had purchased back on the yard boat. Brad pulled a cold case of Schlitz beer from under his ammo crates, and we lustily popped tops and slugged down all kinds of relief. All of us, I should say, except Tim Witherspoon.

Tim crouched on his haunches, at the after end of Honey's hull, constantly scanning through the twilight glint from the ugly brown water. He seemed disgusted as we cracked wise about how he was contemplating the physics of the water flow and broke into uncontrolled fits of laughter. I knew what must have really been going through his mind. Tim was mad at us, for getting so messed up that we might decrease his chances of catching that flight back to life. But he was too terrified of Dutch, by then, to even suggest that he would squeal us out. Dutch would have fragged him for sure, or Bradley would have slit Tim's throat with his cherished machete.

I had put away a couple of brews, and shared the benefits of three reeds, when I suggested that we wind the old girl up again and head in to berth. In the back of my mind, I was already imagining a bar girl. As I was reaching for the throttle, I saw the tattered sampan struggling to make a quick turn into a side channel, about a thousand yards upstream.

That sight alone would have aroused my suspicions, but the capper was seeing one of our Zippo boats trailing the sampan, her engines spitting fire in hot pursuit. We called them Zippos, after the lighters, because their main armament was a napalm-spewing nozzle that could fry an acre of jungle in fifteen seconds. And it had to be Viet Cong they were chasing, because of the way the sampan was running. No piece of Vietnamese shit like that boat should have been able to stay ahead of our Zippo.

"Well, lookee there," I laughed.

Dutch studied the scene for less than a heartbeat.

"Yes, sir, Loot. Looks like we got us some action. Let's fire this bitch and follow them boys."

"Battle stations, guys. Get those pots on your heads," I yelled as I shoved Honey's throttles to the firewall. "We got a date with Charlie tonight."

Russell was nodding satisfaction at the powerful roar of the diesels he had so tenderly maintained. We fairly skipped over the water, like a flat stone chucked by a powerful arm, glancing and throwing spray in all directions as Honey's bow smacked and flew.

Bradley scrambled into his mount, and yanked the magazine levers on his destructive twin guns with the aplomb of a hardened veteran. Dutch stood behind me, his M-16 resting on the awning over my head, and I could see that he was stroking the weapon's stock.

Witherspoon was leaning into my shoulder, and screaming over the straining blast of Honey's cylinders.

"Do we have to do this, Loot? I'm really short, man. Do we really have to do this?"

"What the fuck, Tim? This is what we're here for."

"Yeah, but you guys are wasted, and I'm really short."

Dutch clamped his meaty paw on the kid's shoulder, and pulled him back from me. His clenched white teeth were frightening in the fading light.

"Get your God damned weapon ready, college boy, or I'm going to shred your worthless ass."

I didn't have time to get involved in that short skirmish, because it took only seconds to reach the channel. With practiced skill, I swerved Honey right down the throat, and we entered an overgrown waterway of hanging vines that twisted tortuously in all directions. For quite a while, I couldn't see either the sampan or our Zippo friends, because there were so many tight turns in the stream. Demonstrating my practiced skill as one of the finest PBR pilots in history, I hit every one without skipping a beat, and I could see Russell's proud grin from the corner of my eye. Yeah, they all knew they were riding with the best. Russell went into one of his rebel yells, hollering at the top of his lungs.

Dutch was talking to himself, repeating over and again a single phrase:

"Come on baby ... Come on baby ... Come on baby ..."

About the time that I realized that we were in an ideal location for an ambush, I heard the zipping of hot rounds slashing into the branches, and thunking into tree trunks on the bank. Acting on reflex, I hunkered deeper into the pilot's seat and rested my free hand in front of my genitals.

With the rounding of a final bend, we suddenly saw both our Zippo and the sampan, and I figured the pursuit was over, and we would soon be harvesting contraband weapons and interrogating obstinate Viet Cong. It took several seconds for the weirdness to register, and Dutch noticed at about the same time I did.

"What the hell we got going on here?"

The Zippo's props were still turning, but she had wedged herself onto a sandy bank, and her napalm nozzle was aimed at the sky, throwing sheets of flames like a useless Roman candle. Then I saw some of the members of the Zippo's crew, sprawled and contorted on her deck. The co-pilot was missing his head, and the pilot lay back in his chair, as if he were examining the awning above his command chair.

It was an ambush, and the enemy fire was coming from VC nestled in the brush on both shores. Our buddies were getting raked, mercilessly, and we had bumbled into the trap right behind them.

Without thinking, I threw the wheel over, splaying wash at the beached Zippo, and screamed my order to open fire at the top of my terrified lungs, even though some part of my mind told me that it was probably too late.

Misreading the signs, Bradley sprayed the decoy sampan with unleashed vengeance. Dutch, at least, had the savvy to aim at flashes from AK-47 muzzles that lanced out from behind the trees. Russell stared at me with wide eyes, the whites visible all the way around, and his entire face was a question mark. When I twisted in my seat, I was thrilled to see that Tim had joined the fight, and his face was a mask of concentration, and determination. Nobody was going to stop him from going home.

The world was filled with the cacophony of battle, from the whine of bullets to the plinking reverberations of empty shell casings rebounding from Honey's deck. Trying to minimize the hits, I swerved and twisted my boat, gracefully dancing between the chocolate columns of water thrown up by heavy enemy fire. The stenches of cordite and burning flesh flooded my nostrils.

But there were too many of them, and they were too ready for us. When it came, the rocket propelled grenade seemed to move in slow motion, a burnt orange basketball churning straight for us. I couldn't turn in time to protect Honey. With a sickening thump, that grenade pierced her bow, and sliced fourteen feet into her engine compartment before exploding.

Looking back at it, I'm sure only seconds elapsed, but those seconds dilated into what seemed like agonizing hours. Bradley was catapulted over the starboard side, and I can still see his spread-eagled form high in the air, his helpless arms grasping at nothingness. My hearing was blunted, and it sounded like a million gnats were buzzing through my brain, my men's voices distorted as if they were coming through a blown speaker. I tried to sit up, and when I turned, I saw that Russ was in bad trouble. His arms were on fire, from his elbows down, and his rebel yell had become a panicked scream. He looked at me as if I should be able to tell him what to do about that. Behind me, Dutch was in worse shape, his hips pointed at impossible angles away from his chest, with a smoking fragment of the rocket's tail protruding from his back, and his feet lying flat on their outside edges on the deck, no longer functioning portions of his body.

"Get us out of here ... Get us out of here!"

It was a pleading, fragile voice that quavered, that I never would have expected to come from Dutch's mouth. I wanted to reach out to him, but my vision was flooded by shades of red as blood from my torn scalp poured into my eyes. Honey's controls and dials were spinning around my head. With the engines stopped, the PBR's way paid off quickly, and we slid back on the sluggish current at a snail's pace, trapped in a maelstrom of screeching enemy fire.

At that moment, when we were surely doomed, the kid aft

showed us how much of a man he really was. Witherspoon jumped up out of his turret, to slash down the awning from over my head, and to smother Russell's flaming forearms in a graceful, coordinated swoop. Aware of the fact that our burning engines made us easy targets, Tim extracted the extinguisher from beneath my seat, and had the flames out in seconds. Without any orders, he shoved Dutch into the aft gunnery well, to get him out of the lanes of fire.

When the Cong saw all of this motion on Honey's deck, they renewed their shooting with gusto, and the rounds bounded through the cockpit and ricocheted from her punctured hull.

"Rest easy, Loot. You're gonna be okay," Tim reassured as he pressed my fatigue jacket against the rip in my scalp.

I heard the dull plunk of another round entering flesh, and Witherspoon's shoulder gouted blood as he rocked back on his heels. He staggered, but he refused to fall.

"Rest easy, Loot. We're gonna make it," Tim said through a steeled jaw. "I'll be right back."

I can still see that image of Witherspoon dropping over the side, and I was sure, for a few minutes, that he was running out. I thought that he would leave us there to save his own skin. With all of the strength I had left, I rolled over to starboard, carefully avoiding Russell's charred flesh, and tried to find Tim in the water. It was then that I learned what this guy was made of. With a bloodied hand, Tim grasped onto Honey's hull by his shattered arm, and he hoisted Brad Johnson by his good shoulder into my outstretched hands, and I was able to drag Johnson back aboard. The tough man from Watts was nearly unconscious, and certainly would have drowned in a matter of minutes, but Witherspoon had saved him from that awful end. Johnson coughed and sputtered, and I piled him into my chair before I reached back for Tim.

But Tim was gone. The Cong saw me and opened up again. I knew it was only a matter of time before they launched another rocket propelled grenade at us. If they found the mark a second time, it would be our final curtain call.

What was Witherspoon trying to prove? My mind was racing, and my capacity for rational thought was failing. I imagined that Tim hated us so much that he had put us all into a single easy package for Charlie to nail.

Pain arrived like a tidal wave, washing over my entire body as I rolled onto my back, blood trickling into my ears to add irritation to the agony. But when I craned my neck, I saw Tim Witherspoon hauling himself onto the deck of the beached Zippo. I had no idea what he was up to.

I watched as Tim checked the reclining pilot's neck for a pulse, before he unceremoniously dumped the man overboard. He sat in the pilot's vacated seat, and brought the Zippo's engines back to life. As he cranked the boat into reverse, much of the enemy fire got diverted from us to the Zippo, in hopes of preventing its escape. In spite of the forceful thumps of entering bullets, Witherspoon successfully backed away from the sandy bank. At a slow speed, he aimed for Honey.

But Witherspoon didn't leave it at that. Braving enemy fire, he got out of that cockpit and dodged onto the Zippo's foredeck, so that he could turn that flaming nozzle on the enemy sampan.

At first, I didn't understand that action, and I was sure that Tim had caught another couple of rounds for doing that. Surely he knew that most of the enemy fire was coming from the shore away from the sampan. But Tim was persistent, and he didn't leave that nozzle until the sampan was aflame. I heard the smack of fresh bullets impacting with Tim's chest. But the sampan was burning, and raising billowing clouds of black smoke. My foggy mind took quite some time to decipher Tim's intention, but realization dawned as that dark shroud of oily smoke enveloped Honey, making us nearly invisible to the snipers on the shore. The whistling rounds were coming less frequently, and I thanked God that we had acquired a "college boy" gunner who knew how to use his brain.

I was beginning to fade in and out at that point, near shock if not in it, because the next thing I can remember is the picture of Tim Witherspoon gently nudging the Zippo into Honey's side, and whipping a dredge chain around her forward sponson. Without saying a word, he was back at the Zippo's helm, and he spun the wheel hard over as he accelerated smoothly away, back down the channel into the fading twilight, towing us through all of the bends and sweeps with a skill I knew that I could never have matched.

The cracks of enemy rifles became fewer and fewer, and then stopped. Each turn brought a shriek of agony from Russell as his charred flesh slapped against the metal hull, and Dutch was grunting with his efforts to breathe. But I was still conscious when we felt the transition to the smooth and welcome current of the Mekong River.

"The kid's got guts ... the kid's got real guts," Dutch croaked from the black expanding lake of his own blood.

In the little last light of that awful day, I can still see Tim, framed by the dark waters of that filthy river, his face drained white by the loss of blood from his many wounds. His big glasses are cocked at a funny angle, because one of the earpieces is missing. I'm looking at a sideways image of the man, because I'm still flat on my back on Honey's deck, unable to pull myself up to thank him.

For me, Tim Witherspoon will always be in that Zippo's cockpit, seated next to a headless co-pilot, grinning a tight smile of sadness, knowing that his life is leaking away.

"Damn it, Loot ... I was so short."

After they shipped us home, I never tried to look for Dutch. He never tried to find me either, as far as I know. Unlike the other wars that had gone before, our countrymen wanted to forget about us, and the fact that we had ever been there. Very few of us sought out reminders of the time we were encouraged to avoid mentioning. We concentrated on erasing those haunting images.

A few years after the war, I heard that Bradley had been killed in some gang brawl back in Los Angeles. Russell went country gentle, and married some debutante who bought him a stable of stock cars to look after. Russell wouldn't jeopardize that standing by keeping company with fellow "baby killers" from his past.

It was eighty-nine when I ran into Dutch, quite by accident. I had made the trip to D.C. because I knew that I would never sleep right again until I touched the kid's name. Tim Witherspoon had won the Silver Star, but it would never sparkle in front of his eyes.

Dutch was in his chair, his atrophied legs spindly on their rests, sickly contrasting with the heavy upper torso and still magnificent arms that draped down over the big wheels. He had taken a job with the Veteran's Administration, and spent weekends volunteering at the Vietnam Memorial, talking to the crowds of tourists gathered to experience this granite monument to wasted lives.

Without needing words, we embraced for a long time, and tears streamed into Dutch's gray moustache. Finally, he shook his head and grunted.

"Give me a couple of minutes here, Loot. Got something I got to talk to these fine people about."

I stepped back from my old comrade, amazed at how he had faded to such a weak shadow of what he had once been.

But Dutch smiled and crinkled his entire, mischievous face, and lifted the microphone to his lips as he reached back to stab at Tim Witherspoon's stone etching.

"Ladies and gentlemen, I want to tell you a story about the bravest man I ever knew. He kept saying that he was really short, ... but they don't come any taller."

CARA CHAMBERLAIN
My Mother's Legs

A GIRL WITH SHINS BARE AND DOWNY BETWEEN BOBBY SOCKS AND the hem of her dress kicked through alkali, salt roses and stars, on the seasonal pond's dry bed. She was afraid of horses, hogs, poultry, and cattle, but she liked cats (not, of course, the mean barn mousers). She liked dressing two of them in doll clothes, but now they had run away—Isabelle and tailless Stubby. Still, they were tame and wouldn't go far, and, sturdy and quick as she was, she found them soon enough near the blacksmith shop, but the small rose-print gowns made of her grandmother's worn batiste were lost forever.

Despite her feline companions and the freedom to run anywhere she wanted, my mother was glad when her parents left Six Mile Ranch near the Utah-Nevada border and moved to Salt Lake City. She liked the city. She went to the movies (5-cent matinees) and to Neighbor's Grocery Store (pronounced "nayguhburrs" by the locals), but the new school and the new children were city-tough and made fun of her answer to the teacher's question: What is your religion? She wasn't LDS. That was all anyone remembered. I doubt my mother as a child was self-conscious about her appearance (she was a beautiful girl, though her grandmother had once called her "moon-faced" and the comment stuck with her for the rest of her life), but my mother always felt herself second-rate in school. And it wasn't just because she was a "gentile." Her handsome older brother was a better artist and athlete—everyone's favorite, in fact. Even if she'd be teacher's pet one year in Home Economics class, boys were privileged and generally superior.

Her parents seem to have thought so, too. Crossing her street when she was only seven and still unused to traffic, she didn't see the Model A until it struck her. The driver carried her home, but, this being the depression and she only a girl, no one called a doctor. She propelled herself with her arms as she sat on a piece of cardboard until she healed enough to walk again. Sixty years later, a titanium rod had to shore up her arthritic hip and damaged femur.

As a young woman, my mother learned to be undeniably chic, seeking a Hollywood-style glamour, wearing in a brownie camera photograph one of those alluringly modest 1950s halter swimsuits with shirred front and tiny skirt. Her legs are young and fit, though the ankles are thick even then. "Prussian," my dad would call them, perhaps in genuine admiration of their sturdiness. In this early photograph he took, unmarried as yet, she stretches her legs long and smooth on the white beach of the Silver Sands resort on the Great Salt Lake. In those days, she proudly owned a pink silk-lined shaving kit with an electric razor (though apparently in perfect condition, it no longer worked when I was old enough to pretend to use it).

She loved the Big Band look but not the music itself. She loved silk stockings and high heels, and wore a girdle that made her appear more slender than she already was, but she paid for early ranch poverty with dental problems and was almost as ashamed of her crooked teeth as she would later be of her legs, thick ankles and hammer toes (the latter, she told me, the result of the mail-order shoes she wore at Six Mile that never quite fit). In a fine linen suit and black pumps, she walked home by herself from the dentist's office after tooth extractions and gum surgery.

Perhaps years of feeling ostracized by the dominant religion of her chosen home wore on her. Or perhaps her various tacit marital frustrations came to rest in animosity toward the part of herself she could easily observe. At any rate, by the time she was 35 or 40, my mother stopped wearing shorts and bathing suits. And, of course, she never wore sandals. Her skirts became full and her heels sensible. She said her thighs were fat, her legs and feet embarrassing. The word we learned was a French neologism: cellulite. Diets came and transformed into other diets. Exercises evolved. She danced while the potatoes boiled: "Shuffle off to Buffalo." Jack LaLanne followed, and then leg lifts, and finally a stationary bicycle.

She walked everywhere, even to the grocery, my sister mortified since everyone else's mom could drive. My mother took the bus and walked. Shanks mares, she called her legs. She walked in heels to parent-teacher conferences and medical appointments, and in Keds to the library and Grand Central Drug. My dad took the car to work and met us at the store every other Friday on paydays when there were too many groceries for us to carry. We could have afforded a second car, but my mother didn't want to drive and did not earn her license or get a part-time job or buy her Ford Fairlane until 1980. She was never fat, but she had come to abhor her legs. And so she walked.

After hip replacement and craniotomy, she still marched to the store and the bank, crossing the six-lane street she'd once told me never to go near, scaring me so much when I was little that I long thought 33rd South could spontaneously kill anyone, not just a careless child or an old woman with balance issues. She walked to the post office and to hair appointments. And she walked her dog, a demented corgi who accidentally pulled her down once outside the LDS ward. No one helped her. Perhaps no one saw. She was proud to have kept hold of the leash and saved the dog. She was probably pleased, also, to have something new to hold against the Mormons—a swollen knee.

No matter what, she wouldn't carry the cell phone I'd bought for possible emergencies on her rambles, though it fit in her pocket. "Easily," I said.

"Who would I call?" she'd countered. My sister in California and I in Montana were certainly not in a position to rescue her should she tumble in Utah.

Eventually, when the brain tumor returned and she required a variety of medical devices to help her stand, she walked in the nursing home until her therapist deemed the exercise too dangerous. Still, she never gave up hope that she would "get back in shape" one day.

Dying at 83, she was turned every hour so she would not develop bedsores. The aides admired her pure white skin and the absence of varicose veins. No mottling, even at the end. "Her legs are beautiful," they said with genuine envy.

SHANN RAY
City of Hunger and Light

"In each family a story is playing itself out, and each family's story embodies its hope and despair."—Augustus Napier

CHAPTER 1
The Family

AT DAWN IT WAS A CLEAR DAY, NO WIND, BUT BY THE TIME HANK picked the boy up from school a grey stroke of cloud met the horizon to the north. On the barren Highline of Montana they went with the windows down in the green Chevy Malibu up the highway beyond the town until the buildings faded and the scrap yard appeared on the left side of the road. Hank slowed and drove past the structure, a tall two-story rectangle with metal garage doors right of the front window. Mr. Olaf owned the place and parked a long brown Cadillac in front, chub-faced man with dark teeth and chew stains at the corners of his mouth. He slept upstairs.

Hank pulled into the dirt parking lot then around to a fenced area in back. The gate was wider than a bus, a closed ten foot high expanse in the larger fenceline. A makeshift tangle of barbed wire lined the enclosure and inside were a dozen or so burned-out cars, some on blocks, some flat on the orange steel of rusted rims. Jakob had his elbow out the window, his chin at rest on the crease of his arm. He noticed the blown windshields of the nearest two vehicles, both sedans, big American models from the 70s. A few shards of glass in the frame. He saw the dark insides, the seats perhaps, or just blank shapes of steel. At the back of the enclosure, the sun flashed from the roof of an angular storage shed made of sheet metal.

Jakob was bored so he thought of guitar rhythms, hand heel to mute the strings, clicking out one-twos, ta-tat-tats, with a wood slap every fourth beat. He pushed the rhythm with his fingers on the dash. He was small, but music, unlike sports, didn't ask his height. A freshman in high school, five-foot two inches tall, Nordic looking with shoulder-length dirty blond hair, he weighed ninety pounds.

In front of the gate Hank put the car in Park and revved the engine.

Jakob looked at him.

"Watch," Hank grunted.

Hank chewed the inside of his cheek. Idiot, Jakob thought. Around his mom he called Hank "Pops" but from day one Hank received it without acknowledgement, expressionless as a slab of concrete. Jakob had thought of naming him Bull, he nicknamed all her men, but he'd settled on Heifer, preferring to see Hank as a dense-headed cow that ate fields to the nub, dull-eyed chewing his cud, leaving a trail of excrement ankle-deep. Later when Jakob found the word 'heifer' in a dictionary during English class he put the book to his mouth and laughed out loud.

"There," said Hank, pointing to movement at the storage shed.

Two dogs emerged, big males, some strange Doberman-Rottweiler mix. Jakob heard them too, and he pushed himself back in the seat, the dogs on a dead run, a roar more metallic than animal from their mouths, like a train, he thought, or like the jets that flew from the Air Force base at Glasgow. Barking, they ran for the gate and launched, rapping their snouts into the metal's diamond pattern, standing back, growling. Their jaws made a ridiculous racket, Jakob thought, as he pressed his head back into the headrest.

He had a great fear of dogs.

These two were higher than his waist. Probably closer to his chest, he thought. The Doberman was in the legs mainly, but the rest was Rottweiler, thick bodied, block-headed.

"Come with me," Hank said and took Jakob by the wrist, jerking him across the seat and out the driver's side door. Jakob held back but Hank pushed him forward, taking him by the shoulders and positioning him before the gate not three feet from the dogs. Jakob felt strengthless and loathed himself. The near one had a ragged left ear, the flap entirely missing, just a crownlike edge to it. He smelled dirt and car oil, tangy body odor, the scent of alcohol from the pores of Hank's body. Jakob's eyes felt raw. He tasted, more than he smelled, Hank's breath, dank and sulfurous, heavy, overpowering. It was something Jakob's mother pointed out about Hank, sometimes publicly.

"Your breath smells like feces," she'd say, and Hank would eye her like murder.

The dog's teeth clicked as the jaws snapped. Their harsh, hollow breaths rose from deep in the chest. They want to eat me, Jakob thought. Behind him, Hank's jaw popped as he chewed his cheek, which meant the Heifer was excited and needed more snuice. Despite Hank's breath and the weight of his hands, for a moment Jakob almost felt ready for what might come.

"Watch this," Hank said loudly.

Then Hank hollered, "Down pigs!"

The dogs fell prostrate, faces on forepaws, bodies flat. Everything was quiet but for the hum of the electric lines, and the flight of a grasshopper in the scrub grass along the fence.

"Up!" Hank said, and the dogs jumped up, bellowing, lunging again.

"Pretty cool, huh?" Hank shouted in Jakob's ear, and Jakob had the odd feeling of being close to Hank.

"Power," Hank said, "I've got it."

Hank's voice sounded distorted so near the boy's face, and Jakob noticed the lock then, a masterlock almost directly in front of him, shiny silver with a round black face. Small white numbers. Smaller white notches.

Shouting again, Hank said, "Back pigs."

The dogs shut up and trotted back through the husked-out cars. They were high-chested animals, barrel-shaped with large stonelike heads. Like warlords, thought Jakob. Like wolves.

Hank retrieved a white sheet of paper from the car. "Gotta get my time slip to Olaf," he said. He motioned toward the office with his chin.

Jakob sat on his heels and eyed the fence. Heifer, he thought. Mean as a boar. With the mind of an idiot. He heard Hank from the front of the building, overly loud, glad-handing with Olaf.

Jakob stood and took the lock in his hands. In front, the two men belly-laughed in unison. In the scrap yard all was quiet. He held the lock, his fingers on the bright silver casing. Then he went back to the car and sat in the driver's seat with his hands on the wheel. Heifer, he thought again... power. Power of the cow, maybe. Not power of the dog. On the radio he found Foreigner, Lou Gramm's high-edged vocals. A song called Emergency. In the ashtray he fond a scrap of paper, the numbers 20-42-12 in blue ink. He took the paper with him and got out again and approached the fence. He held the lock face, cleared it and cycled the numbers—20 right, left two times around to 42, back right to 12. When he pulled down, it popped like a knuckle. He expected noise from the back of the enclosure but none came. Quietly he slipped the lock's metal loop free, pulled the handle up and drew the gate an inch or two open. He moved the handle back down and set the lock back in place, leaving the gate unlocked and slightly ajar. He pressed the lock together again.

He went back and sat in the car.

Perfect, he thought, the gate looks closed.

CHAPTER 2
The Family Bent

IN THE CREASE BETWEEN THE DASH AND THE WINDSHIELD A half-eaten bag of pistachios was pressed betwen the blackened remnants of old t-shirt sleeves and an unwrapped Twinkie on a square of white cardboard. As Hank returned, Jakob stared at him in the rearview mirror. Never much for cleanliness, thought Jakob. Old goat parted his hair in the middle so it hung limp to each side, black as coal above an overgrown beard. His eyes were down as he plodded toward the car. Jakob chalked up against him his obesity, his head hooded by hair, his greasy bloated face. Jakob hated him.

"Glad I showed you those dogs?" Hank said as he got in.

"Not really," said Jakob.

Jakob knew the Heifer was trying to be nice, but Jakob wasn't interested. Hank didn't notice the lock, just looked over his shoulder and backed the Malibu out.

"Thought you had to work," said Jakob.

Hank looked at him, detected Jakob's sullenness, and shouted, "Sometimes I do, sometimes I don't."

Jakob glared.

Hank backed the car into the street, stopped, jammed the works into drive and turned back toward town. He drove with his left hand and with his right he reached out and clutched Jakob's chin, and pushed the boy's face in the opposite direction. "Look that way," he said. "I don't like your face."

Staring out at the fields Jakob knew why he had opened the gate. He wanted the dogs to be free, not walled-in or chained to something ugly like he was. And he hoped someone would get hurt, a thought he had often but rarely had the courage to act on, unless it was to harm himself—he bit his nails to the quick, he despised school, and last year there was the mess with Pat Stone in another no-name city like this one. City of hunger. City of light. Lines from a song he'd written. And people, he thought, like cities themselves.

Jakob rolled his window up to cut the dust as Hank drew the Malibu into a circle of dirt on the side of the highway. If someone got hurt, Jakob hoped it would be Hank. The Golden Spur stood angular with a low roof, painted brown, a structure wholly unelectrified, nondescript even in daylight, narrow dark windows either side of the door. Hank made Jakob wait in the car while he went inside, played Keno and drank beer. A dog to his own vomit, he thought—a line he'd stolen from the biology teacher, Ms. Micken, a manlike woman who wore spiders encased in glass around her neck. Jakob wedged his head between the shoulder of the seat and the vinyl bumper of the door. He pictured the dogs attacking the Heifer, ribboning him. He was stuck again, controlled by Hank's agenda, and so he thought, as usual, about guitars—this time about owning his own. The band teacher, Mr. Mason, had the guitar Jakob wanted, a clean Gibson Signature

Jakob coveted incessantly: Sitka spruce surface, maple on the back and sides, 11 mother of pearl stars on an Indian rosewood fingerboard and headstock. A rhythm guitar, Mason had told him, first created for the Everly Brothers in the mini jumbo body style set with double pick guards. Straight from the factory in Kalamazoo, Michigan in 1971 and then through two previous owners before Mason got it. Mason was a self-proclaimed guitar aficionado and whenever he played a solo during class he liked to call himself, "The Unacknowledged Axeman of Montana." He was bald and kept a soul patch like a dime of grey under his lower lip. He like to pull out his Strat and lay down some Stevie Ray Vaughn, or Hendrix, Zeppelin, or Van Halen's Eruption. Said he hated to part with the Gibson. It was one of seven guitars he owned. "One too many though," he told the class, on account of his newborn son.

"Two hundred and twenty-five bucks," he said. "Won't find anything like it for that price."

It wasn't too far away, Jakob thought, if he could just bide his time. He'd been lifting money from Hank's pants pockets from where they hung over the chair in his mom's bedroom. Hank passed out in his mom's bed. Jakob hated this town, the eleventh of his life if his mom's calculations were correct, excluding stints of one or two months, summers, when she'd worked construction. Baronville, it was called, northern oil outpost on the Montana/ Canada border. A sign on the highway said Edward Baron struck oil in the late 1800's and made ten thousand dollars. Hank took them here for a supposed job that would get the family back on track after Jakob had "publicly humiliated" the family. Pipechecker or line worker or some other dumb thing, who knew, thought Jakob. Another move, the third in less than two years, and nothing changed. Jakob knew no one and no one knew him. Except if he counted deaf Mr. Elhaven two doors down with the fenced backyard, or crazy Binder next door, the middle-aged ex-military man with the jarhead crew cut.

Jakob's mom had met Elhaven at the store and pointed the old man out once on the street. "Be nice to him," she'd whispered. "He's deaf." Jakob shook the man's hand, noticed the grey velcro-stripped tennis shoes he wore, saw kindness in his eyes. But Binder, Jakob had run from when the lunatic threatened him with a shotgun. The man stood in his clean-cut backyard, green square of grass with no fence, screaming at Jakob to stay off his property.

He hadn't even been on Binder's property. Only walking the alley, making his way home.

IN THE SLANT OF LATE SUN JAKOB FELT THE DULL PRESSURE OF THE door on the frontal bone of his forehead. Hank had no care for how long he made him wait. Jakob remembered their first year together, Hank's and his mom's, and how he'd lie in the narrow hall outside their bedroom door, late at night or in the early morning. Hank would step over him on the way to the kitchen for alcohol or to the bathroom to pee and Jakob would reach up and touch the man's ankle and Hank would grunt or say nothing. At some point Jakob had stopped doing that.

He sat up in the car seat and looked out above the straight edge of the bar. In the depths behind the building the sky had narrowed, darkening toward night and a gathering storm. He had to get out, he told himself. He just needed a way. He wished he could sing, stand with a fist in the air and pipe lead vocals for a real band. He looked in the rearview mirror. He had the face for it, a pretty face he thought, like a rich boy's face. He slumped back in the seat, convinced lead was not possible, it being too up front and requiring more than he had. But guitar, rhythm guitar preferably, not lead singer, not even lead guitar, though Mason told him his scales were dialed in, even said Jakob, "broke off difficult riffs smooth as butter." No... two steps back from the front, he could do that. And write songs. He looked out the window. It'd be a pretty penny to get that guitar. Pretty Boy, they'd call him, and he'd like it. Pretty Boy punching the rhythms on the Gibson Signature. He'd find the money, make the purchase, and be gone.

Hank walked from the bar, his face full and red, his neck purple. The two drove home in silence.

LATE NIGHT, THE SILENCE GONE, HANK AND JAKOB'S MOM STOOD face to face downstairs, carving into each other with their words. Upstairs in his bedroom, Jakob picked his pencil off the floor, sat down at his makeshift desk, fiberboard table, wood stump chair, and hastily sketched another guitar, a Flying V this time. It was 11:47 pm. A table Hank had claimed from the dump. He gripped the upper portion of the table legs where they swelled like tiny, elongated calf muscles, and twisted them slightly so a birdlike sound eked from the leg holes. He'd gotten Hank to curse him this way a few nights back. His efforts brought nothing tonight.

He rose and left his room, slamming the door as hard as he could. He walked downstairs and passed through the living room. He walked into the kitchen and stopped where the counter armed out from the wall and squared off the room. Jakob's mom and Hank were in that small space, yelling. Beyond them was a thin card table up against the wall and three high-backed chairs tucked in, the upholstery white vinyl with big orange daisies. He stood between his mom and Hank and put his hands up, one in each of their faces.

"Stop!" he said.

Immediately his mom turned, shouting at him: "Shut your mouth, boy!"

Spittle sprayed from her mouth.

He'd thought he was defending her.

"Bastard!" Hank added and clenched Jakob's neck with one hand. His mother dug her nails into the back of Jakob's arm.

"Get your ass out of this kitchen," Hank said, raising his hand to strike, but instead of slapping him, he shoved him so that Jakob stumbled from the kitchen to the living room and nearly tripped over the line of carpet that met the linoleum.

Jakob's face flushed. His heart felt hot. Head down, back to his mother and Hank, he eyed the undone laces of his Pro-Keds. Shoes bought for a quarter at a garage sale in Glendive, gift from the Heifer. Yellow suede, two-sizes too big. He started upstairs.

In the kitchen the two were shouting at each other again.

She called him lazy asshole. He called her whore.

Back in his bedroom Jakob sat on the floor. The carpet smelled of cat urine.

He looked at his hands. Small hands, but quick, he thought. Quick fingers for chord changes, picking patterns, strum patterns, solos he'd fought to learn... he wanted to be good, real good... he wanted to give people tight slick licks the likes of which the world had never known. He frowned. Pipedream, he told himself.

CHAPTER 3
The Family Broken

JAKOB TAKES THE PICK FROM HIS BACK JEANS POCKET, GRABS THE bandroom loaner guitar, plain low-level acoustic, and turns a three minute riff that makes his head sweat. Like death, he thinks, or death like that—made of absorption and fire, something to be lost in, like wilderness, like rage. He props the guitar against the arm of the couch, and sits back and sighs and wants to cry but won't let himself. He puts the pick in his mouth and feels his face. He lets his mind think of a woman loving him, finding him attractive. His nose like a blade, and his lips small and red. I won't need a voice, he thinks, just a face—good lines and clear good skin, no marks. According to the picture his mom carried hidden in a slot in her wallet it is the one real thing his biological father gave him: a good face, no blemishes.

He pictures how a woman might touch his face, a woman who has seen him play. She'd touch him not for sex, though he wouldn't stop her, but for understanding... to know him more, to be closer to him. He takes the pick from his mouth and smooths it between his thumb and forefinger and puts it back in his mouth.

He covers his ears. They keep yelling.

BARONVILLE. EMBARRASSMENT BLEW THEM EAST ALONG THE Highline due to the pact Jakob made with Pat Stone back in Havre. They'd agreed, he and Pat, to set fire to the school. The detail is what he remembers, simple print on matching blank chord charts:

Let's do it today.

A victory, he thinks now, though it went nowhere. Lunch break. Because of the gasoline the fire burned his teacher's desk near to the ground, but nothing else caught. Tile floors. Concrete walls. He and Pat were arrested and spent two days in jail and in less than a week the Heifer relocated the family, first to Geffin, bald spot in north central Montana, then to Three Horse, uglified reservation town past Wolf Point, and finally further east to Baronville.

"No more stupid black clothes," was all the Heifer said.

UGLY, ALTERED TONES FROM THE KITCHEN. SO CALLED MOM AND dad, he thought. Anathema.

She curses. He slams the door.

She yells at him through the door. In a hard barking baritone he says shut up or I'll shut you up.

Silence.

Jakob leans back and hears the wind, a north wind against

which the house seems to brace itself. A few ticks at the window, the touch of a tree, the beginnings of rain. He cups his face in his hands. He can't recall the last time his mother touched his face.

The Heifer, he thinks, doesn't touch at all.

Or touches with hands hard as rock.

The yelling starts up again.

Jakob stands and wipes his hands on his jeans.

He removes the guitar pick from his mouth, fingers the clear brown-gold, the rounded edges. He holds it over his head and stares through the small translucent window up at the light. He slips the pick into the back right pocket of his jeans. His faded black sweat-top lies in the corner of the room, arms splayed, midsection bent in on itself. He takes it up, puts it on, walks down the stairs and out the front door.

THE NIGHT IS DARKER THAN HE IMAGINED, A PLANK OF CONCRETE like a grey arm in the yard. He leaps down the steps and sprints, jumping the sidewalk, angling toward the highway. He doesn't know where he'll go and doesn't care. A low ceiling of cloud blackens the sky. A drizzle of rain meets his face. He runs hard down the middle of the pavement and meets no cars and sees no one walking. His eyes burn and he cries.

They live in government housing a mile from town. Small squarish houses stand down from Highway 2 on straight lines to the south. They end on fields alternately fallow or brimming gold with wheat, fields he hates, fields quilting the earth from here to middle America. The old streetlamps emanate a dull orange glow, their luminous spheres attached to short metal arms atop half-cut wood-tarred utility poles—dim halos domelike over the sidewalk. Rain enters the outer rim of the light, down in quick jettisons that shine on the ground. Up ahead he sees the otherworldly elongated metal of the highway lights, spidery above the asphalt.

He runs angry, with no plan but to keep running.

Every house is dark, the tall grass slicked with rain. He feels strong, cruising, floating, only slightly cold in the upper body. From up ahead he hears the noise of a semi as it descends the downgrade toward town. He stops at the highway and lets the force of the huge machine, burdened with downshifting, pass him by. A dirty mist sweeps over him and the white trailer fades east into the city. He walks to the middle of the road, turns, and follows the truck.

He keeps running, and drifts some, feeling the downslant of the asphalt, drawing himself back. His ears ring. His nose runs. The road, a two-lane hump-backed straightaway, slits the city east to west. Railroad tracks line the far side, through town and further east to all the other stops on the Highline—Glasgow, Wolf Point, Poplar, through the Dakotas to Minnesota, to Minneapolis, and St. Paul. His shoes are old. He thinks of two words: Mom, Hank. Words he rarely speaks in kindness. His reedy mother, tiny, full of barbs. His step-animal, Heifer, a fat man with vacant violent eyes.

Running, he feels nothing.

A mile or so ahead he sees the lights of the city, a faint red hue on a black underbelly of cloud, and closer the small round headlights of an oncoming car. As the vehicle approaches he moves into the car's lane. The car slows, the driver pumps the high beams. Light consumes Jakob's body. He feels ghostly and bright-headed. He runs toward the dark windshield but the car veers and takes the shoulder, lurching, kicking up stones. A loud honk blares as an old man's face appears, loose-skinned, contorted. Jakob hears a hoarse angry yell, then nothing.

Darkness.

His upper body is hot, his fists icy and hard.

He keeps running.

CHAPTER 4
The Family Lost

THE RAIN THRUMS THE BACK OF HIS HEAD. THE WIND IS A LOUD hush from the north. He considers lying down. Between the big cone-shaped beams of the highway lights lie huge fields of darkness. Dark, he thinks, deep dark. Dark, the absence of light. The highway lights are modern giants compared to the dwarfs that line his small subdivision. They spill bone-white light into the night, and he stares at their long gray necks, ultra high luminaries erected on thin silver poles, slanted at the tip. The lights reach up, out over the road. Above them, the sky is so black looking into it he feels blind.

People don't know me, he thinks. They never have.

Lightning flashes and for a moment the world opens wide.

Houses become vivid behind him, pale shapes in orderly lines. Then blackness swallows everything and thunder booms. He is left with an image in his mind of houses like the narrow elongated bones of forearms or thick-set femurs, the earth around them a grey-white skin that has sloughed off. In the bang of sound he doesn't flinch or grow afraid. He slows to a walk, down the double yellow line. A monumental apathy fills him. He decides to stop.

He believes if he lies down, the pavement will be hard but good, beaten down, and restful. He won't hear the cars, the ranchers' trucks with their loud mufflers, the wide holler of gears from the 18-wheelers. He'll sleep and forget everything.

As he bends down and touches the road with his left hand, something far ahead catches his eye.

ALMOST BEYOND VISION TWO FORMS PASS INTO A BROAD CIRCLE of light. He knows they are dogs, the dogs he himself released, bodies tall and wolflike, but more muscular than wolves. They walk, then begin running toward him. He stands upright, head high, watching until they pass again into the dark. His mouth tastes like metal. He smells asphalt, dirt and the oil ground into it, the rubber of tires, the tar of road crews, gasoline. He hears electricity in the sky, the sweep of lightning flashes and the deep stillness that harbors thunder. He hears the quick rhythm of the dogs' paws on the pavement far away.

The dogs come visible again under another highway light, nearer, five lights ahead now, perhaps five or six-hundred yards. That far away they look sleek and fast. Because they shimmer, they don't look real. His shoes feel heavy as stones. He touches at the outside seams of his jeans.

From the black of Canada and the boundary lands, the north wind rises, and with it the rain comes harder. The dogs enter the darkness again. He knows he should go back to the house; he receives this thought like a strange almost unwanted salvation. But he doesn't move. He keeps staring into the dark. He should go, he tells himself, right now. Closer still, the animals emerge. He sees the pink ribbons of their tongues at the side of their mouths as they run. Dobermans, he thinks. Rottweilers.

The words jolt him and he flies.

The dogs move with their heads down and Jakob lowers his head too, running wild, pumping his fists. But his shoes are almost black now, waterlogged, banging at the road. Behind him the dogs claw the street and when he looks again, lightning flashes, showing their stark faces, the strange ear of the lead dog, truncated, half-eaten. The sky goes dark and Jakob enters the glow of another circle spread wide on the highway. He is halfway across, frantically looking back when they enter the edge of the light one light behind him. He turns, runs to the first house and leaps a small picket fence. K Street: one over from his own. No pavement, just gravel.

I can make it, he thinks.

Across the front yard, along a narrow path at the side of the house, he moves quickly, bumping his shoulder once on the wall. The path opens on a wide backyard picketed like the front. At the far end of the yard he barely clears the fence before turning up the alley.

A minute later he hears the dogs in the gravel, fighting to make the corner. At a house on the left he grips the top of a short chain link fence and hurls himself over. Landing, he falls to his knees and scrambles up. The dogs rise behind him, clutching the fence top, wriggling into the yard. He reaches a gate, unlatches it and slams it behind him. He runs beside the house and comes out onto his own street. His house is at the far end. He runs harder and cusses and starts crying again.

For a moment he hears nothing, just his own rants and hard breathing. He wants to panic. He calms himself. The gate was topped by a curved metal swirl, a length higher than the rest of the fence. High enough, he thinks. He slows. Faintly in the distance he hears snarls and the snapping of jaws as the dogs bang their faces into the gate. Volumes louder the storm surges to an ultimate build, factories of noise in the city of the night. The rain has torn a hole in everything now. Silver and black. Water. Sky. All is nothing, he thinks. He arcs into the street and runs straight ahead and the voice of the dogs dies on the howling wind.

Laboring, he holds his side and slows to a jog.

For a few seconds the wind calms and he hears a bright sound, high, pronounced. The sound of familiarity, of conviction. He pictures the latch on the gate, lifted by the nose of one of them. He pictures the mouth of the lead dog carving flesh from his wrist, jaws hinging open and shut, splintering bone.

When he turns he finds the dogs in the street, running straight for him.

He bolts for Mr. Elhaven's place, the tall fence, a backyard he can rely on, two down from his own. The dogs gain on him as he feints to the side of Elhaven's, to the back where he gathers and catapults himself, slamming bodily some feet up the giant chain link fence, gripping the small metal squares and climbs. Pain registers in his hands as he reaches the top, swings his leg over and drops, letting out a small uncontrolled yelp before rolling sideways on the flooded grass of the backyard. He turns and sits on his haunches and breathes. I'm safe now, he thinks, and when the dogs arrive, he eyes them and gloats. "Pigs," he says. "You won't get over that."

He blows heat into his hands.

Heads down and teeth chalk white, the dogs bellow, bodies black and slick in the rain. He finds them beautiful. They leap. The fence repels them.

Lightning fractures the sky and the night births thunder, mythic sounds as of mountains falling or earth opening, and for a span all is blind and all is changed. In the space between the houses, on the horizon to the north a diadem of light branches upward from the surface of the world. Then a great booming, and more blackness, and the sky alight again, cracked with crooked branches of light, the edge-burn hot and clean.

He sits on his heels, clutching his knees to his chest. Rain pummels him. He is alone in a wide puddle of water that covers nearly the whole expanse of Elhaven's back yard.

Like toy battering rams the dogs keep jumping at the fence, growling, snapping their jaws. "Wear yourselves out," he says and he gets up and walks closer.

At the top of his lungs he yells, "Down!"

"Back!" he screams.

The dogs hit the fence with their heads, bloodying their flat, short faces.

He has no power over them.

They're done, he thinks, tears on his face, they're cooked. But they keep on.

In among the facial bones, in the dogs' wide, thick skulls, the thin slits of their eyes appear buried and narrow. Sitting again, holding his knees in his arms, he puts his head down and waits. But no one comes.

"Go ahead," he yells again. "Knock your heads in."

He likes the heart they have, the appetite, even with him secure behind the fence. "I'm safe," he says aloud, and he feels puffed up, as big as he wants to be, followed by the certainty that he is actually small, the same nothing he's always been, pale and wet in this puddle, full of fear. He is more afraid, in fact, than ever.

He wraps his knees tighter in his arms and considers killing the dogs, but has no idea how he might do so, thin as he is, and without a weapon. He looks around, hoping to find a hard-edged implement or bludgeon, a broom handle or two-by-four, a baseball bat. He finds nothing. In the far corner of the yard is Mr. Elhaven's tool shed, square of tin in an ocean of broken black water, the water beaten to pieces by the rain. The world harbors rage, he thinks. A silver masterlock with a black face seals two white tin doors.

He decides to wake Elhaven but as he approaches the back door of the house the ragged-eared dog trots down the fence-line, slips his snout under the latch of the gate there and enters the backyard. I'm dead, Jakob thinks, and wishes, painfully, he would have been more attentive. The dogs flow into the yard like eels as Jakob breaks for the back fence, splashing wide holes in the water's surface. The dogs are fast, their angle precise.

The lead dog overtakes him as he reaches the fence.

A scream comes unhinged from Jakob's throat.

CHAPTER 5
The Family

NO LIGHT AND NO ONE STIRS. JAKOB'S MOMENTUM CARRIES HIM forward and he scrambles and drags the dog as it jerks convulsively, jaws locked on a bell of denim at the bottom of his right pant leg. The second dog half-climbs the flanks and head of the first but fails to gain purchase, careens and hits the fence left of Jakob.

In a vigorous thrust Jakob moves to the top, makes a quick reach, finds the crossbar and secures a handhold. He hoists his chest upward and throws his arm out, checking another lunge from the second dog, but the dog bites his forearm, tearing a wide hole in his sweatshirt before falling back to the ground. A crescent of blood opens on Jakob's skin and he sees the bite-flap raised and half-mooned before the blood wells and branches down his arm.

He pulls himself up, trying to dislodge the animal on his pant leg. His jeans are tight to his hips, the dog flailing below, heavy as a hay bale. He strains upward feeling the pull of tension in the dog's mouth. The stitching creaks and finally the material shears as the dog rips the denim free and falls, white-eyed, smacking its head and chest on the ground and letting out a single yelp.

The second dog sniffs the lead dog as Jakob draws himself to the fence-top and throws his leg over. He sees his shinbone white as snow in the ragged hole. He pushes his body over the top and the sudden imbalance flings him free as he floats in mid-air, his mind like a lost thing until he lands flat on his back in the alley.

As if he's swallowed a stone he lies holding his stomach. Both dogs are on the other side of the fence, an arm's length from his face as they paw vigorously and splash muck and water behind them. Jakob can't find air. He gags. He lets out a thin groan. Then his chest opens and he sucks in whole breaths, arms wide, legs straight, rain hard on his face. Grit covers his teeth. His hair is set back from his head, starlike, the locks spread and dirty in the gravel.

I've done it, he thinks, I've won.

HIS HOUSE IS ONLY TWO DOORS DOWN NOW, TWO SETS OF GARBAGE cans, then his own weedy back yard, his own back door. Beyond the house lies the mighty field, and beyond the field, darkness, and in the darkness the horizon lit from below as if by fire, a solitary line of light beneath the storm.

He rises, and when he does the dogs leave the fence and run back for the open gate. He knows undeniably they will circle in front of Elhaven's. Try to head him off on the far side of Binder's lawn, the lawn mown tight to the wall of weeds that delineates the beginning of Jakob's backyard. He needs to beat them there. Ahead, he sees the dented metal of Hank's garbage cans in their rotted wood frame.

Running, his eyes wildly search the line of weeds between his house and Binder's but before he gets there the dogs emerge low and quick, and Jakob ducks behind Binder's tall silver trash cans. A dream, he thinks. The sleek fur of their bodies oiled as a raven's wing. Their solid, blood-stained noses and the silken complexion of the face and neck. The dogs sweep into his yard and disappear into the height of weeds.

From behind the cans, he watches. The lids are chained shut.

Binder's jarhead ways. The weeds are knee-high and wet from the torrent of rain and beyond them he sees the emptiness of the big field and out far the light. He places his hand on the back of his neck, the skin wet and cold. Rain strikes his chest. He imagines Binder the military man, Montana militia, sees him in a shooting stance on the back step, shotgun a double-barreled canon that blows the dogs away.

Think, he tells himself, as the lead dog comes out of the weeds and sniffs the ground on the line between Binder's yard and his. For a moment at least, they've lost him. Downwind, he thinks. When he looks again the dog is on the small slab of cement at the back of Jakob's house. Nose down, the animal paces back and forth in front of a tall metal-framed screen door. The wood door beyond it is open, a thing Jakob's mother does to let the heat out when it's too muggy.

Jakob moves into the gap and enters the yard on a dead run.

The lead dog turns, facing him.

The second dog trots in from behind and Jakob goes stock still.

CORNER OF THE EYE, SPEED LIKE MERCURY, THE DOGS BELLOW AND converge.

Jakob tastes bile in the back of his throat. He wants to flee. He wants a gun. He wants to maim these dogs, kill them. He lowers his head and runs for the screen door.

The lead dog moves straight on and Jakob runs at him, seeing the dog's ear, the nakedness of it. Jakob doesn't dodge or look away even as the dog leaps with such force the impact snaps Jakob's head back and torques his body sideways. The bite carves an opening in Jakob's face from the upper right side of his forehead, across his nose in an S, all the way to the underside of the jawbone. He bends and falls, throwing his forearm, flipping the dog crazily behind him. The second dog's teeth puncture Jakob's calf but he recoils and rolls and in one flawless motion throws the dog aside, rising as he runs and jumps for the screen and breaks through. His cheekbone and hip meet the vinyl floor where he slides and comes to a stop. He scrambles up and throws the door shut.

HEAD DOWN, HE BREATHES. HE WAITS AND LISTENS TO THE DOGS, tearing at each other, clawing the door. Blood spills from his face and pools on the floor.

He sets the deadbolt and looks through a small square-shaped window in the upper portion of the door, watching the dogs leap up. They sense him as they bump the window with their mouths, bloodying it. Madness, he thinks. He fears they might break through despite the height and firmness and smallness of the window. He moves to the sink and touches the edges of the wound in his face. He stands for a long time with his hands at the sink watching the blood slip from his chin into the basin.

In the small chamber of the laundry room sounds are muffled, the bump of the dogs' heads on the outside, the grind of their mouths gnashing, the bigger sound of the storm. He stands over the sink for a long time. He hears nothing from his mother, from Hank. Finally, he turns and when the far wall touches his shoulder he slides to the floor, sets his feet out before him and sits in the semi-dark as the blood drips from his chin to his sweatshirt and blackens a circle wider than a fist. Blood warms the underside of his pant leg. His calf aches. He stares blankly ahead. Strands of his hair stick to his neck. He fumbles in his back jeans pocket, finds the pick, amber triangular disk, lovely, he thinks, iridescent even in the dark. When he sets it on his tongue and closes his lips his mouth feels comforted. His mind is light. He sits still and it seems to him all the blood is running slowly out of him. He thinks he should drink something.

He is too tired to lift himself.

FAR ON, THE LIGHT OF MORNING WAKES HIM.

The dogs are quiet. There is no rain. A shaft of sun from the window places the bright gold shape of a diamond on his chest. He feels warm. His eyes burn. When he stands he hears movement outside. Light headed, he flips the pick with his tongue, moving it to his cheek. His mouth waters. He looks out the window, watching the dogs stretch and stare up at him. He hadn't noticed it before, the faint brown mask on each face in the shape of a butterfly.

The dogs turn and disappear into the weeds before they reappear on the lawn at the back of Binder's yard. They cross the alley, heads high, lips still quiet with sleep. Their faces dark and indistinct, they slip into the corridor between two houses.

They're gone, he thinks.

Taking his shoes and socks, off he walks from the room. His feet dampen the floor. The sun from the front room lights his whole body.

Through the hall he sees the blue-white glow of the television and the couch where his mother lies sleeping. She has her back to him, a small baby-blue pillow tucked beneath her head. He witnesses the slight curve of her body, her tiny feet at rest on Hank's lap. Hank's head is tipped back, the drone of a snore discordant with the smooth hush of the television. Tenderly, Hank holds her feet in his hands.

ANNA PAIGE
Transference

You tell me to breathe
I stop breathing
You pinch between my thumb and forefinger,
Pull the last piece of air from me
The room rolls
My entire name collects underneath your tongue
I carry your energy between sweaty palms,
Through 3 a.m. awakenings and across
Sidewalks curled from this relentless pacing
Across these long distance days
I fall out of bed,
Wake with clutched throat,
Corners of mouth stuck shut
You are not here to remind me
To breathe

Spring

I count days:
33 today
The ache is becoming pale,
Like something I've worn well
The oldest parts of me know this tide
The newest pieces—
Even they feel old
I awaken to frost
Touching the delicate skin of spring,
Killing little bits of itself as it grows
Pale till translucent,
Soon we will cycle as before
To hear spring is to be deafened by winter,
Collect the blankets of warmth and gently
Fold them away
The sun rises to withered flowers,
Too fragile to survive the swing
I believe we already made this agreement,
Many lives ago

Spring, continued

I'm not certain if,
On my 3 a.m. bike ride home,
The scent of apple blossoms has me
Thinking of you
Or if I was already thinking of you
You are not something new,
But rather the air of a season I know
There is comfort in this smell,
As if we'd bloomed before
And will bloom again
It is as though we are just emerging
From such slumber

ALLEN MORRIS JONES
A Remembrance

Building Fence

Meadowlarks square faint
arpeggios of wheat; dogs piss
on street signs; me I clang metal
to metal, pounding posts the way
sleep pounds us or maybe grief.
A hard unlovely bell pealing the
world to pieces: Mine. Mine. Mine.
Yours.

I SAID, "THAT BIG BULLET WENT RIGHT ON THROUGH, DIDN'T IT?"
It was too cold to snow but still it was snowing; a thin sheet of gauze twisting around the porch light. Buddy kicked through frozen marbles of blood, scattered at them, swept them aside with

Excerpted from the novel *A Bloom of Bones* (2017, Ig Publishing) his boot. He knelt and rose, hoisting the body across one shoulder. Voice muffled by a wool scarf, he said, "Leaking?"

"What?"

"Is he leaking anywhere?"

"I don't see it.

"All right then."

"That big bullet went plumb through, didn't it?"

"Will you quit with the goddamned questions? Just for once?" A gentle man, Buddy rarely cussed, seldom rebuked, never raised his voice. I stood abashed, one breath from tears. He inhaled hard through his nose, shifted the body on his shoulders. "Let's just get this done."

He set off toward the county road, walking fast. I ran to catch up. To the east, it was fifty miles of dirt until you hit the two saloons and five churches of Jordan; to the west, nothing but the Musselshell. At two in the morning, and barring high school kids off on a jacklighting drunk, there'd be no traffic. We had the road to ourselves.

I huffed along beside him. "You ain't taking the truck?"

"You want Pete's blood all over my truck bed?"

"No. I guess that's right."

He glanced down. "You can get on home if you want. No use for us both."

"I want to help."

"All right then."

"Where we taking him?"

"I was thinking Cherry Creek. All them little eroded holes."

"Oh sure."

Our breath bloomed blue around us.

Up on the road, he said, "We don't want to leave no tracks. Careful just to step in the ruts."

"All right."

"Just step where I step."

"Okay."

He shifted the body. "It sure turned cold on us didn't it?"

It was so quiet. The squeak of our boots on the snow recalled nails twisting in boards. We were the first or last men on the earth. Lone survivors of an epidemic, an ice age.

Eye level in front of me, bouncing against Buddy's back, Pete's shock of hair had frozen into a stiff brush of frost, a rigid, cartoonish explosion of fright. His eyes were open, and a rime of snow had collected in the lashes.

After a time, Buddy left the road. He stood waiting for me to open the gate. Grabbing the post, my gloves came away scaled silver with hoarfrost. He led us a hundred yards or so into the pasture before dropping one shoulder, letting the body slump off into the snow. He stretched at his back and studied the sky, the stars showing through. "Looks fair to clear."

It was a porous ground around us now, hidden under the drifted calluses of old snow. A honeycomb of ditches and pipes carved before the spring had been piped and controlled. Buddy began walking in circles, kicking at drifts. "That good round one's around here someplace." After a time, his boot broke through, revealing a vertical chimney as straight as a small highway culvert set on end.

It was deep but narrow. Pete's legs, cocked to the shape of Buddy's elbow, were going to make him half again too wide. Buddy pressed down hard on the knees, trying to force them straight. But the combination of freezing and rigor kept bouncing them back. Finally, Buddy pulled off a glove and reached into his overalls. "Haul one a them legs up here."

I grabbed a heel and raised it, with difficulty, to my waist. Both legs came together, paired in a posture of obeisance. Buddy blew into his fingers, unfolded his knife. He forced the blade under the cuff of Pete's frozen jeans and started cutting. One hard cut up, then another, then he was sawing freely through the wrinkles.

Above all other things, Buddy was a pragmatist. He knew how to keep calm during a crisis. When the grease popped hot across the pan (his own words), he prided himself on approaching the world with the coldest kind of eye.

Now he folded the fabric back to expose Pete's hairy shin and calf. The skin gray, freezing. When he pressed his blade to the soft patch of flesh below the kneecap, that place where a doctor tests the reflexes, the skin split into a narrow, bloodless mouth.

I could see that Buddy had expected this to be a good start, for the skin to pull loose as it did with elk and deer. But human skin, it seems, holds to a tighter standard. He worked his knife hard around the knee, grunting. "Damn if old Pete ain't about as hard to skin as some old beaver. Beavers, now, there's some tough skinning."

Eventually, the blade cracked hard into the joint, popping

between cartilage and bone. Buddy worked at it until the leg wobbled loose in my hands. He motioned me away, taking the foot and bracing it on his lap, twisting it hard, heel to toe. Tendons popped and snapped. He twisted it again, then again. Then the leg span freely, caught now only by a remnant of fascia. He cut these last strands away and tossed the leg into the hole: boot, hairy calf, loose athletic sock. Then he treated the other leg just the same.

"Can I close his eyes?"

Buddy touched his dripping nose with the back of his hand. "Help yourself."

Bending down to Pete, I found his pupils fixed and white, frozen opaque. Closing his lids was harder than you'd expect. It wasn't like the movies where all it took was one magic pass of the hand. No. The lids rebounded with a slow, stubborn resiliency. A stitch of thread was needed, or barring that, a pair of coins. I had a quarter and a penny.

The quarter wanted to slide down his cheek. I spat on it and held it in place until the spittle froze. Then I treated the penny just the same. Given the way his mouth was hinged slightly open, the lopsided shine of the coins, his face was given a waggish leer, a wink and grin. He was sharing some private joke. Maybe I was the butt of it. Pete had always hidden his insults inside a jibe. This felt like a proper face for him to take to the grave.

Buddy tilted the body over into the hole, lighter now without its legs, and began stomping at the sides of the hole, shearing off frozen plates of clay with his heels. "We'll come out here in a day or two with a shovel, finish the job. Maybe turn out a few steers to chop up the ground some."

It didn't take long, only a few minutes. Already it seemed impossible that Pete should be down there, legless and dumb.

I watched, surprised, as Buddy next unbuttoned his trousers, dug through his layers of long johns. Finally stood taking a heavy piss into the half-filled hole. Steam rose as if from a crack in the earth. As he turned back, tucking himself in, I expected a grin, a joke. But he only looked old; he looked tired.

Later he handed me the pocket knife he had taken from Pete's trousers. A little deer horn, lock-blade Buck. "Put that in your pocket. You'll need you a remembrance."

As if I would ever be able to forget anything about that night. Or what came before.

PRECIOUS McKENZIE
Know This

—for J.D.

Will I? You will. You will kick cancer's ass.
As you prepare, know this though,
the battle will be long and terrible.
Wispy lock loss, bone-sore fatigue, days
squandered hovering near the toilet, praying
to a faceless god that you never had much faith in before.
You will be angry, ultraviolet angry, screaming, thrashing inside
before
you will truly hurt. You will see. The body's betrayal and loneliness
is terrible.
You will weep, sometimes without tears, sometimes with, for
days.
Typical side effects, they claim. You will want to surrender, to die
though
You are afraid of death. You will feel like an ass,

curled like a bereft child on your sofa, promising and praying.
Cliché it seems, such bargaining, such praying.
It isn't a matter of if but when the terrible
dread disease will manifest in us all, stealing days
from innocent souls, frightened children-- before
we spoke of it in careful whispers. Know this though,
It is in you now but, for all of us, you will kick its ass.
Circle your wagons, cover your ass,
Keep your loved ones close before
the physicians inject you with poisons so radioactive, so terrible.
Refuse to be a victim, praying, praying, praying
for their mercy. Fight. Scream. Rage if you will. Surrender to me
though,
be enveloped in love, to battle for your earthly days.
You will need a ride home on treatment days.
Borrow my spunky neon headscarf; you are praying
that no one will notice your bare scalp. How terrible
it is to hide. Even worse to die though.
Know what is coming, to help you before
you will be knocked flat on your ass.
My little sister fought it until she had a boney ass
and cryptic arms. I have faced fear so terrible.
Trust me. I know this. I have seen it before.
Death hovered close, always, always left unspoken though.
To remind her of her almost forgotten carefree days,
we swam in cool spring water, a baptismal font, praying.
Know this though, during your darkest days, we are praying
before you. You are a marked foe most terrible
to face. Know this. Now go kick cancer's ass.

Iridescent

My world is iridescent because of a little girl—
all ruffles and sequins, "Twirl! Twirl! Twirl!"
she squeals and performs pique turns across the floor.
She'll hop a horse, scale a fence, and yell for more.
She's action, momentum, and adventure.
She's so much more than sequins and smiles, this girl.
She's tender-hearted rosebud cheeks and curls,
pink framed glasses and sapphire eyes that explore.
My world is iridescent because of a little girl.
She titters and teases, "I speak bird."
And I believe her, petite chicken wrangler.
Stitches, bumps, bruises, and Band-Aids, or
hours of earnestness, "I will live with you forever,"
she promises, kisses me and then the dog, her eyes upturned.
My world is iridescent because of a little girl.

CARRIE La SEUR
Colt the Bull-Riding Hasid

THE OLD COWBOY TWISTED WITH A GRUNT AND A WHEEZE TO retrieve a dented green metal Stanley vacuum bottle, missing its cup lid, from behind the driver's seat of the F-350 flatbed dually. He felt around his feet and came up with an apparently clean heavy white cup with a gold scroll detail around the rim, the sort of thing my mother might bring home with a full table service for eight in a re-taped box from the discount store for one of her endless charity drives. I didn't care. Ice tendrils had formed in my nostrils and I wanted a hot cup of coffee like I wanted an extra pair of Mama's handknit wool socks.

We'd been standing in the creeping, diabolical chill of a March morning outside Merle's corrals, watching younger men – and somebody's twin teenage daughters, quiet girls and strong – rope and lever January calves flat for the branding iron, castration, dehorning, and vaccination. I could tell that the affable Hutterite cowboys expertly heeling calves were cold too by the way they tucked their hands into the armpits of their collarless homespun blue coats and snuck envious looks at my heavy black wool rekel and black felt hat. The similarity among them, the plainness and heavy beards, lent us a look of relationship born of the same deep religious roots. Common humility before God. They blinked watering blue eyes against the wind and smiled at me without speaking or approaching.

Merle Emerson, my companion in the dirty pickup, had a bad hip and could no longer do the tough labor of branding. He joked about this all morning. "Time to put me down," he'd say when his hip slowed an instinctive lurch toward a straying calf, then a few minutes later he'd lean through the fence rails and instruct his nephew with a shout and a curse on getting the brand straight. Every person who arrived or left made a point of shaking Merle's hand.

All this was novel as science fiction to me. My rebbe needed someone to observe the handling of grass-fed cattle destined for the new kosher slaughterhouse in Billings, Montana, that advertised itself as a source of high quality, humanely raised beef for Orthodox communities across the U.S. After stumbling across some disturbing feedlot videos on YouTube, Rebbe Grossman wanted written notes on conditions at each of the ranches involved. It was a chance for me to leave Crown Heights and settle with blissful anticipation into one of the cramped steel tubes that sailed above us, carrying lucky strangers to destinations I had dreamed of all my life. Montana. It even sounded sunlit and handsome. But visiting the shochet, the kosher butcher, watching at close range the prayer followed fast by the slice and bleed, shining steel machinery rocking the nervous steers into place like so much wild-eyed meat, had left my stomach clenched and my taste for steak an uncomfortable memory.

At last, mid-morning, Merle gestured to me with a finger and led me to the shelter of the cab. "Cold as a witch's tit out there," he said as we slammed the doors. The diesel engine rumbled like Prospect Expressway at rush hour without the honking, soothing me. Heat dumped out the vents onto our feet, almost liquid in density.

"I'm so glad to hear you say that," I said. "I thought I was just underdressed."

I looked out to see the crew going back to work after observing our retreat. Every time I moved they looked up, like I was the most interesting thing they'd seen all month. I thanked Merle with a smile and nod as he offered me the first sip of steaming weak coffee.

"I've only got the one cup," he said. "Hope you don't mind just drinking out the other side."

A primitive sort of hygiene, I thought, accustomed as I was to living with two kitchens to observe dietary laws, but probably not dangerous to health or soul. "It looks as if you don't have many of my kind around here," I said.

What would have been a minor throat clearing in a younger, healthier man was a long and loud process of phlegm extraction for Merle. He opened his door and spat a long stream – not tobacco, just the contents of his lungs – with exceptional force and accuracy.

"Not in a while," Merle answered when he'd shut the door, "but I've been meaning to tell you about another fella like you we had out here in the Powder River country, years ago when I was a green kid. We called him Colt. Champion bull rider."

"A Hasid named Colt?" I was incredulous. "Here?"

"His name was Calev, but we called him Colt."

I reflected. "Calev, the spy Moses sent into Canaan. Appropriate. But why Colt?"

"He looked kinda like a colt, to tell you the truth." Merle took back the coffee cup and duly sipped from the opposite side. "All arms and legs, put together just a little wobbly. I gotta hand it to that fella, though, he was the cleanest bugger I ever met. Had to bathe every goddamn - 'scuse me, rabbi - every morning, even when it meant running through the snow and jumping in the river. He had a word for it, but I forget. He had a different word for everything, all in that – whaddya call it...."

"Yiddish?" I said. Merle insisted on calling me rabbi when he had to call me anything, although my given name is Zevulun - "to honor" in Hebrew - and he'd used it to introduce me to a dozen people. I was only a student, but if it made him more comfortable to think of me as a religious leader, I wouldn't contradict him. My ingrained habit was to defer to my elders. Rabbinical studies were my mother's obsession for me. I felt no certainty that I would emerge successful from that gauntlet - perhaps the reason why Rebbe Grossman had assigned me this peculiar journey. The strategy was beneath his usual standard of subtlety: exposure to such a macho environment would surely stamp out the part of me that had borrowed chic clothes from a friend and snuck into Fashion Week runway shows to suck in my breath at the workmanship and sketch ideas for my growing design portfolio.

"That's it. Yiddish. Sounded kinda like the Hutterite fellas, but they couldn't understand each other."

"And you say he was a champion bull rider?" My toes had begun to speak to me again and Merle was warming to his tale. There was no solar gain in the pickup on that cloudy day, but getting out of the wind was a respite to cherish. He shoved his black wool Scotch cap – rather similar to mine – up a little on his head, scratched the mat of white hair beneath, then drained the coffee cup, filled it for me, and settled back in his seat for the tale-telling just as one of our white-haired Brooklyn storytellers would do. The same sigh of fulfillment and tug of chin hairs.

"That's the tragedy of it. He couldn't compete for the championship half the time, because there was usually at least one round on Saturday and he couldn't ride on account of it being his Sabbath. Well, cowboys are God-fearing folk. We understood that. Made allowances. But there was one year, the fourth of July fell on a Saturday. Cowboy Christmas, we call it." He glanced at me sidelong with rheumy eyes, serious. "Not Colt, I don't suppose." I repressed a laugh at Merle's flawless comic timing.

"Why Cowboy Christmas?" I asked. I was willing to play straight man to a bred in the bone storyteller as long as we could stay inside drinking coffee. The bawling of cows and crying of calves was floating my nerves to the surface to the point where every new outburst made me shiver, cold or no cold. Even in the pickup the smell of blood, burnt hair and skin, sweating men and horse, was a penetrating mist I couldn't help but breathe. I was alternately nauseated and intoxicated - and at a loss as to how to report this experience to the rebbe. So much violence, but respectful and to a clear purpose, performed in community as tradition - a whiplash of contradictions, like so much of my life.

"Whole slough of rodeos all in one week and enough prize money to keep a guy going all year. Around here you've got the Cody Stampede, Red Lodge Rodeo, Cheyenne Frontier Days – granddaddy of 'em all. Cowboys fly from one to the next in little planes to make as many events as they can. Your boy Colt, he was on a tear. Would've qualified for the NFR that year if it hadn't been for the Saturday thing."

I must have shown my puzzlement because Merle tagged on, "National Finals Rodeo, son," in a tone of reverence.

"Where did he come from? I've never heard of a Jewish cowboy. Well, except for Kinky Friedman, and I'm not sure he counts. He's more of a hippie," I said. My parents sheltered me carefully, but I'd snuck abandoned periodicals into my bedroom regularly and the world of Orthodox Judaism is a rather small town. Surely I would have heard of such an extraordinary thing. The possibility that Merle was pulling my leg suddenly bloomed in my thawing consciousness.

Merle pulled off his gloves and examined fingers as big around as quarters, stained and scarred, the right thumbnail half-missing and the tip gone from the middle finger of his left hand. "He was from New York, like you. Not the city, but somewhere upriver. A farm, he said. That's where he learned to ride, and he taught himself to rope. I guess they told him to go to Montana and get it out of his system and that's exactly what he did."

Was this a common solution then, sending questioning youth west to show us how harsh the world could be outside the cocoon of New York, or had Calev acted out of more self-determination than I had? What would that be like, to renounce the life my family had so carefully prepared me for? I removed my rekel and rubbed my ears to get the circulation going. "So he couldn't compete on Cowboy Christmas that year?"

"Nope. Saddest kid you ever saw the week before, out working the cattle with a face like somebody shot his dog. He needed the money, see, to stay out here another year. His folks were on him to go back east, get married, work at his old man's business – but he wanted one more year on the range. Cowboy heart, he had, more than anybody I ever knew."

The world Calev had chosen was the last place I would settle. A sunny July in this place might be enjoyable, but March was the sort of suicide expedition Captain Shackleton – another of my secret heroes – would have embraced. And somehow Calev had resisted the force of what I felt sure was a formidable mama. My estimation of him was growing. "What did he do?"

"Came to me a few days before the fourth, beside himself with excitement. He'd done some figuring about the Cody Night Rodeo. Starts at 8 p.m. – an hour before sunset, and some booster had thrown in cash for a big pot. He reckoned if he entered and won every event after dark, he could make enough money to hang around. Wanted me to help him trailer down there with his horse and join him in the team roping for a share of the winnings. I thought we had a decent shot together, so I said yes.

"I'll never forget the night. I had to get the horses there because Colt couldn't work on the Sabbath, and then he set up this ritual of his on the tailgate that had half the parking lot looking over his shoulder before he was done. Chanting in Hebrew, wouldn't you know? Never seen the likes of it. Other cowboys thought he was voodoo cursing them but I said no, that's just Colt, praying his way."

"It was the Havdalah," I said. "The prayer to end the Sabbath."

"Well, you know that," Merle answered, "but it wasn't the most diplomatic thing for Colt to do in that time and place, if you know what I'm saying. People get keyed up before a big event and ain't nobody more superstitious than a rodeo man. Anyhow, Colt finally put away his candles and whatnot and got on his horse, and I tell you son, that kid rode."

I was carried away now by the enthusiasm in Merle's stoic face. A guy named Calev, a guy like me, competing with the hardened ranch hands I saw here, living a dream he'd conceived and realized entirely on his own. It was thrilling to imagine. "He did it? He won?"

Merle held up a finger. "It all came down to the last event. We took the team roping, Colt won the calf-roping, the bareback and the saddle broncs. He was the star of the show, until there was just one event left. What everybody waits for: the bull-riding." Merle delivered a perfect, practiced dramatic pause. "The bull he drew was this mean old Brahma I'd seen before. Toughest bull on the circuit. Hard draw. But Colt got right up there and rode his heart out. Gutsiest ride I've ever seen until that bull tossed him near into the stands. Slammed him into the boards."

"Was he okay?" I clutched the dash, the cold forgotten.

Merle's shoulders slumped and he exhaled in a heavy gargle. "I ran for him, straight past the clowns, but he was gone by the time I got to him." He gripped the steering wheel in both hands and stared straight ahead with moist eyes. "Broke his neck clean in two."

"Oh." My heart had been riding with Colt. Now it fell, cold and still. I had expected a final twist in Colt's favor, a Jewish miracle, but old Merle shook his head, looking a little away from me.

"I know what you're thinking. You're thinking it's a tragedy. But Colt died doing what he loved. He was a true cowboy. He died a cowboy's death. It's what he would have wanted."

My throat was closing. I curled my arms around myself and sat in the quiet of the cab for a while, listening to the calves' cries and the cowboys' shouts, choking on the fragility of life and the ephemera of rare dreams. Perhaps I should tell Mama this story. Maybe it would reconcile her a little to my own illicit obsession, which as much as she hated it was unlikely to snap my neck. Merle broke the silence.

"They came out to get him, you know. His people. Your people. They wanted to take him and bury him in Israel. Had relatives there, they said. Wanted him to lie with his family. The body was in a funeral home in Cody, waiting for them, and I took his mother to see him. She'd come over from Germany after the war. Tough lady. Didn't speak a lot of English and she didn't cry. Told me she'd cried all her tears. We talked, she and I, mostly me, about how Colt loved Montana. When we were done she went back to the others and told them – in English mind you, so I'd hear – that Montana was his promised land, and they needed to bury him here. Big fuss in Yiddish then, of course, but in the end it seemed like they listened to her."

I could picture Merle trying to be gentlemanly to his dead friend's mama, with no earthly idea who she was or what she came from, but traditional people both. Dignified. They must have looked at each other the way the Hutterites and I did, with a glancing light of distant recognition. Their halting conversation, the family's confusion and objections. I could write the script. "Is he buried near here?"

"No idea. He'd probably be in the Jewish cemetery in Billings. It's the closest one, but I don't know if they really kept him here. We offered to put him in the family burial plot on our land, but I guess that was taking things a bit far even for Mama."

My flight left from Billings after two more days of grueling ranch tours. I watched, took notes and photos, but even as I talked to others I walked in the company of Merle's words, the vision of Calev's broken end consuming me. Back in Billings, before going to the airport I took one of the city's peculiarly casual taxis to the Jewish cemetery—a small, flat plot beside the sprawling Catholic cemetery on a street busy with pickups and old cars. I felt silly seeking Colt here. What chance was there that they'd really buried him in Montana, that I would find the marker? And what would it mean if I did? I stepped through the well-oiled gate aware of my own absurdity, ready to go back and submit to my rebbe's discipline, my mama's plans.

But there, not twenty feet from the gate, was a stone with the name Calev Aronsen above the years 1937 and 1958 and a single word: Cowboy. I stood in the crusted snow staring at it long enough for the cold to resume its march on my extremities. The cab waited. The sun was as white as the clouds and seemed to give no heat. A few cars slowed to observe my solitary vigil. At last, while I still had enough feeling in my fingers to push buttons and with Calev's courage emboldening me, I pulled out my phone and dialed my mother.

STELLA FONG
Blowing Wind

I DID NOT LIKE WIND. AS A YOUNG CHILD, I SCREAMED, "ROLL UP the window," from the back seat of my Dad's Comet. I hated the blasting force pushing against me tossing my long black hair in every which direction. The whipping strands of black not only obscured my view of San Francisco as we emerged from the Yerba Buena Island tunnel but creviced into my mouth straddling the edges of my lips. The sharp strikes against my face not so much hurt, but were more annoying. The cold moist air carried car exhaust fumes along with saltiness from the bay's waters.

"Not so loud," Mom sternly said, lifting her hand to bat away my complaint.

I saw Dad's eyes in the rear view mirror smile as he glanced back at me while cranking the window back up. As I smoothed down my hair, pulling threads from my mouth and loosening tangles, I took a deep breath. We were once again sealed into the calm and quiet of our car. "Sorry about that," he said gently, "I needed to adjust the mirror. It will be all okay."

In high school, right in the beginnings of Title IX, Mrs. Phyllis Delavergne quickly broke the rules of traditional physical education. Jumping jacks and square dancing were supplemented with riding our bikes through the Posey Tube. She was ahead of her time in demanding cars share the road with bicycles as our group of girls pedaled in the traffic lanes into this 4.5-mile tunnel under the Oakland-Alameda Estuary. Needless to say we were pulled over by the police while making our way back to Encinal High School. I do not know what transpired next, but I do know that no paddy wagon showed up to pick us up.

Mrs. Delavergne next took us to Oakland's Lake Merritt where we learned to sail El Toros. We jumped into rigged boats without a lot of instruction. I was excited to be on the waters where I had stood on the shores many times with a bag of old bread crusts feeding the ducks. Now I was gliding the lake with them.

I mimicked the movements of my sun bleached haired teacher. Our group followed her around like little chicks. But it was the light breeze brushing against my cheeks that stroked away all anxiety. Then in a blink, the ripples on the water intensified in front of me. I felt the sail tug heavily on the sheet I was holding in my hand. The force became stronger and my reaction was to fight back, to hang on, to pull in tight.

"Let go of the sail," Mrs. Delavergne yelled. "Let go."

No, I was going to hang on. As I gripped tighter, the boat started to heel over and my sail touched the water. Soon I was wet as I slid into the lake. As I bobbed high in the water with my life jacket boosting me up, my boat miraculously righted itself with the boon flinging and settling back with the sail fluttering. I swam to the boat and hefted myself into the cockpit, embarrassed. But I was not the only one who went swimming as several of my classmates joined in christening the waters.

I may have been cold but not dismayed. I was more proud of myself for being able to hoist myself back into the cockpit of the boat. Once everyone settled back into their sailboats Mrs. Delavergne led us back to the dock.

I am grateful to this teacher for exposing me to an activity I always watched from afar. Growing up in the San Francisco Bay Area where winds blew from the land to the Golden Gate especially in the summer, sightings of sailboats gliding across this ocean's pocket were not unusual.

"Let the sail out when it gets too windy," Mrs. Delavergne reminded me when were we standing on land. She reminded me that Mother Nature was much more powerful than I and I should not fight her. I needed to work with her. The next times we sailed, I learned to better cooperate. I confess to being reminded of this time whenever I neglected to practice my teacher's advice as I have been dumped many times out of boats in later times.

The winds blew my husband and me to Montana. It began with our whipping up the waters, exploring the rivers through fly-fishing. I quickly learned that casting a tiny-feathered fly was much easier with no wind, and if Mother Nature was exhaling, having her breath at my back was much better. Her air and my mediocre casting, when I neglected to work with her, resulted in a hook caught in a tree branch or worst yet, in my eyebrow or in my left fourth finger.

During one of our annual trips to the Big Horn River at the end of November, after spending a few days watching The Travel Channel and a handful of other channels, we finally were able to emerge and fly fish. The wind blew so strongly that we could not be outside without feeling as though we would be lifted away. Temperatures hovered in the mid 30s with winds darting around 15 mph. At the time we stored a drift boat here so I fished as my husband rowed us down river. The fishing started out well with a few hookups right at the Afterbay but then the wind became more constant. Though I was adequately dressed, I was cold. When my husband pulled over to the shore to see if he could throw out a few casts, I felt an overwhelming need to sleep. I curled up against a rock with my back to the wind just wanting to warm up. My husband scooped me up, and as quickly as he could, paddled us downriver into the wind.

On another trip in Livingston, we stopped for gas. My husband warned, "Be careful. It is really windy so hang onto the door." Almost immediately I forgot, opened my door and it was quickly ripped from my hand. The door swung open all the way but fortunately, our car was parked far enough away from the pumps so nothing was damaged. My husband gave me a compassionate knowing look as I now gingerly stepped out of the car. After pushing the door closed tightly, I clutched the lapel of my coat around my neck and was literally blown into the convenience store.

I knew I had been in Montana long enough when I was at The

Grand Hotel in Big Timber. A woman stepped out from the front lobby and onto the sidewalk. Immediately she came back in to say to her travel companion, "Honey, it's really windy out there." My instantaneous thought was, when is it not windy in Montana, much less in Big Timber? Wind funnels up the Boulder Valley and shoots through the Crazy Mountains.

For years, my husband and I made the annual trek to Burns Lake, a 30-acre reservoir on the ranch of Horatio Burns right below the Crazy Mountains to fly fish. He allowed four rods on the lake daily where big brown, rainbow and brook trout could be caught. On the days when the winds gusted to 20 mph, fishing almost became impossible, not only for casting the line but simulating smooth movement for a nymph or mimicking a real flying insect with a dry fly. I have on several occasions stood at the edge of the shore and asked, "Mother Nature, would you just please let up." A kind ask became a plea, and then a frustrated declaration evolved to discouraged angst. I could not believe that our want of just minutes of relent went without answer.

I wanted Mother Nature to hold her breath when I rode in the Multiple Sclerosis Bike Ride from Billings to Red Lodge and then back to Billings by way of Columbus. In 1980, snow changed the course of the ride, and when we did ride the alternative route, wind was not our friend. Here I was reminded of the importance of how we as humans must collaborate and coordinate to survive her forces. With the wind gusting at above 15 mph we needed to form a line to pull each other along, drafting into the wind for the miles we were to travel.

Most of my encounters with Mother's breathing had been through my own choosing. I elected to be outside in the elements instead of stagnating indoors, because I wanted to play in Mother Nature's playground to inhale her fresh air. I never had to work in nature like many do such as ranchers and farmers. Growing up in the San Francisco Bay area was easy compared to life under the Big Sky.

Wind flattened fields of wheat to a rippling carpet. Wind obscured the markings on a highway pushing snowdrifts over the man-marked roads. Wind came in the form of a tornado on Father's Day in 2010 damaging businesses in Billings. In March of 2015, high winds stoked a fire in Shepherd burning over 2,000 acres while a fire started near the Red Lodge ski area with winds blowing embers from a brush fire started on private land.

When I first moved to Montana, the dust nature swirled around convinced me I could no longer wear contacts and I resorted to wearing my very thick eyeglasses. One of the first times my sister came to visit me after I moved here, we took her and her husband to the rodeo in Cody. Wind blasted through the stadium. After almost an hour, my sister finally requested heading back to the hotel room to remove her contacts. I was surprised she did not ask earlier.

Wind warms the air in the winter, changing temperatures from negative numbers to positive ones. Wind quickly dries the wet ground, transforming mud to hard packed ground. Wind pushes off the clumps of snow weighing down tree branches.

When traveling with the wind in a car or in a sailboat, there is a calm, a somewhat haunting silence as opposed to forcing into it. Wind keeps the black flies and mosquitos away. Casting a line downwind with a light breeze fools me into believing I am a pro. In sailing, having wind is better than a dead calm on any day.

I gravitate to the spaces on the earth where wind can circulate. These are places where there is nothing to block its travel. Up valleys, across plains, and above mountain peaks the wind blows, and also over lakes and oceans. The sky is vast above these unencumbered landscapes. The openness allows for viewing, for seeing beyond unobstructed. There is room to think.

I think I have gained much respect for Mother Nature's breath. I think I must continue to learn to work with her. I think I have come to like wind.

BERNARD QUETCHENBACH
Baboon Mountain

Water

Behind the Cabin

> Draped across the clearing
> Baboon Mountain
> clutches what's left of its snow.

*

Time to Leave Bridge Creek

> Through the cascade,
> thunder.

*

Conundrum of the mountain thunderstorm

> Walk faster.
> Takes longer.

*

River

> Up all night
> > talking about the rain.

*

Boulder River Road

> A beach party!
> Siskins and sparrows
> > around the flooded potholes.

Animals

Darwinian

> Look behind you,
> > church camp:
> > Baboon Mountain.

*

Roadside Thistles

> Siskins
> > work in purple flowers,
> > setting stars adrift.

*

Unresolved

> Hermit or Swainson's?
> Thrush hides her tail.

*

Nature

> Eating horseshit,
>> doe and spotted fawn.

*

Outhouse

> Going in:
>> Deer stares from the meadow.
> Coming out:
>> Deer stares from the meadow.

Trees

Emergence

> Is that you
>> between those firs,
>> Baboon Mountain?

*

Clearing

> The dead
>> among the living
>> and the dead.

*

Branches

> They
> > catch their falling comrades
> > when they can.

*

"What Do the Trees Say?"
—*William Heyen*

> How could I know?
> I'm not the wind.

*

Gray pines

> How did you die?
> Was it me
> > this time?

Sky

Faith

> Baboon Mountain
> clouds
> above the chapel.

*

Our Time

> Summer haze:
> > Smoke?
> > Rain!
> And smoke.

*

Orange

    Smoke
        from burning forests
        tints a treeless moon.

*

Ironic

    Sun
        escapes from clouds,
        sinks behind the mountain.

*

Full

    Not many stars.
    Moon sparks the cliffs
        before it rises.

JON HENN
The Happiest Man on Earth

AN OLD WOMAN WITH A HOOK NOSE AND A FACE THAT WAS SO wrinkled it made dried prunes look smooth, placed the final item she was buying on the Walmart conveyer belt at checkout register number 5. *Hillary Clinton Gives Birth To Alien Baby*, the *National Enquirer* headline seemed to scream in bright, bold letters. *My Steamy Nights In UFO Love Nest.* Trey, a young cashier with brown tousled hair, picked up the supermarket tabloid and scanned it. *Oh, lookie here. The gossip police strike again with all the bizarre news that's unfit to print. How can people believe this hogwash? It's completely bazinga.*

"So, tell me ma'am," Trey said jovially, scanning a quart of prune juice. "Do you think this story about Hillary Clinton's alien baby is true or just a bunch of baloney for human dummies?"

The Old Woman spoke through thin lips. "What's the matter, sonny boy? You don't believe aliens are amongst us?"

Trey scanned a bottle of Geritol. "Well, most scientists believe that life exists on other planets. But any aliens we meet would be so mentally advanced we would be morons next to them. Why would they care about us? I mean, how much time do you spend reading books with your goldfish?" he chuckled, bagging a tube of denture adhesive.

The Old Woman sat on an electric cart, breathing air through a plastic tube from an oxygen cylinder. "After the Bible, the *Enquirer* is the only source of truth left on the planet," she said heatedly.

Oops. Better pull the plug out before she has a heart attack and ruins our yearly employee bonus. Trey smiled. "Yes, Ma'am. I was only kidding. The *Enquirer* can tell no lies." He scanned a bag of disposable incontinent underwear. "Hillary's fortunate to have alien sex. We should all be so lucky. I can't even find a nice girlfriend on this planet, let alone one from fifty light years away." He chuckled at his little joke. The Old Woman glared at him.

Trey put the groceries in her electric cart's basket. "There you go, Ma'am. It's snowing outside. Would you like some assistance carrying that out? We haven't got any robots with artificial intelligence available, but if a squishy human brain will suffice I'm sure can scare one up for you." He smiled broadly.

The Old Woman frowned, adding even more wrinkles to her already furrowed brow. "You're a super creepy young man. Get away from me." She gripped the motorized cart's handles, and sped out into the main corridor nearly hitting another cart with a baby basket.

"Out of my way, unbelievers. Rot in hell," she cursed on her not-so-merry way.

"Thanks for coming to Walmart," Trey said, waving goodbye as she rushed off into the distance.

A finger tapped his shoulder. Turning, a Customer Service Manager stood behind him wearing a yellow Walmart manager vest. Trey knew he was in trouble, again.

"Trey," Margarita said in a Spanish accent. "I've told you twice today that you're taking way too much time talking to customers. Now cut the gab or there will be consequences."

"Yes, Ma'am," Trey replied. "I was just trying to make the customer happy."

"I want you to train a new associate. Her name is Sue Ling. She's a foreign exchange student who will be a new part time cashier."

Oh, happy day. He smiled dutifully. "Of course, I will. I'm a team player. Always happy to oblige."

As Margarita left, a short woman appeared behind her. Sue Ling stared at the floor, her head bowed. She was young, in her mid-twenties, with shoulder length, dark brown hair. She raised her face, her brown doe eyes met his.

"Hello," Sue Ling said in a quiet voice. "What are your orders, sir?"

Trent's lips curled slightly upward. He felt strangely happy.

THAT EVENING TREY ATE DINNER WITH HIS COLLEGE PROFESSOR parents. It was hamburger helper night with tater tots, cole slaw with salsa, and wine. Lots of wine. *If it doesn't come out of a package or a wine bottle, Mom won't fix it. Maybe I should learn to cook. Anything would be better than this.*

His dad must have thought so too, for the instant his father put the casserole into his mouth he grimaced. "Oh, my god, this is awful," Dad said, downing half a glass of wine. "Terrill, how can you be such an insightful Professor of Psychology and such a terrible cook?"

His mother drained her wine glass. "I have to be at my battered women's shelter group in less than an hour, Tom. Be grateful I take the time to cook anything for you lazy men."

Dad poured himself more wine. "You could at least bring home some take-out for dinner rather than force us to eat this pre-packaged garbage. That's very insensitive of you."

"Are you saying helping abused women with their psychological problems is a waste of my time? Shame on you, Tom. That's very insensitive of you."

"Why do you always take the opposite side of whatever I'm talking about?" Dad protested.

"Because we're married, you inconsiderate oaf. Now shut up and let me eat. You're making me late."

Trey could almost see steam rising off his parents' reddening flesh. He knew what was coming next. *Oh, no. Here comes the lava from Mt. Chardonnay ... again.*

"I read Hillary Clinton gave birth to an alien baby," he blurted out.

His mom and dad ceased their quarrelling and gazed wide-eyed at their only son. "Well, I mean, uh," Trey stumbled under their judgmental gaze. "It was in the *National Enquirer.* I thought it was kind of funny," he tittered making tiny circles with his fork.

His mother attacked. "Trey, if I wasn't the one who gave birth to you I would be convinced your mother slept with the village idiot. What's wrong with you?"

"You're twenty-three years old, son. Why are you still working at Walmart?" his dad demanded. "That's for people without an education. Why do you reject a higher standard of life? You're completely irresponsible."

As his parents tore into him, Trey felt like he was shrinking. *Oh, my aching brain cells. Mt. Chardonnay is spewing lava down on me. And I'm the one who set it in motion. Am I stupid or what?*

HALF AN HOUR LATER IN HIS BASEMENT BEDROOM, TREY PLAYED A video game on his X-box – Lord of the Rings: Return of the King. Killing digital orcs, he wished virtual reality technology was more advanced so he could be surrounded by more realistic action. Upstairs, his parents argued at Defcon One. *Mom's going to miss her meeting.* The crash of a dish hurled at the floor confirmed his thoughts. He vigorously scratched his hair wishing they would just shut up.

The timer on his cell phone went off. Time for his favorite radio program on conspiracy theories. Tonight's topic – the Titanic's sinking was totally planned. Trey smiled. *The owners substituted a sister ship, the Olympic, which had been damaged in a collision and claimed it was the Titanic. Fifteen hundred people died in an insurance fraud scheme.* Having heard this theory before, Trey turned off the radio and went back to his X-box game while his parents squabbled and screeched above him. Finally, he could not stand it anymore. He bolted to his feet, and shouted, "Shut up! The purpose of intelligence is not to destroy your marriage by fighting until death or divorce do you part! You're both acting completely bazinga!"

The screeching stopped. Had they heard him? Trey's hands covered his lips.

"What did you say?" his mother shouted. "We didn't hear you."

A chill shuddered down Trey's spine. "Nothing," he yelled. "The radio was up too loud."

THE NEXT THREE WEEKS WERE JUST LIKE THE PREVIOUS ONES. *Why is happiness so hard to find? It's like the universe is out to get me.* The only exception was training Sue Ling.

THE NEXT EVENING, TREY SAT IN HIS LIME GREEN CHEVY SPARK hatchback in the Walmart parking lot in the freezing, snowy weather. The tiny, two door car was the only place he could escape from his parents' constant fighting. *My life is a cesspool of darkness. Every day I feel like Frodo beaten down by the ring of power. My parents are Sauron the dark, my managers are the Nazgûl crying out with the voices of death. My soul is corrupted. Where is my Gandalf? Where is my Gollum? How can I free myself of this burden and be happy?*

It was eight o'clock. Time for his soul salvation—conspiracy theory radio. The broadcast exposed that blood-drinking, shapeshifting, extraterrestrial reptilian humanoids had taken over our world leaders and Grammy award winning singers. They planned to enslave the human race as a source of livestock. They loved the color turquoise. *I knew it. Our leaders suck. I'm just a cow to worldwide evil. Buffy the Vampire Slayer, where are you when the world needs you?*

The narrator announced that David Lee Roth and Beyoncé were alien blood suckers. Trey imagined himself as Gollum, a wretched soul, offering himself to the reptile Beyoncé dressed in a sensuous gown. She sank her jagged teeth into his scrawny neck, drawing his 'precious' blood in a scarlet stream of helpless servitude to the shapeshifting tyrants of turquoise. *Beyoncé having her bloodthirsty way with me. Wow. I could get used to that. She's hot!*

He felt a trifle cold so he turned up the car's heater. *At least I can use my creative mind to free myself from the harshness of everyday reality. A little fantasy role playing sure beats wallowing in utter despair.* He rubbed his hands together in front of the warm flowing air.

A cry of pain ripped out from something in front of his car. Trey turned on the windshield wipers. As the snow was brushed away he saw a person who had slipped and fallen on the concrete. The person's hoodie blew back. It was Sue Ling. She was hurt. Her knee was bloody.

Alarmed, Trey opened the door. The cold air whipped at his face as, jacketless, he rushed to help her. "Sue Ling. Are you okay?"

She raised her eyes towards him. "Please, help me," she said, her voice colored in misery.

Trey picked up her frail form and carried her to the front

passenger seat. As he scurried around to the driver's side he noticed she had dropped a letter. His breath steaming, he retrieved it, nearly slipping on the icy ground.

Inside the car, Sue Ling was curled into a ball, crying softly. "Walmart has a medical kit," he said. "Or do you need me to take you to the hospital?"

"No," Sue Ling whispered. "I bang my knee. Just give me a minute. I be all right."

Trey gave her the space she wanted. The letter in his hand bore the seal from the U.S. State Department. Trey could not control himself. He read the letter.

"We regret to inform you that your request to extend your F-1 foreign student status has been denied. You can remain in the United States for no more than sixty days after completing your current program of study. At the end of sixty days, you must return to your country of origin or be deported."

Trey dropped the letter as if it were a hot potato. He understood why she was crying. "Sue Ling," he spoke softly. "Can I do anything to help you?"

Sue Ling nodded. "Please take me home. My knee hurts. I can't walk and I have no car."

TWENTY MINUTES LATER, TREY AND SUE LING WERE INSIDE her small apartment. While she cleaned up her wound in the bathroom, Trey sat on a worn sofa in the nearly empty living room. *Wow. She doesn't even own an X-box. Now that's what I call poverty.*

Sue Ling emerged from the bathroom, her knee wrapped in toilet paper with plastic tape around it. Entering the kitchen area, she put water into a tea pot and turned on the stove. "I make us some tea."

"Oh, you don't have to do that," Trey said. "I'm fine."

"But I must," Sue Ling replied. "In my culture it is rude to not treat your guest with kindness and hospitality. It is our highest calling in life to bring joy to ourselves and others."

"That's amazing," Trey replied. "I've been studying the nature of happiness in my car, lately, but I don't really know how to turn it into reality."

"Tell me about it, please. I am interested in such things. I believe we spend too much of our lives being unhappy when we have the power to create joy despite adversity."

For the next several hours, Trey and Sue Ling spoke of the nature of happiness. He talked excitedly about the theories of Hedonism, Desire, and Meaningful Life. He laughed when she said that he sounded like a learned college professor.

"I know a ceremony which brings joy to your being. Would you like to try it?" Sue Ling said.

"That's a no brainer," Trey replied. "It sure beats listening to my parents argue all night long."

"First, I must make us some more tea."

THEY SAT TOGETHER IN HER FURNITURE-BARREN BEDROOM ON A soft mattress on the bare wooden floor, drinking tea. The warm liquid tasted like peaches and mangos. Delicious. Trey opened his mouth to ask what it was, but Sue Ling put a finger to her lips for silence. She opened a box beside her labelled Alpha Brain Wave Sphere, placed a globe on the mattress and turned it on.

Sue Ling smiled. "Close your eyes, and breathe deeply." Trey did so.

A soft ringing, like a gong, sent waves of relaxing energy that penetrated his body. Soon, he felt peaceful. Something stirred deep within him. Something wonderful. He hadn't felt this good in a very long time. Sue Ling took hold of his hands. Her touch was thrilling. He felt her energy mingle with his, filling him like an empty glass, making it full.

Holy guacamole, he thought entering into a sublime state of being.

THE NEXT MORNING HE WOKE UP ON SUE LING'S MATTRESS WITH her sleeping beside him, his arm around her waist. He realized they were both naked. *Oh, my gosh. What happened last night? Did we do the bump and grind? I can't remember a thing. Am I a rapist or just a cad taking advantage of her in her weakened condition? Should I turn myself into the police?*

Sue Ling woke up, her soft eyes staring up at him with a dreamy expression. She kissed his lips with deep feeling. *Well,* Trey thought, *I guess I don't have to call the police.*

They spent the entire day in bed. Trey called in sick to Walmart for the first time in several years.

THIRTY DAYS BEFORE THE IMMIGRATION DEADLINE, TREY ASKED

Sue Ling to marry him. She said 'yes.' She would be his wife. Trey moved out of his parents' 'House of Blame' and into her apartment. He used Walmart's education program to study for a degree in psychology. He wanted to teach people how to use their intelligence to make themselves and others happy.

IT WAS ELEVEN P.M. AT WALMART. TREY TURNED OFF THE LIGHT showing his register lane was now closed. It was time to go home. He wished Margarita, the female Customer Service Manager, a blessed evening, and left the store. He overheard her say to another manager, "Trey's become our best cashier since he got married. He's happy all the time now."

TWENTY MINUTES LATER, TREY OPENED THE DOOR TO THE apartment. "Sue Ling. I'm home."

Sue Ling entered the living room from the bedroom, her face downcast.

"What's the matter, precious?" Trey asked. "Is something wrong?"

Sue Ling sobbed. "Trey. I haven't been entirely honest with you. I married you, not just because I love you, but because I would have been deported."

"Oh, I know all about that," Trey said, waving his hand. "I married you, not only because I love you, but because I didn't want you to be deported back to Japan. So we're even. Right?"

Sue Ling shook her head. "I lied to you. I'm not from Japan."

"So, China, North Korea, Thailand ... it doesn't matter to me where you're from."

Sue Ling's body began to glow. The light was so bright Trey had to shield his eyes with his arm. When the light subsided Sue Ling had transformed. Her beautiful brown hair was gone, she was completely bald. Her skin was pale green, her almond eyes were blue. A jewel glowed in the center of her forehead.

"I'm from the planet Zoomba. I didn't want to go back when my visa expired so I used my forehead tasp to bond with you, and make you love me." Her eyes glistened with tears. "The Alpha Wave machine is a fake. The tasp is how my race promotes matrimony. If you wish to dissolve our marriage I will understand and go back to my home planet." She bowed her head.

Trey took a step backward. "You're an alien shape-shifter?"

"Yes."

"And that tea ceremony we did. You entered my mind and filled it with happiness?"

Sue Ling nodded. "I can transport us to any place that you can imagine in a mutually guided meditation that's so completely realistic you won't be able to tell it from reality."

Trey thought a moment. She had admittedly used him for sex. She had also used him for marriage. If he acted like his parents he should be outraged. Still, he was the chosen one. That had to count for something. "Can I give it a try with me in charge?"

"I'd be delighted to bring you joy, my human husband."

MINUTES LATER, TREY AND SUE LING SAT ON THE BEDROOM mattress holding hands. The crystal in Sue Ling's forehead glowed. "Go wherever you wish," Sue Ling said. "Indulge yourself."

Trey imagined himself on an alien planet in a luxurious bedchamber with tall curtains of shimmering fabric. Beyond a large, round porthole was an exotic landscape with a star-filled night, and an enormous moon bathed in the light from a nearby nebula. He gazed into a full-length mirror. The image of Gollum from his Lord of the Rings video game looked back at him. *Wow. This looks completely real. Color me Gollum the wretched soul.*

Sue Ling shapeshifted into a reptilian Beyoncé wearing a sensuous turquoise gown. Slithering seductively, she wrapped her scaly arms around his wiry chest and kissed his sallow lips. Trey felt giddy. This was awesome. They could do anything they wanted, be anything they wanted. In their union he felt loved. Unconditional love wrapped up in the ultimate role playing universe. He didn't even need an X-box. Together, they were the X-box. It was even better than virtual reality. *Together we're like Romeo and Juliet without the dying. How cool is that?*

Beyoncé sank her reptile teeth into his scrawny Gollum neck, flooding Trey with waves of bliss. It was a weird fantasy, he knew, but it was also a creative illusion which inspired him. *I will not be like my parents. I will use my intelligence to choose joy, not misery, even if it's a bit strange and geeky.*

As a trickle of imaginary blood flowed down his make-believe Gollum chest, Trey Waterson became the happiest man on Earth. Sharing virtual ecstasy with his alien wife, unbidden words came to his mind.

God bless the National Enquirer. It tells the truth. Treasure your steamy alien love nest, Hillary. Go completely bazinga.

JACI WEBB
Peddling Montana's Stories

A SCARED BLACK BEAR CLUNG TO A PINE TREE IN A LAUREL YARD.

It was 1983 and I was fresh out of college, writing business briefs for *The Billings Gazette* and dreaming about working my way up to obits.

All the veteran reporters had left for lunch when the scanner spit out the details of the bear sighting. There was an awkward moment between myself and the city editor, Pete Fox, who finally gave me the nod to chase the story and the bear.

I saved that front page byline for years until my basement flooded and it grew mold. Like a business owner's first dollar, that story was the start of something for me. It's been a beautiful, nerve-racking, exhausting career, and I wouldn't change more than a few days of it.

The newspaper business has changed since the glory days in the 1980s. But I still wake up most mornings, a bit more cranky and lot more creaky, and marvel that I get paid to write about people, Montana people.

Sure there were a couple of bank robberies, a murder or two, President Ronald Reagan's epic arrival at MetraPark in a stagecoach, and some traffic fatalities to cover. But mostly I've peddled the softer side of news—Virginia City's Brothel Days, Miles City's Bucking Horse Sale, and profiles on Montana legends like Ben Steele, Sue Hart, Evelyn Cameron, Deborah Butterfield and Ivan Doig. I am one of the last of the feature writers left at *The Billings Gazette* and possibly the last cultural reporter left in Montana.

There will always be a niche for human interest stories, but it's a wobbly precipice I walk. One of my favorite writers, Sherman Alexie, once wrote how soul-endangering it is to write stories only to please people. I've railed against that idea and pondered it, but in the end, I am proud of telling the story of Montana through its people.

Interestingly, the biggest battle I ever had with a source was a row over a monster truck. The owner, a small man, had said, "I like to tease the kids down on the Point with this."

He was referring to Burning the Point in downtown Billings, a fad that went out in the mid 1980s. He actually wrote a formal letter to the city editor, the same Pete Fox who had given me the thumb's up just a year before to write a news story.

Pete questioned me about the quote and I pulled out a notebook, and said, "See, it's right here."

Pete then ripped the letter of complaint up very dramatically and tossed it in the trash.

I never forgot how good it felt to have an editor support me, and I learned to save notebooks. That explains why two of the three drawers in my file cabinet are so stuffed, they won't open anymore. But if I get another complaint, I'll grab a crowbar and wrench that sucker open.

In an era where reporters are no longer the heroes and newspapers are often viewed as out of touch, I keep telling stories and celebrating every time one lands on the front page.

Some of my favorite assignments were covering the two centennial cattle drives, one in Montana in 1989 and the second in Wyoming in 1990. I had to take horse riding lessons from a Rocky Mountain College equestrian student so I could ride a horse one day on the trail between Roundup and Billings. I still remember the pain in my knees after sitting on that horse for what felt like a month, but was only a few hours. I now understand why cowboys walk bow-legged.

The Wyoming Centennial Cattle Drive was a week long and I got to sit in a wagon. The coolest part of the drive was dancing under the stars at its end at the fairgrounds in Powell, Wyo., when Willie Nelson performed my favorite of his songs, "Blue Eyes Crying in the Rain."

It was surreal thinking that Willie was playing for just a few hundred people in the middle of nowhere.

There were weird moments in my career, too, like the breast-feeding interview.

The story I was working on was one of only two I wrote about North Dakota. My nephew, Aaron, was graduating from New Leipzig High School, one of 13 guys and no girls in his class. I thought it would be a cute human interest story, focusing on the fact that the fellas had to drive to other towns to find dates for their prom.

I did the entire interview over the phone while I was breastfeeding my oldest daughter Phoebe. She didn't mind, I didn't mind, and the fellas I interviewed didn't know.

The second time I wrote a North Dakota story was when my youngest daughter, Chrissy, and I traveled to the Standing Rock Sioux Reservation over Thanksgiving 2016 to cover the protest over the DAPL pipeline.

It was the first time in my career that I faced such a quandary over an assignment. Do I wear the required long skirt to honor the traditions of the tribe or keep my jeans on to stand apart from the movement? I opted for the skirt.

We felt awkward pulling into the Oceti Sakowin Camp that November day, trying to figure out who we were. We felt like two white girls pretending we understood the hundreds of years of oppression Native Americans have felt. In the end, I went into my reporter mode because that's my comfort zone. No, I couldn't spend the day chopping wood to help the camp, but I could use my words and the bullhorn I have as a member of mainstream media to try and tell the Native story. Did I tell it correctly? I struggled with that question and lost many hours of sleep over it.

Crow tribal member Jared Stewart said to me a week later, "Remember, they will always talk about you if you try to do something, but if you don't try, nothing ever gets done."

My stories are never perfect, but they exist because I did something.

DAVID CRISP
Hope This Works

THE AUTHOR AND TITLE HAVE LONG SINCE BEEN LOST TO MEMORY, but the message was unforgettable: Montana was the last state in the Union to enjoy the blessings of the First Amendment.

I had just been invited to a job interview at Montana's largest newspaper, so I trundled off to the Texas A&M library to see what I could learn. I read an unhappy story, with what appeared to be a happy ending.

I learned that Montana newspapers had been dominated for decades by the Anaconda Co., which mined copper from the Richest Hill on Earth in Butte while running roughshod over Montana politics and journalism. The papers, under the thumb of Anaconda headquarters in Butte, were timid, underfunded, understaffed, and largely unread.

But things had gotten much better, I read, since the papers had been sold to Lee Enterprises, a publicly traded corporation based in Iowa.

That was good enough for me. My wife and I flew to Billings, were treated to huge steaks at the Grizzly Bar, and I wound up taking the job.

That was nearly a quarter century ago. While what I had read about Montana newspapers turned out to be mostly true, the business now faces challenges that may well equal those that editors faced back when the Copper Kings were battling for control of the state. Montana journalism remains understaffed, underfunded and dominated by a few large companies. While the growth of the internet threatens to break up the old oligopolies, the economy of Montana journalism remains on rocky ground where new ventures still struggle to find purchase.

Not that journalism has ever been a lucrative venture, at least not for its practitioners. It's a heartbreaking business, hard on family life, with unpredictable hours, a chorus of critics and pay that, at least in Montana, averages from 6 percent to 14 percent lower than the median salary of all U.S. occupations. In 2015, CareerCast listed three journalism-related jobs among its ten-worst jobs: broadcaster, photojournalist and, dead last among 200 jobs, newspaper reporter.

My own newspaper career started out at a modest $175 a week in Palestine, Texas. The paper hired so many talented young reporters with worn-out cars that we used to joke that our employment ads should read: "Wanted: Reporter for daily newspaper in East Texas. Experience preferred, reliable transportation required." An ad in *Editor & Publisher* actually did read: "Overpaid? Underworked? We can solve both problems."

I eventually figured out that with the help of the G.I. Bill and a fellowship, I could make more money going to graduate school than working for a newspaper. I bounced around between college and journalism for a while, edited a couple of small dailies in Texas, had an ugly showdown with a cruel boss, and was teaching at A&M when the job in Montana came up.

That was a few years before Dennis Swibold, a journalism professor at the University of Montana, published "Copper Chorus," a magisterial account of the days when the Anaconda Co. owned most of Montana's daily newspapers.

"Anaconda journalism stifled competition, muzzled reporters and editors, and delayed efforts toward enterprise and professionalism," Swibold wrote. "In the end, it was bad for democracy, bad for journalism, and bad for the company itself."

Even Swibold wasn't able to track down exactly when Anaconda's dominance began or how extensive it was. The mastheads of company-owned newspapers didn't mention that fact, and the company didn't talk about it. *Missoulian* editor Martin Hutchens once characterized those critical of the Anaconda Co.'s influence on its papers as "hare-brained demagogues, political castoffs and incendiaries of a particularly vicious type."

But Swibold was able to quote a muckraking reporter who said that by the end of 1912, all but one of Montana's dailies "was subject in policy to the control and influence of copper combine management." This showed up in numerous ways.

When Jeanette Rankin spoke in support of striking miners in Butte in 1917, she drew a crowd of more than 8,000 people—but almost no news coverage from the company-owned papers. Reporters who wrote a complete (but unpublished) story for the *Anaconda Standard*, including the full text of the speech, were fired the next day.

In World War I, the daily press supported a bill by the Montana Legislature making it a crime to speak, write or publish "any disloyal, profane, violent, scurrilous, contemptuous, slurring or abusive language" critical of the nation, its government, its soldiers or its symbols.

During World War II, legendary Montana historian K. Ross Toole wrote, a subsidiary of the Anaconda Co. was convicted of wartime fraud. Four employees went to jail, and the company was fined more than $1.6 million. "The company press completely ignored it," Toole wrote.

When the governor of Montana was jailed for drunkenness in New Orleans in 1950, the story got nationwide coverage—except in Montana, where only the *Miles City Star* reported it, according to John H. Toole, author of "Red Ribbons: A Story of Missoula and Its Newspaper."

With admirable candor, John H. Toole, a former state legislator, relates that when he was cited for careless driving in connection with a 1953 traffic accident, he was able to get the editor of the *Missoulian* to kill the story.

"We'll squelch it," the editor told him. "But in the future remember what we did for ya!"

Numerous sources suggest that it wasn't the stories the Anaconda papers killed that hurt the most. It was all the stories that nobody ever bothered to write in the first place that made the papers consistently boring and unprofitable.

Local controversies over streets and sewage were ignored. Editorials opined about events across the ocean but ignored issues at home. Montana papers gave readers little information about what was going on in their towns and even less reason to care.

Even then, there were bright spots. The *Anaconda Standard*, founded in 1889 by Copper King Marcus Daly, brought in national talent and built a daily that was four times larger than the population of the city where it was published. With vituperation typical of its time, *Standard* Editor John Durston attacked a competing newspaper: "It must disgust any reputable man to be the object of a prostitute's compliments; it must insult any man to be made the object of pleasant mention in a newspaper so base in its purpose, so contemptible in its methods and so outrageous in the deliberation of its false testimony as the Butte Intermountain has proved itself to be."

In Butte, the *Montana Free Press* published a daily list of company-owned newspapers and regularly attacked the Anaconda Co. in editorials. The *Free Press* tried to establish a daily in Billings in 1928 to compete with the *Gazette*, "a paper so complacent that it rarely published editorials for fear of stirring the public's emotions," according to Swibold.

The *Billings Free Press*, however, was unable to break the *Gazette*'s stranglehold on both the AP and UPI news wires. The *Gazette* caught the *Free Press* stealing its stock market listings by listing "Nelots" on its stock pages one day, then pointing out that the *Free Press* ran the same listing, failing to notice that the stock was "Stolen" spelled backward.

In Helena, the *People's Voice* championed liberal causes from 1939 to 1960. John H. Toole, a conservative Republican, disliked the *Voice*'s politics but admired its spunk, noting that it regularly referred to the Anaconda Co. as an "unspeakable serpent" and Gov. Roy Ayers as a "company stooge," a charge that Toole conceded was true.

Eventually, the Anaconda Co. grew tired of the high criticism and low profits that resulted from its tight grip on Montana journalism. Even near the end of its ownership, in 1957, a national survey ranked Montana 47th in legislative news coverage among the 48 states.

So it was good news to many Montanans when Anaconda sold its papers in Billings, Missoula, Helena, Butte, Anaconda and Livingston to Lee Enterprises, which promised not to dictate editorial coverage or to quickly sell off any of the papers.

In a final blow to the prestige of the Anaconda papers, news of the sale to Lee Enterprises first broke in *Time* magazine. Breaking the story in Montana was the *Montana Kaimin*, the student newspaper at the University of Montana. On June 2, 1959, the sale finally was announced in the new Lee newspapers.

Don Anderson, a Montana native who brokered the deal for Lee, said, "It was just like freeing men from slavery." Swibold wrote that on the first day Lee owned the papers, the *Montana Standard* covered union negotiations with the Anaconda Co. metal workers. It was the first time similar negotiations had been covered in Butte. One reporter told a colleague, "By God, Bill, at last we are newspaper men, not company whores."

When I arrived in Billings in 1992, the Anaconda Co. was long gone. Lee became the third newspaper chain I worked for, and it was clearly the best of the bunch. The first two chains, Harte-Hanks Communications and Worrell Enterprises, are out of the news business. Worrell sold 29 publications to Media General Inc. in 1995 for $230 million. Within 15 years, Media General was valued at only $70 million.

A third tight-fisted newspaper company with strong holdings in rural Texas, Donrey Media Group, also sold off all of its papers after years of squeezing out profit margins of up to 40 percent.

"Donrey would rather make 30 percent of $10 than 20 percent of $100," a Donrey editor once told me.

Lee was strictly anti-union, but it had good benefits with an excellent retirement plan. Money was in the budget for bonuses and training—heady stuff for survivors of the Worrell sweatshop. Maybe chain ownership wasn't so bad after all, I began to think, even if Lee and Gannett, the nation's largest chain, between them controlled some 80 percent of Montana's daily newspaper circulation.

Still, Lee had its critics. Some of that was the result of the bad reputation Montana papers inherited from the Anaconda Co., former *Missoulian* Publisher David Fuselier asserted in an interview with *American Journalism Review*.

"Anaconda employed an enormous number of people and

owned all the daily newspapers," he said. "While providing economic underpinning, it was viewed as the bad guy who controlled the state. Well, Lee bought the Anaconda papers, so Lee by default became heir to the bad reputation."

Other critics were less sympathetic. Nathaniel Blumberg, former dean of journalism at the University of Montana, launched the *Treasure State Review* in 1991, skewering Lee Enterprises on practically every page. Blumberg, who died in 2012, could be both merciless and charming, as one might expect from a veteran of the Battle of the Bulge, which he was. Blumberg had an acerbic wit and razor-sharp writing style that drew readers from across the region.

His close ties to former students still working in Montana gave him inside sources that he acknowledged in every issue with special thanks to those "who for honorable reasons wish to remain anonymous."

When Blumberg wrote about how the *Great Falls Tribune* butchered the column of humorist Dave Barry, Barry responded by mailing Blumberg a postcard with a quarter of it scissored off. "This card was a bit longer before the Trib got hold of it," Barry wrote.

Blumberg was usually generous to working journalists, but he was pitiless on the failures of Lee Enterprises, on everything from its emphasis on profits to inept management to out-of-date baseball box scores.

"Its papers are widely recognized in Montana for their daily flow of inaccuracies, poor copy editing, failure to proofread and other deficiencies—all the result of management's refusal to provide enough reporters and editors to do a professional job," Blumberg wrote.

Occasionally, Blumberg accused Montana's new corporate giants, Lee and Gannett, of continuing the bad old days of Anaconda journalism. When Blumberg outlined his case against corporate journalism in 1997 at a conference celebrating the 25th anniversary of the 1972 Montana Constitutional Convention, one Lee paper didn't run an Associated Press story about the talk at all. The Gannett-owned *Great Falls Tribune* ran the story but edited out paragraphs about corporate control.

I became a faithful subscriber to the *Treasure State Review* and started reading too many books about the corporate takeover of American journalism: Ben Bagdikian's *The Media Monopoly*, which chronicled the growing concentration of media ownership in fewer and fewer hands; James D. Squires' *Read All About It: The Corporate Takeover of America's Newspapers*, which argued that the news business was combining the culture of television with the conscience of Wall Street; Robert McChesney's *Rich Media, Poor Democracy*, an indictment of corporate journalism by a professor whose other books include *Will the Last Reporter Please Turn Out the Lights?*; Noam Chomsky's *Manufacturing Consent*, a leftist's view of media corruption; and Doug Underwood's *When MBAs Run the Newsroom*, which argued that newspapers had been "reshaped by newspaper managers whose commitment to the marketing ethic is hardly distinguishable from their vision of what journalism is."

Meanwhile, life kept getting tougher at Lee Enterprises. I had once worked at a newspaper that moved into a building previously occupied by a grocery store. We liked to fantasize that our jobs corresponded to supermarket jobs. The business reporter, rifling through a pile of news releases, said he was in the canned goods section.

As a region editor at the *Gazette*, I was definitely in the butcher shop. The paper published four editions a night in those days (it announced in February 2017 that it was cutting back to two), and my fellow editors and I might have to edit, lay out and write headlines for as many as 20 pages apiece some nights. From the time I walked in the door in early afternoon until the last page of the city edition went through the window at 12:15 a.m., there was rarely a moment for reflection, much less careful editing.

After five years I had had enough and started a weekly newspaper of my own, *The Billings Outpost*. The time seemed ripe for an urban weekly, like those that had been sprouting up all over the country. But nothing about it sounded easy. The *Missoula Independent* celebrated its fifth anniversary a year before the *Outpost* started with a piece from co-founder Eric Johnson that said, "Statistics show that most people who try to start newspapers fail miserably, losing their money and breaking their hearts."

In 1997, Johnson and fellow co-founder Erik Cushman were ordered out of their offices by new owner Jeff Smith, who had pumped in some $70,000 to keep the paper going over the years, according to a story in the *Treasure State Review* by Printer Bowler, whose family history in Montana journalism traced back to the 1920s, and even showed up in his name. When Smith took over the *Independent,* he told Bowler, the paper was $150,000 in debt and six weeks behind in payroll and operating costs.

On the *Indy's* 10th anniversary, Andrea Barnett, the paper's first full-time reporter, wrote, "I lied my way into my first job at the *Independent.* The paper was only six months old, and when publisher Erik Cushman asked me if I knew design and layout, I said yes. For that sin I was hired. My days I spent cleaning rooms at the Red Lion motel, but one night every other week, I sat on the sixth floor of the Montana building, struggling with the computer from midnight to sunrise."

Barnett was one of the people I consulted before starting the *Outpost.* In her 10th anniversary column, she wrote about that meeting, "I had little to give. 'Walk away,' I wanted to say.... Starting a newspaper is the most difficult, painful, rewarding task I can imagine."

The *Independent* was sold in 2017 to Lee Enterprises. Brad Tyer, who had edited the paper from 2000 to 2007 and then again beginning in October 2016, wrote this about how the paper changed in the meantime: "The page count is leaner. We used to have a bureau reporter in the Flathead. We don't have a staff photographer anymore. Just this year the editorial department has taken a 15 percent budget cut. I negotiated our already negligible syndicate fees for Free Will Astrology and The Advice Goddess to half-price. We cut our copy editor's hours by two-thirds.

"The point is that all the arrows were pointing in the wrong direction, and the *Independent* had neither the reserves nor the resources to either turn it around or ride it out."

In 1995, Paul Friend, formerly of Billings, founded the *Idaho News Observer* in Wallace, Idaho. It was a short-lived but feisty sheet published under the slogan, "It's my paper, and I'll pry if I want to." One unforgettable headline that ran in huge type across the top of the front page was on a story about a law enforcement officer who was cleaning his gun when it discharged into the freezer compartment of his refrigerator: "Freeze or I'll shoot!"

The *Great Falls Great Times,* founded in 1996, lasted only a year or so. The *Butte Weekly,* which started a few months before the *Outpost,* is still going under its fourth owner after recently closing its downtown office. The *Outpost* helped inspire Cathy Siegner's *Queen City News*, which was published in Helena for eight years.

Given all of that history, starting another weekly in Montana sounded like a fool's errand, and I was just the fool for the job. I was tired of bitching about cheapskate publishers, and quickly became a cheapskate publisher myself—although for all of the right reasons.

Roger Clawson, a longtime *Gazette* reporter and columnist— and later a columnist for the *Outpost*—warned me, "You can get more work done in 80 hours than you can in 40, but you can't get twice as much done."

Clawson liked to say that he once "committed capitalism" by starting a weekly in Columbus with former *Gazette* editorial page editor Gary Svee. It took them 10 days to get out the first issue, he said, adding, "It occurred to us that if we were going to be a weekly we were going to have to pick up the pace a little."

Over the 18 years the *Outpost* was in business, I learned a lot about picking up the pace. Sixteen-hour days were common, and many days were longer. The first time I pulled an all-nighter, *Outpost* sales manager Lee Ullom told me, "It's about time you put in a full day's work."

She was one of the fiercely dedicated employees the *Outpost* seemed to attract, people always willing to help in a pinch, coming in nights, weekends and holidays to handle whatever the crisis of the day was. Some were willing to wait weeks for a paycheck to clear; some people in the community volunteered to help for no money at all. My wife and daughter helped out, and so did my daughter's boyfriend, and so did her boyfriend's mom.

We also attracted our share of misfits. One graphic artist went to lunch one day and never came back. One, on a bad day, emptied a whole desk onto the floor. Once we were just settling in for a job interview with a young woman when two police officers knocked on the door, armed with an arrest warrant and handcuffs. She didn't get the job.

Lee Enterprises took notice of us in a big way. We kept hearing rumors of extraordinary price breaks offered to our advertisers if they would stick with the daily paper. We had to drop our original plan of free home delivery and buy newspaper racks to distribute the papers around town.

Gibson, feeling some of the same pressures at the *Independent* in Missoula, started handing out copies of Richard McCord's *The Chain Gang: One Newspaper Against the Gannett Empire.* McCord detailed the fight his Santa Fe, N.M., paper waged against a competing Gannett daily, as well as fights against Gannett in Little Rock, Ark., and Green Bay, Wis.

The part that stuck with me was when McCord's printer in Santa Fe told him he had never had a customer so far in arrears. The paper survived, but McCord's marriage did not.

"All those midnight cans of soup," he wrote, "all the invitations we turned down, and movies that we missed. All those days, nights, and weekends when we were 'down at the paper'—or too tired to do anything if we were not."

Like McCord, we cut expenses to the bone. While other papers were sending electronic PDFs to the printer, we were still pasting the paper together on a jury-rigged light table, using X-ACTO knives and wax. Our printer told us the *Outpost* was used to train new pressroom employees who had never seen a hand-assembled paper before.

When we finally turned a small profit in our fifth year, we invited investors to dinner and celebrated with steaks and drinks. The very next year, we got an amazing opportunity: The Lee-owned *Thrifty Nickel* had cut sales representatives' commissions, and practically the entire staff defected to the *Outpost*: three sales reps, two delivery drivers, a graphic designer and a classified ad specialist.

Practically overnight, we were printing twice as many pages, with twice as many ads, a bigger location, new equipment and a delivery area that extended into northern Wyoming. It was astonishing; it was beautiful; it was a disaster.

Lee brought in out-of-state sales teams to shore up the *Thrifty Nickel.* Customers of the weekly shopper were allowed to run their ads in the *Gazette* at prices not even we could afford to sell ads for. The new investment money we had brought in disappeared, and soon we were left, once again, small, weary and broke.

Yet we carried on. We slowly staggered back to profitability and paid down a bunch of debt. But we never really got healthy. Sometimes I would find myself sitting all alone in the office late at night, wondering whom I was kidding by pretending to be a newspaper publisher.

We could see the internet taking a growing chunk out of newspaper revenues but had few resources to do much about it. In 2003, I started the Billings Blog, the first blog by a working journalist in Montana. Our website brought in just enough money to pay for itself, but only because we spent almost nothing on it.

To keep a little money coming in, I taught courses in journalism and writing at Rocky Mountain College and in German at Montana State University Billings. I tutored a little, graded papers all weekend, and still delivered copies of the *Outpost* to 85 or so stops each week. Perhaps as a warning sign, I got an infection that put me in the hospital for four days—but still managed to get a paper out.

On one of those long, weary days I ran into Swibold, who was giving a talk about his *Copper Chorus* book in Billings.

"You're doing the Lord's work," he told me.

"Well, I wish the Lord would help out a little," I replied.

After a weak 2015, with diminishing prospects for both the *Outpost* and the newspaper industry as a whole, I decided to shut the paper down. The *Gazette* mentioned the closing in a business brief.

Once again, McCord's words came back to me: "But years of battling a relentless foe had given me my fill. Taking on the largest newspaper chain was like taking on Big Oil or the military-industrial complex: A skirmish could be won now and then, embarrassment could be caused—but in the end the giants kept right on doing what they were doing before."

I kept hearing more stories about the increasing toll newspapers were taking on their employees. Sherry Devlin, former environmental reporter and then editor at the *Missoulian*, told the Institute for Journalism and Natural Resources in 2003 that many reporters were relying on a spouse's paycheck or a second job to make ends meet. Devlin eventually sued the *Missoulian*, arguing that she was forced out of her editor's job because of her age and gender. The suit was later dropped.

As a freelance writer, Ron Selden broke the biggest scoop the *Outpost* ever had: astounding allegations that Crow Tribal Chairman Clifford Birdinground was taking kickbacks from a Billings car dealership. No other paper in the state touched the story for a full year, until the chairman was finally indicted.

Selden eventually went into public relations for the Montana

Department of Fish, Wildlife and Parks. He died in 2014, at age 58.

Robert Struckman, formerly a correspondent for the *Outpost* and a reporter for the *Gazette* and *Missoulian*, wrote about his reporting experiences in Montana in an article for *Dissent* that was reprinted in the *Outpost*. Struckman said that he was threatened with firing after talking about starting a union at the *Missoulian* in hopes of improving a paycheck that was tiny despite his master's degree and an internship at *New Yorker* magazine.

"But in the hectic pace of my life in those days," he wrote, "I now see myself avoiding my growing sense of dread and desperation as the prospect of vacations and new cars and a college education fund for my son slowly receded, slipping away insistently, relentlessly."

Struckman did some research and found this: "From 1975 to 1995, the average news reporter's wage [in Montana] increased every year, starting at a rate of about 5 percent and trending down to about 3 percent. Then something amazing happened: over the next ten years, the average wage paid to reporters in Montana actually declined by 1 percent per year in real dollars. None of these figures are adjusted for inflation.

"In the same time period, the ten years ending in 2006, total revenue at Lee Enterprises (which owns four of the five major dailies in Montana) grew at more than 11 percent a year."

Kathleen McLaughlin, who worked in Montana for the Lee State Bureau, wrote recently that she supplemented a poorly paid *Missoulian* internship by taking a second job as a waitress. One morning she interviewed the mayor and city manager, then served them lunch a couple of hours later.

She sees a steady decline in local news coverage in Montana, in part because the internet has focused so much more attention on national rather than local issues.

"Local press isn't dead, but it's fragmented and weakened," she wrote. "Talk to readers, and you'll find they believe local news these days is both less enticing and less accessible—and thereby less likely to be shared on Facebook, that great master of content."

McLaughlin quotes Theresa Manzella, a Tea Party Republican who serves in the Montana Legislature: "What I have seen is since the onset of social media, we have so much more control and capability over our own message and the destiny of our messages.

I like the fact that I can control the message. I can control my words and the emotion I convey."

A report by the Institute for Journalism and Natural Resources in Missoula reported in 2003 that only about 30 of the American West's 285 daily newspapers remain independently owned. In Montana and in six other Western states, just two companies owned at least 65 percent of newspaper circulation.

Those who follow Montana journalism are exposed to a regular diet of stories about layoffs, consolidated operations and cutbacks in coverage. Lee Enterprises, saddled by debt it took on when it acquired Pulitzer Inc. in 2005, went through bankruptcy in 2011. In an effort to cut costs, it has moved some ad-building and page-design chores to overseas companies.

In 2015, Lee let go of two veteran reporters at its Capitol Bureau, Chuck Johnson and Mike Dennison, and replaced them with less experienced, and presumably cheaper, reporters. Between 2010 and 2013, Lee cut 26 percent of its staff nationwide. Newsprint per subscriber went down 14 percent.

Gannett, Montana's other corporate heavyweight, announced in October 2016 that it was cutting staff nationwide by 2 percent. Atlantic magazine's website reported in 2016 that 40 percent of newspaper jobs nationwide have disappeared. While media jobs actually have increased in Washington, D.C., and Los Angeles, they are decreasing in smaller cities with regionally important newspapers.

McLaughlin wrote, "Most of these missing newsroom employees were not working at the national newspapers where our post-election journalistic worries have fixated. They toiled in local and regional newsrooms, in the teams that long covered often mundane but critically important workings of cities, towns and states. Newsrooms and state bureaus are decimated, and staffed with younger, cheaper talent—equally stretched and hard-working but missing much of the institutional knowledge and confidence critical to successful journalism."

The *Missoula Independent*'s Matt Gibson said at a newspaper editors' meeting a few years ago that the weekly is turning toward other revenue sources, such as sponsoring concerts, to stay afloat. The only companies really making money off online news, he said, are Google and Facebook.

Alternatives to newspapers are slowly welling up in Montana.

In Billings, I have been working with Ed Kemmick at *Last Best News*, an online publication that scoops the daily paper with disturbing regularity. Kemmick and I had worked together on the region desk at the *Gazette* and were grateful for the chance to work together again. In Missoula, Martin Kidston is doing similar work with the *Missoula Current*.

Bloggers at Intelligent Discontent and Montana Cowgirl often break stories of their own. If the reporting is one-sided, it also demands attention.

In Anaconda, something of the spirit, if not the resources, of the old *Anaconda Standard* lives on in the Anaconda Double Standard, a blog dedicated to "exposing the truth about government corruption in Anaconda, Montana."

Still, despite the upsurge of new ventures, media concentration continues at the national level. Some 90 percent of media in the United States are now owned by just six companies, a statistic that would horrify Ben Bagdikian, who died in 2016. Eighteen of 20 alternative weeklies lost circulation or just held steady last year. Despite newspaper cutbacks, newspapers still provide a third of reporters in Washington, D.C., and 38 percent of reporters in state legislatures.

Many observers see news coverage slipping back in time to a day when news was far more partisan and far less reliable than it is now. We face an age of contradiction and paradox, one that might have looked familiar to Thomas Jefferson, who famously said, "were it left to me to decide whether we should have a government without newspapers or newspapers without a government, I should not hesitate a moment to prefer the latter."

Less famously, he also said, "Nothing can now be believed which is seen in a newspaper. Truth itself becomes suspicious by being put into that polluted vehicle."

The polluted vehicle that the Anaconda Co. once used to control Montana putters on. As always, the survival of Montana journalism depends on the willingness of a few brave souls to risk their money and their hearts.

KEITH McCAFFERTY
Aphrodisiac Graveyard

Preface

I FIRST HEARD ABOUT ERNEST HEMINGWAY'S STEAMER TRUNK OF fishing tackle, the lost treasure chest at the heart of this novel, from his oldest son, Jack. At the time, some thirty-odd years ago, Jack and I were contributing editors for *Field & Stream*, and friendly colleagues, if not close friends. It was a blustery November day, easy to recall because all November days on British Columbia's Thompson River are blustery, and we were the only fishermen along a stretch of the river known as the Graveyard, just down the hill from the old white crosses where all the graves face north. On toward dark, Jack hooked a steelhead of fifteen or sixteen pounds, which I landed for him in the tailout after a long fight. We admired this great seafaring trout for a few seconds before releasing it, and celebrated with a thermos cup of hot chocolate into which I laced peppermint schnapps, in honor of my father.

After toasting the fish, I asked Jack if he thought his own

father would have liked this kind of fishing—that is, wading on slippery boulders in a river haunted by the dead, casting hour after hour in miserable weather, and considering yourself lucky to hook up once every few days and manage not to drown. He said that Ernest would have enjoyed the challenge but that he'd lost the heart to fly fish after a steamer trunk containing all his valuable gear was stolen or lost from Railway Express in 1940, en route to Ketchum, Idaho, where he was a guest at the Sun Valley Lodge. In fact, Jack could only remember his father fly fishing once after the loss, in the Big Wood River. This was an interesting insight into the famous author's psyche, but at the time I was more interested in casting my own fly rod than the fate of another man's tackle or the sentiments it evoked.

Years passed, and I had no reason to recall the story until my wife, Gail, persuaded me to set a novel in northwestern Wyoming, where Hemingway stayed at the L-Bar-T Guest Ranch during five summers and falls in the 1930s, hunting, fishing, and writing. By then Jack had died and I sought to verify the details of his story with Patrick Hemingway, Ernest's sole surviving son, who lives in my hometown. I spoke with him at a local screening of the PBS *American Masters* series film *Ernest Hemingway: Rivers to the Sea*. Patrick was kind enough to indulge my questions and said he recalled the lost trunk, adding that it probably contained best-quality bamboo fly rods and reels ordered from the House of Hardy catalog. Hardy was the premier London maker, and Patrick remembered helping his father convert the prices from pounds sterling to American dollars.

Today, only one piece of Ernest Hemingway's fly fishing tackle survives in intact condition, a Hardy rod in a model called the Fairy that he had with him when he first went to Idaho. It is displayed at the American Museum of Fly Fishing in Manchester, Vermont, along with a letter to *Field & Stream* that Jack wrote about the missing tackle.

As concerns that tackle, and as for the possibility that the steamer trunk contained Hemingway treasures unrelated to piscatorial pursuits, and perhaps of far more value?

Pour a drink, light a fire, and turn the page. I have a story to tell.

Chapter One
The Aphrodisiac Graveyard

IT HAD STARTED THE NIGHT BEFORE, WHEN THE SNOW SIFTED DOWN onto the carcass of his horse and there was no sound beyond the intermittent release of its gases and no stars to wish upon. That's when he began to "What if" it to death, going back to the morning, kissing her face and feeling the flutter of her eyelashes that, as he'd helped her from the saddle only a couple hours later, a small woman made smaller by the immensity of the country and the fourteen hands of her horse, were already icicling with frost.

Too long in bed had given them a slow start, their breakfast hurried, the Sunday edition of the *Bridger Mountain Star* outside the mudroom where the paperboy had tossed it. If he'd picked it up he would have checked the back page for the weather. What kind of Montanan were you if you didn't keep an eye on the sky? But he had a pannier in each hand and they were in too much of a rush to get to the property where they pastured the horses, and then to the trailhead with dawn breaking, a sifting of snowflakes she caught on her tongue, but dead calm, just cold enough that the horses blew steam from their nostrils.

It was called the Aphrodisiac Graveyard, a series of wind-scoured openings on a south-facing slope some few miles west of the wilderness boundary. Here the bulls shed their great antlers in February and March, and Freida Toliver, who had a business making antler chandeliers, wanted to get them off the ground while the beams were still that rich dark mahogany and the tines ivory tipped, before porcupines gnawed them and the weather blanched them of their value.

That was before three kisses became four, before the fairytale snowfall turned into stinging shards of ice and the temperature dropped thirty degrees in an hour.

He couldn't really say where they made the first wrong turn. Like most people who became lost, he thought that he knew where they were for some time after he didn't. It wasn't just the visibility, which had dropped from twenty miles to as many yards, but the wind blew the snow into a sea of scallops, dulling colors and swallowing landmarks to the point where it might have been a different country, or, rather, no country at all. A trail that he remembered as crossing a low saddle seemed to have vanished, along with the saddle, and so they took another trail—"This is it, right, Freida?"—and she shook her head yes, feeding into his confidence, willing it to be so. An hour of lying to themselves later, it became obvious that it wasn't.

"I thought you were an Indian," he said, trying for a smile, and failing.

Where the hell are we?

It was a gamble, giving the horses their heads, trusting that they would find their way back to the pack trail. And their hearts lifted when they thought they had found it, only to discover that it was an elk trail that branched like a strong man's forearm veins, some bleeding back into each other, others not. The horses followed one of those veins down into a creek bottom, and it was there, in the dark heart of the mountain, and no longer sure even which mountain, when he'd made the first attempt to build a fire. But the pack of bar matches he found in a pants pocket were damp, the heads only smearing against the chemical strip.

What if I hadn't given up smoking and had my lighter, he'd think. *What if?*

"I might have some in my fishing vest," she'd said. It seemed absurd now, the notion that they might do a little fishing in one of the high-altitude tarns. "It's in the saddlebag," she told him. But her hands shook so badly she couldn't undo the buckle.

"Here, let me." He rummaged through the vest.

"Try the inside zipper pocket, the one with my license."

"I did."

He lifted his shoulders and let them fall. She looked at him, and did exactly the same. Like she was his echo. That's what they were to each other. He even called her that, Little Echo. She was Northern Cheyenne and had taken to it. Told people it was her tribal name.

He bent down and hugged her. He felt the frost of her eyebrows melt against his cheek and thought of the morning, holding her close, feeling her heart beat.

"I don't want to die," she said.

"Nobody's going to die. Don't even think it."

It was the way they had together, one strong, then the other.

I could try to start a fire with the gun, he thought. It was something he'd read about, possibly in the same issue of an outdoor magazine where he'd read about a hunter who'd survived a night of thirty below zero by crawling inside the carcass of a moose.

He pulled the handgun from the holster, the single-action Ruger Blackhawk that was her birthday present to him when he'd turned fifty. Five cylinders loaded, the chamber under the hammer empty. He tried to recall the procedure. You formed a tinder nest with cloth, dried grasses, anything that was flammable. Then you pulled the bullet from a cartridge case, dumped half of the powder and stuffed a piece of cotton cloth over the remaining charge, and fired it into the tinder nest. The idea was that the smoldering cloth would catch the tinder aglow, and you could lift up the nest and coax it into flame with your breath. In the illustration, it had looked like the man was praying, lifting his hands to heaven, exhaling fire.

He had a multi-tool in one of his saddlebags, fifty feet of parachute cord and a roll of duct tape in the other. A Montanan's holy trinity. You could do anything with a kit like that—mend fence, haul a deer out to the road, splint a broken arm. Maybe even start a fire.

He broke a handful of the tiny branches that quilled the lower trunk of a pine tree and collected some larger wood to feed in later. Tinder took more thought, and she was the one who suggested that he unravel wool threads from the tops of his socks. He wadded up the threads as she searched her pockets and came up empty.

"Did I see you put on the panties with the hearts?"

She nodded, too cold to frown at the question.

"Oh, right," she said, the shoe dropping. Nothing burned like cotton.

"I'd use mine, but they're poly."

She said okay, but her hands were so numb she couldn't trust them. "I might stab myself," she said. She had bitten through her tongue from the shuddering of her jaws and her voice was thick with the blood in her mouth.

"I'll do it," he told her.

He worked her zipper and carefully cut a patch of cloth from the top of the panties. Under his fingertips, he could feel her abdominal muscles crawl from the ice of his touch.

"We're going to laugh about this someday," he told her.

She nodded, but didn't speak. The cold had started with her hands and feet. Then it had crawled up her arms and legs. Now it had settled like a pick in her chest. Even the drawing of breath was an effort. She turned away and spit blood onto the snow.

"This is going to do the trick," he said.

He tore thin strips from the cloth and wove them into the tinder nest. Pulling a bullet wasn't easy—the hard-cast .41 Magnum loads were crimped into the case necks so they wouldn't shift during recoil— but by rapping on the neck to expand the brass and twisting the bullet with the pliers on his multi-tool, he managed. He placed the nest at the base of a big pine so it wouldn't be blown over by the gas escaping from the barrel.

The first shot from the heavy revolver resulted in a brief glow in the center of the nest, but it went black before he could pick it up.

A little more powder? The second try was better, producing an orange-limned marble of smoldering tinder that died slowly enough to give them heart, but died all the same.

"What about the flies?"

"What are you talking about?"

"You can shave off the hair and the feathers. It will burn."

"Trout flies, you mean?"

She nodded. "I packed my vest in the pannier. Those big dries, the golden stones and the salmon flies, they have lots of wing material."

"You know, that's a really good idea," he said. "I knew I married you for some reason."

It looked like modern art, a softball-sized bird's nest of dried grasses, rusted pine needles, bits of cloth with pink and purple hearts, all of it woven together with ginger neck hackles, bucktail and marabou stork fibers dyed in a half dozen hues.

"That ought to catch fire just looking at it," he said.

Then the .41 spoke and for a time there was a new color on the mountain, a molten candle of hope. The matchstick-sized sticks caught fire and the flames licked up as they used their hands for wind blocks. But the ground was cold and it sapped the fire even as they fed it.

Come on. Come on. They blew on the struggling licks of flame.

"Not so hard. You're blowing it out. This needs a woman's touch."

That's my girl, he thought.

But it was like the CPR he'd once performed on a victim of lightning strike. You kept pressing the breastbone and sharing your breaths, even after the heart under your hands grew cold.

She had been waving her hat to coax the flames and pushed the frozen clumps of her hair out of her face.

"Eoseeton'eto," she said. *It's really cold.* And to him, "I'm freezing."

He knew soon as she went to the people's language that he'd lost her. She never did that unless she was at wit's end.

"Maybe he was right," she said.

"Who was right?"

"The man, the one I told you about. With the cat. He said that April was the best month to die."

"He's just a crazy old loon. You said so yourself."

"Yeah, I guess."

But that's when it had really sunk in, and looking down at her—she was in the dark, the fire was out—he had a thought. *This is how it ends. You wake up with the woman you'd searched all your life to find, who changed her name for you and who you couldn't think of going on without, and that night you lie down with her and die. There are no premonitions. You're just another victim of nature's impersonal calculus.*

He told himself to stop it. After all, there were still two bullets in the Ruger. He tipped out the cylinder to double-check. And thought of the horses. They were Rocky Mountain horses, not the biggest of their breed, but just as big as a moose.

He shook the cartridges into the palm of his left glove to show them to her, sensed, rather than saw, the recognition take shape in her face.

The brass gleamed in the light of his headlamp.

"Time to decide," he said. He meant they could try again to start fire or—the unthinkable. The unthinkable that had started as a halfhearted joke only an hour before, but was far from it now.

"I don't think I can do it."

"What? Shoot old Henry? You always said he was nothing but a mule with short ears."

"Either of them. They're our family."

He looked at her, her eyes squinted up against the cold, the frozen creeks of tears that ended in beads of ice.

"I'm sorry it's come to this," he said. "It's sure enough my fault."

"I'm the one with the damned business. I'm the reason we're here."

True, but little solace.

"I know what you're thinking and you can just stop it right now, Mister J. C. Toliver."

The paisley scarf she'd pulled up over her mouth was frosted from the exhalations of her breath and her voice shuddered, but the words held out a note of hope. "I thought maybe if we could just get them to lie down, we could snuggle up between them."

"You know they won't lie down in this kind of weather. Hell, old Henry barely lies down ever. And when's the last time you saw Annabel off her feet? It's the only way. If we can ride out this storm, we can walk out of here tomorrow morning."

"I know." For a moment the wind that swirled in the treetops died and they listened to the horses blow.

"All right," she said. A harder edge to the voice, another woman speaking now, the part of her that he was counting on.

"If we're going to do this, let's do it while it's still light enough to see. But I'm not shooting my own horse. We're shooting each other's. Down in that little witch's heart." She gestured toward a patch of tangled timber. "If you can pull the trigger, I guess I can, too."

"All right then." And again: "It's the only way."

"I just need a minute, that's all. Just a minute with her. Go down there and wait for me."

"We don't have long."

"I won't be long. I just have to say goodbye."

He'd never seen her after that. He'd called out for her. He'd gone looking. He still had the gun and the two bullets. After a while, he used one of them.

LAURA PRITCHETT
What I Would Have Asked You

LAST NIGHT IS THIS: MAY I COME IN YOUR TENT? CURL BESIDE YOU?
Together conjure that power of a first kiss? Or have we, in our
late age, come to the place where we only note the stirrings of our
bodies? Aware, as we are, of the troubles that such desires bring?

As I listened to you put away your harmonica, which you had
been playing in the dark to lull us to sleep, I tried out phrasing
for such questions, and I listened for any noise you, across the
small meadow, might now make. Me single and lonely, you newly
widowed and lonely. Me pulling the sleeping bag to my chin, you
likely sprawling on top of yours, hands folded at your chest as you
regarded the nightsky. The both of us camping with a cadre of old
friends, various tents dotted along the river.

My ears ached with listening. I heard the purr of water. The
zing of crickets. The chilling of the earth and the deepening of the
sky. I heard murmurings of others as they got settled, including

one loud bark of laughter. I listened to the most simple things, such as my pulse and breath, because, of course, love is a way of knowing, a way of looking at the ordinary until it becomes special and looking at the wondrous until it becomes common. Desire both amplifies and reduces our lives. My breath was biting me like the stars bite the sky.

I hoped you would come to me, that I would hear your footfall, but I was also willing to come to you once I got the phrasing right, but the correct combination of words eluded me. Only a few syllables, really, but the basic question implied so many others. For starters, would you want to sandpaper off the edges of our skin that keeps us so separate? What a question to burden you with, with others nearby! How were you to respond kindly, if the answer was no? And if the answer were yes, well, then there were others: Do you have any STDs or condoms? What constitutes the basic theology of your sex life? How quiet can you be?

Since I could not figure out how to ask all that in some brief-and-orderly fashion, I got up and tiptoed to the river, to the place where we'd seen a rattlesnake at dinner. It must have been close to midnight, and by the light of the moon, I saw an apple sitting out on the battered picnic table, next to the empty bottles of wine. I felt like leaving a note, William Carlos Williams style: Forgive me, but I am hungry in more ways than one, and this fruit was available and delicious.

So, this is just to say, as I drove away from the river this morning, away from the harmonica and the friends and geology of that deep canyon, back into this very loud and bright world, that I wish I'd asked you the old cliché question on our last night together, that same one humans have been asking one another beneath the star-spattered sky forever: What else is there, exactly, except for love? Why is it, exactly, that we want to curl up next to someone so much?

Had you invited me into your tent on the outskirts of the meadow, beneath that large cottonwood tree, and had we made love, perhaps we would have curled like grapevines and spoken a great deal and slept very little. Nonsense would have ruled, as it always does when such feelings are allowed to surface. We would have unlocked mischief and we would have felt like we'd gotten away with something—an extra slice of life, for instance. We would have discussed much: past loves, future empty space, how hard it is to go for long times without sincere and rousing touch. Life is lonely: on that we would have agreed. Relationships are tricky: dwindling kindnesses, the inevitable and immutable taking-for-granted diminutions. Even the relationship we have with ourselves. We humans have not progressed so far in this regard; perhaps, even, we have gotten worse at sincere connections as time has gone by on this spinning planet of ours.

Last night, when the apple was finished, I walked back to my tent. Halfway there, I stumbled over a rock and fell and rose up, gasping so as to absorb the pain. It hurt so very much. There was nothing to do but bear it. Let it dissipate. When I was back in my sleeping bag, I jammed my jacket under my head and I considered Cassiopeia, visible from my screened window, and I formed words to try to ask you. I made little 'w's' with my lips, trying out sounds. I did hear little murmurings and sighs from one tent over and that's when I decided, finally, to merely walk to your tent and say your name, with a question mark attached. Or perhaps I would have said: Lovers are in the hurt business, to be sure—but do you feel any urgency, do you think you'll live to be a hundred? Wake up and live with me, for just a moment!

But I did not. I became afraid. Afraid you would be sleepy. Afraid you would be unkind. Afraid that you saw nothing in me worth loving. Afraid of the old story, which is that last night, when I looked up the canyon, at the moon, which was at its apogee, tears flew into my eyes because I was conscious that my life, too, is at its apex and that like the moon, my life is floating, ready to change direction, and I am afraid of growing old, and I am afraid that the deep and raging hungers of the flesh are perhaps too much with me and yet it has been some time since I have been desired.

Now, on the highway, my car picks up speed, and the wind rocks it a bit. I am not sorry I ate that last apple in the moonlight because it was good and my mouth needed consoling. But I am sorry I never found the words to ask you one question in particular, one that I thought that maybe, just maybe, you'd have the answer to: Given my silence, how is it that the remainder of my life won't only be a series of sad dreams and appetites that will occupy me, night by night, until my questions are gone?

CONTRIBUTORS

 **Dave Caserio** is the author of *This Vanishing* from CW Books and *Wisdom For A Dance In The Street*, a CD of poetry and music from Gazoobi Tales. A recipient of a Fellowship in Poetry award from the New York State Foundation of the Arts, Dave works with various community outreach programs, such as the Humanities Montana Conversations and Arts Without Boundaries. He has produced a series of poetry-in-performance events—A Feast For The Hunger Moon, WordSongs, Arc of the Communal, and I Conjure A Stubborn Faith—that combine poetry, music, dance and the visual arts.

Cara Chamberlain is the author of three books of poetry, *Hidden Things, The Divine Botany*, and *Lament of the Antichrist in a Secular World and Other Poems*. Her poems have appeared in numerous journals, including *Nimrod, Boston Review, Passages*

North, Crab Orchard Review, and *The Southern Review*. She has received four Pushcart Prize nominations and has been a finalist in the Ashland Poetry Press, Lo-Fi Novella, and Blue Light Book Award contests. She lives in Billings, Montana.

Lorraine Collins has been a freelance writer, columnist and commentator in the United States and abroad for many years. Her first job in journalism was an editorial researcher for *Time* magazine in New York. As a freelance writer, she wrote features, profiles, and humor for national magazines and newspapers. When she lived abroad she wrote for publications in Asia and England. She is the author of a book of humor and of mystery and suspense stories. She has contributed short stories and poetry to anthologies published in her home state of South Dakota. She now lives in Billings.

David Crisp has been a journalist for more than 30 years. He was the editor of two Texas daily newspapers before moving to Montana in 1992. He worked for the *Billings Gazette* until 1997, when he founded the *Billings Outpost*, a weekly newspaper. He folded the *Outpost* in 2016 to work with Ed Kemmick at *Last Best News*, an online newspaper. Crisp has a bachelor's degree from Stephen F. Austin State University in Nacogdoches, Texas, and a master's degree in English from Texas A&M University. He teaches writing classes at Rocky Mountain College and German at Montana State University Billings.

Connie Dillon is a full-time artist and owner of Gallery Nine in Billings. Besides exhibiting in the gallery, her work has been included in juried shows at Yellowstone Art Museum's annual auctions, Paris Gibson Square in Great Falls, Missoula's Zootown Arts Community Center, Radius Gallery & E3 Convergence Gallery, and galleries in New York and Maryland.

 **Stella Fong** writes, cooks and plays in Billings, Montana. For seventeen years, she has called Montana's Trailhead home after relocating from San Diego, California. Fong shares her love of food through her contributions to *Yellowstone Valley Woman Magazine, Big Sky Journal, Blue Water Sailing, Western Art and Architecture* and *Magic City Magazine*. Her radio show for Yellowstone Public Radio, *Flavors Under the Big Sky: Celebrating the Bounty of the Region*, talks to those behind food, wine and production. Online, her blog postings can be found at the lastbestplates.com, lastbestnews.com, venography.com and stellafong.com. Her articles have also appeared in *Cooking Light, Fine Cooking* and the *Washington Post*. For years she taught cooking and wine classes for MSU Billings Foundation, Sur La Table, Williams Sonoma, Macy's Cellars and Gelson's Super Market.

Jamie Ford's debut novel, *Hotel on the Corner of Bitter and Sweet*, spent two years on the New York Times bestseller list and went on to win the Asian/Pacific American Award for Literature. His work has been translated into 34 languages. His  new novel, *Love And Other Consolation Prizes*, will be published September 12, 2017.

 **Pete Fromm**'s latest book is the memoir *The Names of the Stars* (St. Martins, 2016). He is a five-time winner of the Pacific Northwest Booksellers Award for his novels *If Not For This, As Cool as I Am*, and *How All This Started*, his story collection *Dry Rain*, and the memoir *Indian Creek Chronicles*. The film of *As Cool as I Am* was released in 2013. He is also the author of four other story collections and has published over two hundred stories in magazines. He is on the faculty of Oregon's Pacific University's low-residency MFA program and lives in Montana.

Stephen Germic teaches writing and literature at Rocky

Mountain College. His work has appeared in a number of journals, and he is currently completing his book-length manuscript titled *Again, This Fable*. He divides his time not quite equally between Montana and Upper Michigan.

Sid Gustafson writes novels and practices veterinary medicine in Bozeman, Montana. He had the good fortune to be raised by horses under the Rocky Mountain Front with the Blackfeet Indians, to whom he returns time and again to find another story. His latest novel is *Swift Dam*.

Tami Haaland is the author of two books of poetry: *When We Wake in the Night*, and *Breath in Every Room*, winner of the Nicholas Roerich Prize. Her poems have appeared in a variety of periodicals and many anthologies, including *Poems Across the Big Sky I* and *II, New Poets of the American West, The Ecopoetry Anthology* (Trinity University Press) and *Literature: An Introduction* (Pearson). Haaland's work has been featured on *The Writer's Almanac, Verse Daily*, and *American Life in Poetry*. She served as Montana's fifth poet laureate and teaches at Montana State University Billings, where she currently chairs the Department of English, Philosophy and Modern Languages.

Jon Henn trained at UCLA in novel writing and is a founding member of the Creative Writer's Studio in Billings, Montana. His stories contain his love of science fiction and drama mixed with quirky comedy, highly imaginative plot lines, and endearing characters. He has worked on over 50 movies and media shoots in Hollywood as a co-producer, cameraman, lighting director, etc. He was also a makeup artist for the San Francisco Opera and a special makeup effects artist for low budget movies. He has directed five theatrical plays, including *A Midsummer Night's Dream, What the Butler Saw*, and *Play It Again, Sam*, and acted in over 30 other shows. He graduated in theater at San Francisco State University and went to the San Francisco Theater Academy.

 **Allen Morris Jones** is the author of two novels, *Last Year's River* and *A Bloom of Bones*; a work of nonfiction, *A Quiet Place of Violence: Hunting and Ethics in the Missouri River Breaks*; and co-editor of *The Best of Montana's Short Fiction*. He is the publisher of Bangtail Press, based in Bozeman, and editor of the magazine *Big Sky Journal*.

Danell Jones's poetry, fiction, essays, and reviews have appeared in various publications including the *Denver Quarterly, Gingko Tree Review*, and *The Virginia Woolf Miscellany*. Jones has a Ph.D. from Columbia University where she won a Whiting  Fellowship in the Humanities for her work on Virginia Woolf. She was awarded the Jovanovich Award for Poetry from the University of Colorado and was chosen as a finalist for both the Bakeless Poetry Prize and the PEN/Nelson Algren Award for Fiction. She is the author of *The Virginia Woolf Writers' Workshop: Seven Lessons to Inspire Great Writing* and *Desert Elegy* as well as a founder of the Big Sky Writing Workshops.

 **Craig Lancaster** is the author of eight works of fiction, including the High Plains Book Award-winning *600 Hours of Edward*. His work has also been honored by the Utah Book Awards and the Independent Publisher Book Awards. His essays and fiction have appeared in periodicals such as *Montana Quarterly* and *Magic Magazine*. He lives in Billings with his wife, novelist Elisa Lorello.

Carrie La Seur's debut novel, *The Home Place*, won a High Plains Book Award and was a finalist for the *Strand Magazine*

Critics Award for Best First Novel, an IndieNext pick, a Library Journal pick, one of *Great Falls Tribune*'s Top 10 Montana Books for 2014, and a *Florida SunSentinel* Best Crime Fiction pick for 2014. Her writing appears in *Daily Beast, Grist,* the *Guardian, Harvard Law and Policy Review, High Country News, Huffington Post, Kenyon Review, Mother Jones, Salon,* and *Yale Journal of International Law.* Carrie maintains a part-time energy and environmental law practice in Montana, where her ancestors settled in 1864. A licensed private pilot and committed introvert, she loves to hike, ski, and fish the Montana wilderness with her family. Her new novel, *The Weight of an Infinite Sky,* comes out January 16, 2018. Carrie is the founding Board President of This House of Books.

Elisa Lorello is a Long Island native, the youngest of seven children. She earned her bachelor's and master's degrees at the University of Massachusetts Dartmouth and taught rhetoric and writing at the college level for more than ten years. In 2012 she became a full-time novelist. Elisa is the author of seven novels, including the bestselling *Faking It,* and one memoir. She has been featured in the *Charlotte Observer* and *Last Best News,* and was a guest speaker at the Triangle Association of Freelancers 2012 and 2014 Write Now! conferences.

Keith McCafferty is the survival and outdoor skills editor of *Field & Stream* and the author of the Sean Stranahan mystery series, including *The Royal Wulff Murders, The Gray Ghost Murders, Dead Man's Fancy, Crazy Mountain Kiss,* which won the Western Writers of America 2016 Spur Award for Best Western Contemporary Novel, and *Buffalo Jump Blues,* a must-read pick by *O, The Oprah Magazine.* His sixth novel, *Cold Hearted River,* will be published by Viking/Penguin Books in July 2017. Winner of the Traver Award for angling literature, Keith is a two-time National Magazine Awards finalist, a two-time High Plains Book Awards finalist for fiction, a finalist for the Nero Award for Best

Mystery, and a finalist for the Will Rodgers Medallion Award for Best Western Fiction. He lives with his wife, cat, and, as a wild bird rescue volunteer, various feathered friends, in southwest Montana.

 **Precious McKenzie** has a PhD in nineteenth-century British literature and is an assistant professor of English at Rocky Mountain College. She is the author of over thirty books for children including *Buff Ducks, Now or Later Alligator, Peace, Love and K-Pop, The Mayflower Girl,* and *A Thousand Miles.* Her poetry, for adults, has appeared in *ellipsis, Gemini,* and in Tupelo Press's 30/30 Project. Precious is a founding member of the Billings Bookstore Cooperative and serves as vice president on the board of directors.

Scott Murray grew up in Billings, Montana, and graduated from Billings West High School. He received a Bachelor of Science Degree in chemistry from the University of Texas at Austin. After graduating, Scott worked as an environmental  chemist and participated in leukemia research at the University of Texas. In the next phase of life, Scott attended and graduated from Southwestern Medical School, in Dallas, Texas. He completed his intern year at Parkland Memorial Hospital, and then went on to residency in obstetrics and gynecology at St. Joseph Hospital in Denver, Colorado. After the completion of training, he practiced obstetrics and gynecology in Texas and Colorado, delivering over 4000 babies during that time. Subsequent to a clinical career, Scott went on to teach Pathophysiology, Anatomy, and Clinical Medicine for the Physician Assistant Program at Rocky Mountain College. He also taught undergraduate courses in chemistry, physiology, and environmental chemistry. Scott continued his teaching career at Montana State University, teaching multiple graduate and undergraduate courses in the Health and Human Sciences department. After many years of writing in his spare time, Scott had his medical science fiction novel, *My Brothers' Keepers,* published in Great Britain by the Arts Council of England. He continues to write science fiction and military fiction as time allows. Scott lives in Billings, Montana, with Greta, his wife of thirty-five years.

Anna Paige is a poet and educator and co-founder of Billings Area Literary Arts, created from a desire to connect writers to one another and grow the literary community of Billings. Anna performs spoken word poetry and strives for a collaborative, multi-disciplinary approach to her art. Her past collaborations include a piece in the Billings' Fringe Festival and with Terpsichore Dance Company of Montana. Anna is a former Montana Slam Grand Champion and has been named Best Spoken Word Artist at the Magic City Music Awards multiple times. Anna was also a featured TEDx Billings speaker in 2016 and is the co-host of *Resounds: Arts and Culture on the High Plains* on Yellowstone Public Radio.

Laura Pritchett is an American author whose work is rooted in the natural world. Her five novels have garnered numerous national literary awards, including PEN USA Award for Fiction, the High Plains Book Award, the Milkweed National Fiction Prize, and the WILLA Award. She's published over 200 essays and short stories in magazines (including *The New York Times, The Sun, O Magazine, Salon, High Country News, Orion,* and others), mostly about environmental issues in the American West. She holds a PhD from Purdue University and teaches around the country. More at www.laurapritchett.com.

Bernard Quetchenbach's latest books are *Accidental Gravity*, published by Oregon State University Press, and *The Hermit's Place*, from Wild Leaf Press. His poems, essays, and articles have appeared in a variety of anthologies, books, and periodicals. His poem "Baboon Mountain" developed as the result of an Artist's Residency sponsored by the Absaroka-Beartooth Wilderness Foundation. He is a fellow of the International League of Conservation Writers, and lives in Billings, where he is a professor of English at Montana State University Billings.

Shann Ray grew up in Montana, spent part of his childhood on the Northern Cheyenne Reservation in southeast Montana and has served as a visiting scholar in Asia, Africa, Europe, and South America. His books include the poetry collection *Balefire*, the novel *American Copper*, and the story collection *American Masculine*. He is also the author of a work of political theory called *Forgiveness and Power in the Age of Atrocity*. His poetry and prose have been honored with the American Book Award, the High Plains Book Award, the Western Writers of America Spur Award, the Foreword Book of the Year Readers' Choice Award, and the Bakeless Prize. A former collegiate and professional basketball player and National Endowment for the Arts fellow, Ray now lives in Spokane, Washington, where he teaches leadership and forgiveness studies at Gonzaga University. His work has been featured in *Poetry, Esquire, McSweeney's, Narrative, Big Sky Journal, Montana Quarterly, Salon,* and *Northwest Review*. Because of his wife and three daughters, he believes in love.

Russell Rowland's first novel, *In Open Spaces*, was called "a novel with a muted elegance" by the *New York Times*. His next two novels, *The Watershed Years* and *High and Inside*, were both finalists for the High Plains Book Award. His most recent book  is *Fifty-Six Counties: A Montana Journey*. He lives in Billings.

Vicki Tapia, a closet writer of diaries as a young girl, progressed to keeping journals by the time she was 16. In the mid-80's she designed, edited and published a quarterly journal for La Leche League of Montana. She first saw her words printed in a newspaper in 1995 as runner up in a writing contest for the *Billings Gazette*. In her career as a Lactation Consultant, Vicki wrote and edited numerous case studies for Lactation Journals from 1996 to 2014. A finalist in the High Plains Book Awards, her first book, *Somebody Stole My Iron: A Family Memoir of Dementia,* was published in 2014. "Freedom" is a semi-autobiographical account of the author's memories of her grandfather's last summer at the family farm. It highlights a time in history when people diagnosed with hardening of the arteries or other dementia-type symptoms were often committed to state mental hospitals like Warm Springs. Facilities specifically for people with dementia didn't come into existence until the mid-1970s.

Mark Taylor grew up in Billings. In his 35 year career serving rural eastern Montana, Mark worked in residential child care, operated a mental health center satellite office, and he worked in lots of schools. This story is loosely based on his experiences from the time he worked in Baker. Mark is also a founding member of the Billings Bookstore Cooperative.

Jaci Webb has been a journalist for 33 years, covering everything from business to crime to entertainment for *The Billings Gazette.* She loves getting paid to see rock concerts, plays and art exhibits. Webb has also taught writing for 20 years, the last three years at Rocky Mountain College. She won first place in column writing for the Montana Newspaper Association and has won several first-place awards in feature writing. The award she is most proud of, though, is Adjunct Teacher of the Year in 2013 at Montana State University. Fun fact: She has two dogs, a mutt named Cooper and a wiener dog Satchmo.

Blythe Woolston was born in Missoula, brought home to Milltown, and educated in Potomac, Missoula, and Bozeman. Now she lives and writes in Billings. Her books, *MARTians, Black Helicopters, Catch & Release,* and *The Freak Observer,* are little novels about physics and grief, evolutionary biology, terrorism, and loneliness. Whatever the subject, Blythe's stories are all rife with salty language and ornery outlook—including "The Bone Dowsers." Consider yourself warned.

Elizabeth Hughes Wood is a fourth-generation Californian partnered with a third-generation Montanan. Elizabeth and Wilbur's Montana-born daughter resides in Portland, Oregon. Elizabeth lives in Roundup, Montana, where amidst house-holding, gardening, keeping in touch with friends far and near, and supporting causes she believes in, tries to catch up with the creative part of her life. She has been writing from an early age— poems, plays, short stories. She has been a member of a writing group since 1966 in San Francisco, and these days she deeply appreciates her Red Truck Writers who gather mostly monthly, critiquing and encouraging each other's work.

Wilbur Wood writes, "Poetry is the Sun for me, and other forms of writing—journalism, essay, memoir, commentary, fiction, even research reports, letters, e-mail messages—orbit and feed off that center. For any kind of writing we need to place ourselves: physically, emotionally, mentally, spiritually; we need to find a voice, an audience to listen, a community wherein we can thrive and practice. On and off and on again, for five decades, writing groups have helped me create and refine what I need to say. My first listener is my partner Elizabeth. Our first writing group arose where we met, San Francisco, California. Our present group meets mainly in Roundup, south-central Montana, where we continue to live and work and play."